SNOW COUNTRY AND THOUSAND CRANES

Yasunari Kawahata, winner of the 1968 Nobel Prize for Literature, was born near Osaka in 1899 and was orphaned at the age of two. As a boy, he had hoped to become a painter, an aspiration still reflected in his novels. But his first stories were published while he was still in high school and he decided to become a writer. He graduated from Tokyo Imperial University in 1924 and a year later made his first impact on Japanese letters with *Izu Dancer*. He soon became a leading figure in the lyrical school that offered the chief challenge to the proletarian literature of the 1920s. His writings combine the two forms of the novel and the *haiku* poem, which within the restrictions of a rigid metre achieves a startling beauty by its juxtaposition of opposite and incongruous terms. *Snow Country* (1956) and *Thousand Cranes* (1959) made him known in this country.

Kawabata's *House of the Sleeping Beauties*, *The Sound of the Mountain*, *The Master of Go* and *Beauty and Sadness* have also appeared in English. Kawabata was also eminent as a literary critic, and discovered and sponsored such remarkable writers as Yukio Mishima. Like so many other Japanese writers, he lived in Kamakura. On 16 April 1972, at the age of seventy-three, Kawabata died by his own hand.

Yasunari Kawabata

Snow Country and Thousand Cranes

Translated from the Japanese by
Edward G. Seidensticker

With an Introduction by
Kazuo Ishiguro

PENGUIN BOOKS
in association with Martin Secker & Warburg Ltd

PENGUIN BOOKS

Published by the Penguin Group
Penguin Books Ltd, 27 Wrights Lane, London W8 5TZ, England
Penguin Books USA Inc., 375 Hudson Street, New York, New York 10014, USA
Penguin Books Australia Ltd, Ringwood, Victoria, Australia
Penguin Books Canada Ltd, 10 Alcorn Avenue, Toronto, Ontario, Canada M4V 3B2
Penguin Books (NZ) Ltd, 182–190 Wairau Road, Auckland 10, New Zealand

Penguin Books Ltd, Registered Offices: Harmondsworth, Middlesex, England

Snow Country (Japanese title: *Yukinugi*) first published in the USA 1956
Published in Great Britain by Martin Secker & Warburg Ltd 1957
Translation copyright © Alfred A. Knopf, Inc., 1956

Thousand Cranes (Japanese title: *Sembra Zuru*) first published in the USA 1958
Published in Great Britain by Martin Secker & Warburg Ltd 1959
Translation copyright © Alfred A. Knopf, Inc., 1958

Snow Country and Thousand Cranes published in Penguin Books 1971
Reprinted with an Introduction by Kazuo Ishiguro 1986
10 9 8 7 6 5 4 3

Introduction copyright © Kazuo Ishiguro, 1986
All rights reserved

Unesco Collection of Contemporary Works
These novels have been accepted in the Translation Series of Contemporary Works
jointly sponsored by the International PEN Club and the United Nations Educational,
Scientific and Cultural Organization (UNESCO)

Printed in England by Clays Ltd, St Ives plc

Introduction

Snow Country concerns itself with the life of a country geisha, while much of *Thousand Cranes* revolves around tea ceremony rituals. Some Western readers can be forgiven for feeling a little daunted in noting this; the two short novels by Yasunari Kawabata which follow, it may be anticipated, will be bafflingly foreign.

Some reassurance is in order here. Unfamiliarity with geisha or the tea ceremony will prove a surprisingly small drawback. Begin reading, and you are unlikely to feel the need for encyclopaedias or for large numbers of explanatory footnotes; the novels themselves will supply all the information you immediately require, and are in many ways ideal introductions to these peculiarly Japanese territories.

One should not, furthermore, over-react to the problem of how to interpret the words and actions of these characters who operate by alien social rules. Near the start of *Snow Country*, for instance, you will find the hero asking the heroine, as she serves him in a country inn, to procure for him a geisha for his sexual needs. It may strike you the hero is behaving badly, but then you may stop and wonder if in fact this is perfectly normal Japanese behaviour. While such wariness in applying one's own values to another culture is laudable, the danger here is one of over-respectfulness. Not only would your initial response have been correct, but suspending that response and becoming bemused would have caused you to miss the opening gambit in the cruel and melancholy game the protagonists play throughout the novel. The lesson here is not to be over-intimidated by the purported gulf between Japanese and Western behaviour. Of course, you *will* find characters behaving oddly and obsessively, but this is more likely to be because they are characters in a Kawabata novel, rather than because they are Japanese. One should try and respond as naturally as seems reasonable towards them.

But what of the form of these novels? To what extent can

these works be read as though they were of a Western tradition? Here, a certain amount of trepidation is only proper. It needs to be remembered that Kawabata was a writer who quite deliberately aspired to a 'classical' tradition of Japanese prose-writing pre-dating the influence of European realism – a tradition which placed value on lyricism, mood and reflection rather than on plot and character. Read either of these novels for a tangible, developing plotline – adopt a 'what-happens-next?' attitude – and one is bound to reach the end with the feeling one has missed the point. Kawabata needs to be read *slowly*, the atmospheres savoured, the characters' words pondered for nuances. The settings in which conversations and events take place should never be regarded merely as picturesque backdrops; a setting and an event will have been matched carefully to resonate deeply with one another. Accordingly, Kawabata's descriptive writing – often presented in short, concentrated paragraphs of one or two sentences – should be approached with the respect and close attention one would give translated poetry.

What plots we get are somewhat crude and contrived. In *Snow Country*, the tangle of relationships between the heroine and the background characters who live in the village is unnecessarily complicated and explained hurriedly in a way which is far from easy to assimilate; similarly, the opening chapter of *Thousand Cranes* thrusts at us a mess of triangular relationships from the past at an almost indigestible rate. In both instances, one is tempted to turn from the book and work out diagramatically just who is who and did what with whom and when. These clumsy expositions – reading not unlike the 'story-so-far' sections of magazine serials – are not a manifestation of any Japanese stylistic quirk; they simply represent a lack of deftness on Kawabata's part. But it does indicate the low priority Kawabata gives to 'plot' in the Western sense; it is as if he wishes to clear 'plot' to one side as rapidly as possible, as a kind of chore, so that he can place his emphases elsewhere. The reader should respond in a like-minded spirit. It is important to digest these pieces of exposition in so far as they serve as premises from which the novels can develop. But otherwise, these 'plots' should not occupy us unduly.

It follows from all this that the novelist's ability to evoke images and textures in the reader's mind becomes unusually important. (Sounds and smells, too, play a significant role.) It is here, rather than in respect to Japanese social mores, that many Western readers will be most handicapped. For instance, at the most elementary level, some readers may be uncertain what to picture when told a character has stepped into the room of a house. What does this room look like? The author may describe the light in the room, or mention the cold breeze blowing through it, but, not assuming Western ignorance, will not bother to describe the room itself. This is a simple but fundamental problem which can seriously disrupt the author's method of sensual evocation and undermine the spell cast by many a scene. (It is no bad idea for readers interested in Japanese novels – and those of Kawabata in particular – who find themselves in this position to familiarize themselves with some basic Japanese images from films or photographs.) While exteriors in modern Japanese novels present less difficulty – land- and townscapes not varying so wildly from those of the West – traditional Japanese interiors do differ very fundamentally. Fortunately, there is considerable uniformity amongst Japanese rooms, both within one residence and from house to house. By Western standards, a traditional Japanese room will look sparse and unfurnished. Everything will happen at floor level, and items such as tables, bedding and braziers are introduced only as and when needed. The decor will be simple and stark; the floor will be of square straw mats (tatami), the walls and sliding partitions of paper and wood. The general impression is one of sparseness, of subdued, natural colours. The country inn in which *Snow Country* takes place will be comprised of many such rooms, linked by corridors of polished floorboards with minimal decoration. Do not confuse Japanese decor with Chinese, and certainly take care not to let your imagination conjure up the inside of your local Chinese restaurant with its swirling dragon patterns and rich colours. Japanese interiors are practically the antithesis of this.

It is worth the small effort to negotiate such difficulties; both *Snow Country* and *Thousand Cranes*, in the form of these elegant translations, offer experiences unlikely to be found anywhere else in Western fiction.

Kazuo Ishiguro
April 1985

Snow Country

Introduction

In the winter, cold winds blow down from Siberia, pick up moisture over the Japan Sea, and drop it as snow when they strike the mountains of Japan. The west coast of the main island of Japan is probably for its latitude (roughly, from Cape Hatteras to New York, or from Spanish Morocco to Barcelona) the snowiest region in the world. From December to April or May only the railways are open, and the snow in the mountains is sometimes as much as fifteen feet deep.

The expression 'snow country', then, does not mean simply country where snow falls. It means very specifically the part of the main island that lies west of the central mountain range. It suggests long, grey winters, tunnels under the snow, dark houses with rafters black from the smoke of winter fires – and perhaps chilblains, or, to the more imaginative, life divorced from time through the long snowbound months.

The hot springs, one of which is the locale of *Snow Country*, also have a peculiarly Japanese significance. The Japanese seldom goes to a hot spring for his health, and he never goes for 'the season', as people once went to Bath or Saratoga. He may ski or view maple leaves or cherry blossoms, but his wife is usually not with him. The special delights of the hot spring are for the unaccompanied gentleman. No prosperous hot spring is without its geisha and its compliant hotel maids.

If the hot-spring geisha is not a social outcast, she is perilously near being one. The city geisha may become a celebrated musician or dancer, a political intriguer, even a dispenser of patronage. The hot-spring geisha must go on entertaining weekend guests, and the pretence that she is an artist and not a prostitute is often a thin one indeed. It is true that she sometimes marries an old guest, or persuades him to open a restaurant for her; but the possibility that she will drift from one hot

7

spring to another, more unwanted with each change, makes her a particularly poignant symbol of wasted, decaying beauty.

It is not by chance that Yasunari Kawabata has chosen a hot-spring geisha for the heroine and the dark snow country for the setting of this novel. Darkness and wasted beauty run like a ground bass through his major work, and in *Snow Country* we perhaps feel most strongly the cold loneliness of the Kawabata world.

Kawabata was born near Osaka in 1899 and was orphaned at the age of two. His short stories began to attract attention soon after his graduation from Tokyo Imperial University. He presently became a leading figure in the lyrical school that offered the chief opposition to the proletarian literature in the late twenties. *Snow Country* was begun in 1934 and published piecemeal between 1935 and 1937. In 1947 a final instalment was added, and the novel completed as it stands today.

Kawabata has been put, I think rightly, in a literary line that can be traced back to seventeenth-century *haiku* masters. *Haiku* are tiny seventeen-syllable poems that seek to convey a sudden awareness of beauty by a mating of opposite or incongruous terms. Thus the classical *haiku* characteristically fuses motion and stillness. Similarly Kawabata relies very heavily on a mingling of the senses. In *Snow Country* we come upon the roaring silence of a winter night, for instance, or the round softness of the sound of running water, or, in a somewhat more elaborate figure, the sound of a bell, far back in the singing of a tea-kettle, suddenly becomes a woman's feet. In the best of the dialogue, one brief sentence, often a *double-entendre*, is exchanged for another, much as characters in Japanese romances converse by exchanging brief poems.

The *haiku* manner presents a great challenge to the novelist. The manner is notable for its terseness and austerity, so that his novel must rather be like a series of brief flashes in a void. In *Snow Country* Kawabata has chosen a theme that makes a meeting between *haiku* and the novel possible. The hero is a wealthy dilettante quite incapable of love, and the heroine a hot-spring geisha, clean in the midst of corruption and yet somehow decaying before our eyes. The two try to love, but love can never bring them together. The nearer they are the farther apart they are. Shimamura, the hero, has built himself a half-cynical, half-wishful dream world, occupied by very little that suggests flesh and blood. He is an expert on the Occidental ballet, but he has never seen a ballet. Indeed we are given cause to suspect that he would close his eyes if a ballet were set down in front of him. His love affair with Komako, the geisha, is doomed from the start. Through her he is drawn to Yoko, a strange, intense girl who, in Kawabata's image, glows like a light off in the mountain darkness; but he can take neither Komako nor Yoko as a person. They can bring him no nearer their humanity or his own, and he presently knows that the time has come for him to leave.

Komako, for her part, has missed none of this. 'You're a good girl,' Shimamura says affectionately in the climactic scene of the novel. But when, a moment later, he unconsciously shifts to 'You're a good woman,' she sees that she has been used. She too knows that he must leave. It would be hard to think of another novel in which so slight a shift in tone reveals so much.

The final scene only brings the inevitable. We know, as Komako staggers from the burning warehouse with Yoko in her arms, that Komako and Shimamura have parted. Shimamura will go back to the city and continue to play the cold dilettante, while Komako will, as she herself has said, 'go pleasantly to seed' in the mountains. Yoko is the burden she must bear, and the burden is made heavier by the fact that the two women have twice been rivals in love, once, in a way never clearly defined for us, with the dying Yukio, again with Shimamura. Little of this is stated directly. We are not even told whether Yoko is alive or dead at the end of the novel. If the reader finds the last few pages puzzling, however, he should remember that everything has already been implicitly suggested. The novel has in effect ended with Shimamura listening to the sound of the bell in the tea-kettle. The fire scene, beautifully written though it is, only emphasizes a point that has already been made.

Snow Country is perhaps Kawabata's masterpiece. He has found in Shimamura's love affair the perfect symbol for a denial of love, and he has in the woman Komako and in the shadowy beauty of the snow country fit subjects for the *haiku*-like flashes that bring the denial forth. And, in the final analysis, the very success of the novel becomes a sort of affirmation of the humanity that is being denied.

E.G.S.

Part One

The train came out of the long tunnel into the snow country. The earth lay white under the night sky. The train pulled up at a signal stop.

A girl who had been sitting on the other side of the carriage came over and opened the window in front of Shimamura. The snowy cold poured in. Leaning far out of the window, the girl called to the station-master as though he were a great distance away.

The station-master walked slowly over the snow, a lantern in his hand. His face was buried to the nose in a muffler, and the flaps of his cap were turned down over his ears.

It's that cold, is it, thought Shimamura. Low, barrack-like buildings that might have been railway dormitories were scattered here and there up the frozen slope of the mountain. The white of the snow fell away into the darkness some distance before it reached them.

'How are you?' the girl called out. 'It's Yoko.'

'Yoko, is it. On your way back? It's got cold again.'

'I understand my brother has come to work here. Thank you for all you've done.'

'It will be lonely, though. This is no place for a young boy.'

'He's really no more than a child. You'll teach him what he needs to know, won't you.'

'Oh, but he's doing very well. We'll be busier from now on, with the snow and all. Last year we had so much that the trains were always being stopped by avalanches, and the whole town was kept busy cooking for the travellers.'

'But see about the warm clothes, would you. My brother said in his letter that he wasn't even wearing a sweater yet.'

'I'm not warm unless I have on four layers, myself. The young ones start drinking when it gets cold, and the first thing you know they're over there in bed with colds.' He waved his lantern towards the dormitories.

'Does my brother drink?'

'Not that I know of.'

'You're on your way home now, are you?'

'I had a little accident. I've been going to the doctor.'

'You must be more careful.'

The station-master, who had an overcoat on over his kimono, turned as if to cut the freezing conversation short. 'Take care of yourself,' he called over his shoulder.

'Is my brother here now?' Yoko looked out over the snow-covered platform. 'See that he behaves himself.' It was such a beautiful voice that it struck one as sad. In all its high resonance it seemed to come echoing back across the snowy night.

The girl was still leaning out of the window when the train pulled away from the station. 'Tell my brother to come home when he has a holiday,' she called out to the station master, who was walking along the tracks.

'I'll tell him,' the man called back.

Yoko closed the window and pressed her hands to her red cheeks.

Three snowploughs were waiting for the heavy snows here on the Border Range. There was an electric avalanche-warning system at the north and south entrances to the tunnel. Five thousand workers were ready to clear away the snow, and two thousand young men from the volunteer fire-departments could be mobilized if they were needed.

Yoko's brother would be working at this signal stop, so soon to be buried under the snow – somehow that fact made the girl more interesting to Shimamura.

'The girl' – something in her manner suggested the unmarried girl. Shimamura of course had no way of being sure what her relationship was to the man with her. They acted rather like a married couple. The man was clearly ill, however, and illness shortens the distance between a man and a woman. The more earnest the ministrations, the more the two come to seem like husband and wife. A girl taking care of a man far older than she, for all the world like a young mother, can from a distance be taken for his wife.

12

But Shimamura in his mind had cut the girl off from the man with her and decided from her general appearance and manner that she was unmarried. And then, because he had been looking at her from a strange angle for so long, emotions peculiarly his own had perhaps coloured his judgement.

It had been three hours earlier. In his boredom, Shimamura stared at his left hand as the forefinger bent and unbent. Only this hand seemed to have a vital and immediate memory of the woman he was going to see. The more he tried to call up a clear picture of her, the more his memory failed him, the farther she faded away, leaving him nothing to catch and hold. In the midst of this uncertainty only the one hand, and in particular the forefinger, even now seemed damp from her touch, seemed to be pulling him back to her from afar. Taken with the strangeness of it, he brought the hand to his face, then quickly drew a line across the misted-over window. A woman's eye floated up before him. He almost called out in his astonishment. But he had been dreaming, and when he came to himself he saw that it was only the reflection in the window of the girl opposite. Outside it was growing dark, and the lights had been turned on in the train, transforming the window into a mirror. The mirror had been clouded over with steam until he drew the line across it.

The one eye by itself was strangely beautiful, but, feigning a traveller's weariness and putting his face to the window as if to look at the scenery outside, he cleared the steam from the rest of the glass.

The girl leaned attentively forward, looking down at the man before her. Shimamura could see from the way her strength was gathered in her shoulders that the suggestion of fierceness in her eyes was but a sign of an intentness that did not permit her to blink. The man lay with his head pillowed at the window and his legs bent so that his feet were on the seat facing, beside the girl. It was a third-class coach. The pair were not directly opposite Shimamura but rather one seat forward, and the man's head showed in the window-mirror only as far as the ear.

Since the girl was thus diagonally opposite him, Shimamura could as well have looked directly at her. When the two of

13

them came on the train, however, something coolly piercing about her beauty had startled Shimamura, and as he hastily lowered his eyes he had seen the man's ashen fingers clutching at the girl's. Somehow it seemed wrong to look their way again.

The man's face in the mirror suggested the feeling of security and repose it gave him to be able to rest his eyes on the girl's breast. His very weakness lent a certain soft balance and harmony to the two figures. One end of his scarf served as a pillow, and the other end, pulled up tight over his mouth like a mask, rested on his cheek. Now and then it fell loose or slipped down over his nose, and almost before he had time to signal his annoyance the girl gently rearranged it. The process was repeated over and over, automatically, so often that Shimamura, watching them, almost found himself growing impatient. Occasionally the bottom of the overcoat in which the man's feet were wrapped would slip open and fall to the floor, and the girl would quickly pull it back together. It was all completely natural, as if the two of them, quite insensitive to space, meant to go on for ever, farther and farther into the distance. For Shimamura there was none of the pain that the sight of something truly sad can bring. Rather it was as if he were watching a tableau in a dream – and that was no doubt the working of his strange mirror.

In the depths of the mirror the evening landscape moved by, the mirror and the reflected figures like motion pictures superimposed one on the other. The figures and the background were unrelated, and yet the figures, transparent and intangible, and the background, dim in the gathering darkness, melted together into a sort of symbolic world not of this world. Particularly when a light out in the mountains shone in the centre of the girl's face, Shimamura felt his chest rise at the inexpressible beauty of it.

The mountain sky still carried traces of evening red. Individual shapes were clear far into the distance, but the monotonous mountain landscape, undistinguished for mile after mile, seemed all the more undistinguished for having lost its last traces of colour. There was nothing in it to catch the eye, and it seemed to flow along in a wide, unformed emotion. That was of course because the girl's face was floating over it. Cut off by the face, the evening landscape moved steadily by around its outlines. The face too seemed transparent – but was it really transparent? Shimamura had the illusion that the evening landscape was actually passing over the face, and the flow did not stop to let him be sure it was not.

The light inside the train was not particularly strong, and the reflection was not as clear as it would have been in a mirror. Since there was no glare, Shimamura came to forget that it was a mirror he was looking at. The girl's face seemed to be out in the flow of the evening mountains.

It was then that a light shone in the face. The reflection in the mirror was not strong enough to blot out the light outside, nor was the light strong enough to dim the reflection. The light moved across the face, though not to light it up. It was a distant, cold light. As it sent its small ray through the pupil of the girl's eye, as the eye and the light were superimposed one on the other, the eye became a weirdly beautiful bit of phosphorescence on the sea of evening mountains.

There was no way for Yoko to know that she was being stared at. Her attention was concentrated on the sick man, and even had she looked towards Shimamura, she would probably not have seen her reflection, and she would have paid no attention to the man looking out of the window.

It did not occur to Shimamura that it was improper to stare at the girl so long and stealthily. That too was no doubt because he was taken by the unreal, otherworldly power of his mirror in the evening landscape.

When, therefore, the girl called out to the station-master, her manner again suggesting over-earnestness, Shimamura perhaps saw her first of all as rather like a character out of an old, romantic tale.

The window was dark by the time they came to the signal stop. The charm of the mirror faded with the fading landscape. Yoko's face was still there, but for all the warmth of her ministrations, Shimamura had found in her a transparent coldness. He did not clear the window as it clouded over again.

He was startled, then, when half an hour later Yoko and the man got off the train at the same station as he. He looked around as though he were about to be drawn into something, but the cold air on the platform made him suddenly ashamed of his rudeness on the train. He crossed the tracks in front of the locomotive without looking back again.

The man, clinging to Yoko's shoulder, was about to climb down to the tracks from the platform opposite when from this side a station attendant raised a hand to stop them.

A long goods train came out of the darkness to block them from sight.

The porter from the inn was so well-equipped for the cold that he suggested a fireman. He had on ear flaps and high rubber boots. The woman looking out over the tracks from the waiting-room wore a blue cap with the cowl pulled over her head.

Shimamura, still warm from the train, was not sure how cold it really was. This was his first taste of the snow-country winter, however, and he felt somewhat intimidated.

'Is it as cold as all that?'

'We're ready for the winter. It's always especially cold the night it clears after a snow. It must be below freezing tonight.'

'This is below freezing, is it?' Shimamura looked up at the delicate icicles along the eaves as he climbed into the taxi. The white of the snow made the deep eaves look deeper still, as if everything had sunk quietly into the earth.

'The cold here is different, though, that's easy to see. It feels different when you touch something.'

'Last year it went down to zero.'

'How much snow?'

'Ordinarily seven or eight feet, sometimes as much as twelve or thirteen, I'd say.'

'The heavy snows come from now on?'

'They're just beginning. We had about a foot, but it's melted down a good bit.'

'It's been melting, has it?'

'We could have a heavy snow almost any time now, though.'

It was the beginning of December.

Shimamura's nose had been stopped up by a stubborn cold, but it cleared to the middle of his head in the cold air, and began running as if the matter in it were washing cleanly away.

'Is the girl who lived with the music teacher still around?'

'She's still around. You didn't see her in the station? In the dark blue cape?'

'So that's who it was. We can call her later, I suppose?'

'This evening?'

'This evening.'

'I hear the music teacher's son came back on your train. She was at the station to meet him.'

The sick man he had watched in that evening mirror, then, was the son of the music teacher in whose house the woman Shimamura had come to see was living.

He felt a current pass through him, and yet the coincidence did not seem especially remarkable. Indeed he was surprised at himself for being so little surprised.

Somewhere in his heart Shimamura saw a question, as clearly as if it were standing there before him: was there something, what would happen, between the woman his hand remembered and the woman in whose eye that mountain light had glowed? Or had he not yet shaken off the spell of the evening landscape in that mirror? He wondered whether the flowing landscape was not perhaps symbolic of the passage of time.

The hot-spring inn had its fewest guests in the weeks before the ski-ing season began, and by the time Shimamura had come up from the bath the place seemed to be asleep. The glass doors rattled slightly each time he took a step down the sagging corridor. At the end, where it turned past the office, he saw the tall figure of the woman, her skirts trailing coldly off across the dark floor.

He started back as he saw the long skirts – had she finally become a geisha? She did not come towards him, she did not bend in the slightest movement of recognition. From the distance he caught something intent and serious in the still form. He hurried up to her, but they said nothing even when he was beside her. She started to smile through the thick, white geisha's powder. Instead she melted into tears, and the two of them walked off silently towards his room.

In spite of what had passed between them, he had not

17

written to her, or come to see her, or sent her the dance instructions he had promised. She was no doubt left to think that he had laughed at her and forgotten her. It should therefore have been his part to begin with an apology or an excuse, but as they walked along, not looking at each other, he could tell that, far from blaming him, she had room in her heart only for the pleasure of regaining what had been lost. He knew that if he spoke he would only make himself seem the more wanting in seriousness. Overpowered by the woman, he walked along wrapped in a soft happiness. Abruptly, at the foot of the stairs, he shoved his left fist before her eyes, with only the forefinger extended.

'This remembered you best of all.'

'Oh?' The woman took the finger in her hand and clung to it as though to lead him upstairs.

She let go his hand as they came to the *kotatsu** in his room, and suddenly she was red from her forehead to her throat. As if to conceal her confusion, she clutched at his hand again.

'This remembered me?'

'Not the right hand. This.' He pushed his right hand into the *kotatsu* to warm it, and again gave her his left fist with the finger extended.

'I know.' Her face carefully composed, she laughed softly. She opened his hand, and pressed her cheek against it. 'This remembered me?'

'Cold! I don't think I've ever touched such cold hair.'

'Is there snow in Tokyo yet?'

'You remember what you said then? But you were wrong. Why else would anyone come to such a place in December?'

'Then': the danger of avalanches was over, and the season for climbing mountains in the spring green had come.

Presently the new sprouts would be gone from the table.

Shimamura, who lived a life of idleness, found that he tended to lose his honesty with himself, and he frequently went out alone into the mountains to recover something of it. He

---

*A charcoal brazier covered by a wooden frame and a quilt. Although it warms little more than the hands and feet, the *kotatsu* is the only heating device in the ordinary Japanese house.

18

had come down to the hot-spring village after seven days in the Border Range. He asked to have a geisha called. Unfortunately, however, there was a celebration that day in honour of the opening of a new road, the maid said, so lively a celebration that the town's combined cocoon-warehouse and theatre had been taken over, and the twelve or thirteen geisha had more than enough to keep them busy. The girl who lived at the music teacher's might come, though. She sometimes helped at parties, but she would have gone home after no more than one or two dances. As Shimamura questioned her, the maid told him more about the girl at the music teacher's: the samisen and dancing teacher had living with her a girl who was not a geisha but who was sometimes asked to help at large parties. Since there were no young apprentice geisha in the town, and since most of the local geisha were at an age when they preferred not to have to dance, the services of the girl were much valued. She almost never came alone to entertain a guest at the inn, and yet she could not exactly be called an amateur – such in general was the maid's story.

An odd story, Shimamura said to himself, and dismissed the matter. An hour or so later, however, the woman from the music teacher's came in with the maid. Shimamura brought himself up straight. The maid started to leave but was called back by the woman.

The impression the woman gave was a wonderfully clean and fresh one. It seemed to Shimamura that she must be clean to the hollows under her toes. So clean indeed did she seem that he wondered whether his eyes, back from looking at early summer in the mountains, might not be deceiving him.

There was something about her manner of dress that suggested the geisha, but she did not have the trailing geisha skirts. On the contrary, she wore her soft, unlined summer kimono with an emphasis on careful propriety. The *obi** seemed expensive, out of keeping with the kimono, and struck him as a little sad.

The maid slipped out as they started talking about the mountains. The woman was not very sure of the names of the

*The sash with which a kimono is tied. A woman's *obi* is wide and stiff, a man's narrower and usually softer.

mountains that could be seen from the inn, and, since Shimamura did not feel the urge to drink that might have come to
him in the company of an ordinary geisha, she began telling of
her past in a surprisingly matter-of-fact way. She was born in
this snow country, but she had been put under contract as a
geisha in Tokyo. Presently she found a patron who paid her
debts for her and proposed to set her up as a dancing teacher,
but unfortunately a year and a half later he died. When it
came to the story of what had happened since, the story of
what was nearest to her, she was less quick to tell her secrets.
She said she was nineteen. Shimamura had taken her to be
twenty-one or twenty-two, and, since he assumed that she was
not lying, the knowledge that she had aged beyond her years
gave him for the first time a little of the ease he expected to
feel with a geisha. When they began talking of the Kabuki, he
found that she knew more about actors and styles than he did.
She talked on feverishly, as though she had been starved for
someone who would listen to her, and presently began to show
an ease and abandon that revealed her to be at heart a woman
of the pleasure quarters after all. And she seemed in general
to know what there was to know about men. Shimamura, however, had labelled her an amateur and, after a week in the mountains during which he had spoken to almost no one, he found
himself longing for a companion. It was therefore friendship
more than anything else that he felt for the woman. His response to the mountains had extended itself to cover her.

On her way to the bath the next afternoon, she left her
towel and soap in the hall and came in to talk to him.

She had barely taken a seat when he asked her to call him a
geisha.

'Call you a geisha?'

'You know what I mean.'

'I didn't come to be asked that.' She stood up abruptly and
went over to the window, her face reddening as she looked out
at the mountains. 'There are no women like that here.'

'Don't be silly.'

'It's the truth.' She turned sharply to face him, and sat
down on the window-sill. 'No one forces a geisha to do what
she doesn't want to. It's entirely up to the geisha herself. That's

20

one service the inn won't provide for you. Go ahead, try calling someone and talking to her yourself, if you want to.'

'You call someone for me.'

'Why do you expect me to do that?'

'I'm thinking of you as a friend. That's why I've behaved so well.'

'And this is what you call being a friend?' Led on by his manner, she had become engagingly childlike. But a moment later she burst out: 'Isn't it fine that you think you can ask me a thing like that!'

'What is there to be so excited about? I'm too healthy after a week in the mountains, that's all. I keep having the wrong ideas. I can't even sit here talking to you the way I would like to.'

The woman was silent, her eyes on the floor. Shimamura had come to a point where he knew he was only parading his masculine shamelessness, and yet it seemed likely enough that the woman was familiar with the failing and need not be shocked by it. He looked at her. Perhaps it was the rich lashes of the downcast eyes that made her face seem warm and sensuous. She shook her head very slightly, and again a faint blush spread over her face.

'Call any geisha you like.'

'But isn't that exactly what I'm asking you to do? I've never been here before, and I've no idea which geisha are the best-looking.'

'What do you consider good-looking?'

'Someone young. You're less apt to make mistakes when you're young. And someone who doesn't talk too much. Clean, and not too quick. When I want someone to talk to, I can talk to you.'

'I'll not come again.'

'Don't be foolish.'

'I said I'll not come again. Why should I come again?'

'But haven't I told you it's exactly because I want to be friends with you that I've behaved so well?'

'You've said enough.'

'Suppose I were to go too far with you. Very probably from tomorrow I wouldn't want to talk to you. I couldn't stand tne sight of you. I've had to come into the mountains to want to talk to people again, and I've left you alone so that I can talk to you. And what about yourself? You can't be too careful with travellers.'

'That's true.'

'Of course it is. Think of yourself. If it were a woman you objected to, you wouldn't want to see me afterwards. It would be much better for her to be a woman you picked out.'

'I don't want to hear any more.' She turned sharply away, but presently she added: 'I suppose there's something in what you say.'

'An affair of the moment, no more. Nothing beautiful about it. You know that – it couldn't last.'

'That's true. It's that way with everyone who comes here. This is a hot spring and people are here for a day or two and gone.' Her manner was remarkably open – the transition had been almost too abrupt. 'The guests are mostly travellers. I'm still just a child myself, but I've listened to all the talk. The guest who doesn't say he's fond of you, and yet you somehow know is – he's the one you have pleasant memories of. You don't forget him, even long after he's left you, they say. And he's the one you get letters from.'

She stood up from the window-sill and took a seat on the mat below it. She seemed to be living in the past, and yet she seemed to be very near Shimamura.

Her voice carried such a note of immediate feeling that he felt a little guilty, as though he had deceived her too easily.

He had not been lying, though. To him this woman was an amateur. His desire for a woman was not of a sort to make him want this particular woman – it was something to be taken care of lightly and with no sense of guilt. This woman was too clean. From the moment he saw her, he had separated this woman and the other in his mind.

Then too, he had been trying to decide where he would go to escape the summer heat, and it occurred to him that he could bring his family to this mountain hot spring. The woman, being fortunately an amateur, would be a good companion for his wife. He might even have his wife take dancing lessons to keep from getting bored. He was quite serious about it. He said he felt only friendship for the woman, but he had his reasons for thus stepping into shallow water without taking the final plunge.

And something like that evening mirror was no doubt at work here too. He disliked the thought of drawn-out complications from an affair with a woman whose position was so ambiguous; but beyond that he saw her as somehow unreal, like the woman's face in that evening mirror.

His taste for the Occidental dance had much the same air of unreality about it. He had grown up in the merchants' section of Tokyo, and he had been thoroughly familiar with the Kabuki theatre from his childhood. As a student his interests had shifted to the Japanese dance and the dance-drama. Never satisfied until he learned everything about his subject, he had taken to searching through old documents and visiting the heads of various dance schools, and presently he had made friends with rising figures in the dance world and was writing what one might call research pieces and critical essays. It was but natural, then, that he should come to feel a keen dissatisfaction with the slumbering old tradition as well as with reformers who sought only to please themselves. Just as he had arrived at the conclusion that there was nothing for it but to throw himself actively into the dance movement, and as he was being persuaded to do so by certain of the younger figures in the dance world, he abruptly switched to the Occidental dance. He stopped seeing the Japanese dance. He gathered pictures and descriptions of the Occidental ballet, and began laboriously collecting programmes and posters from abroad. This was more than simple fascination with the exotic and the unknown. The pleasure he found in his new hobby came in fact from his inability to see with his own eyes Occidentals in Occidental ballets. There was proof of this in his deliberate refusal to study the ballet as performed by Japanese. Nothing could be more comfortable than writing about the ballet from books. A ballet he had never seen was an art in another world. It was an unrivalled armchair reverie, a lyric from some paradise. He called his work research, but it was actually free, uncontrolled fantasy. He preferred not to savour the ballet in the flesh; rather he savoured the phantasms of his own dancing imagination, called up by Western books and pictures. It was like being in love with someone he had never seen. But it was also true that Shimamura, with no real occupation, took some satisfaction from the fact that his occasional introductions to the Occidental dance put him on the edge of the literary world – even while he was laughing at himself and his work.

It might be said that his knowledge was now for the first time in a very great while being put to use, since talk of the dance helped bring the woman nearer to him, and yet it was also possible that, hardly knowing it, it was treating the woman exactly as he treated the Occidental dance.

He felt a little guilty, as though he had deceived her, when he saw how the frivolous words of the traveller who would be gone tomorrow seemed to have struck something deep and serious in the woman's life.

But he went on: 'I can bring my family here, and we can all be friends.'

'I understand that well enough.' She smiled, her voice falling, and a touch of the geisha's playfulness came out. 'I'd like that much better. It lasts longer if you're just friends.'

'You'll call someone, then?'

'Now?'

'Now.'

'But what can you say to a woman in broad daylight?'

'At night there's too much danger of getting the dregs no one else wants.'

'You take this for a cheap hot-spring town like any other. I should think you could tell just from looking at the place.' Her tone was sober again, as though she felt thoroughly degraded. She repeated with the same emphasis as before that there were no girls here of the sort he wanted. When Shimamura expressed his doubts, she flared up, then retreated a step. It was up to the geisha whether she would stay the night or not. If she stayed without permission from her house, it was her own responsibility. If she had permission the house took full responsibility, whatever happened. That was the difference.

'Full responsibility?'

'If there should happen to be a child, or some sort of disease.'

Shimamura smiled wryly at the foolishness of his question. In a mountain village, though, the arrangements between a geisha and her keeper might indeed still be so easy-going ...

Perhaps with the idler's bent for protective colouring, Shimamura had an instinctive feeling for the spirit of the places he visited, and he had felt as he came down from the mountains that, for all its air of bare frugality, there was something comfortable and easy about the village. He heard at the inn that it was indeed one of the more comfortable villages in this harsh snow country. Until the railway was put through, only very recently, it had served mainly as a medicinal spring for farmers in the area. The house that kept geisha would generally have a faded shop curtain that advertised it as a restaurant or a tea-room, but a glance at the old-style sliding doors, their paper panels dark with age, made the passer-by suspect that guests were few. The shop that sold sweets or everyday sundries might have its one geisha, and the owner would have his small farm beside the shop and the geisha. Perhaps because she lived with the music teacher, there seemed to be no resentment at the fact that a woman not yet licensed as a geisha was now and then helping at parties.

'How many are there in all?'

'How many geisha? Twelve or thirteen, I suppose.'

'Which one do you recommend?' Shimamura stood up to ring for the maid.

'You won't mind if I leave now.'

'I mind very much indeed.'

'I can't stay.' She spoke as if trying to shake off the humiliation. 'I'm going. It's all right. I don't mind. I'll come again.'

When the maid came in, however, she sat down as though nothing were amiss. The maid asked several times which geisha she should call, but the woman refused to mention a name.

One look at the seventeen- or eighteen-year-old geisha who was presently led in, and Shimamura felt his need for a woman fall dully away. Her arms, with their underlying darkness, had not yet filled out, and something about her suggested an unformed, good-natured young girl. Shimamura, at pains not to show that his interest had left him, faced her dutifully, but he could not keep himself from looking less at her than at the new green on the mountains behind her. It seemed almost too much of an effort to talk. She was the mountain geisha through and through. He lapsed into a glum silence. No doubt thinking to be tactful and adroit, the woman stood up and left the room, and the conversation became still heavier. Even so, he managed to pass perhaps an hour with the geisha. Looking for a pretext to be rid of her, he remembered that he had had money telegraphed from Tokyo. He had to go to the post office before it closed, he said, and the two of them left the room.

But at the door of the inn he was seduced by the mountain, strong with the smell of new leaves. He started climbing roughly up it.

He laughed on and on, not knowing himself what was funny.

When he was pleasantly tired, he turned sharply around and, tucking the skirts of his kimono into his obi, ran headlong back down the slope. Two yellow butterflies flew up at his feet.

The butterflies, weaving in and out, climbed higher than the line of the Border Range, their yellow turning to white in the distance.

'What happened?' The woman was standing in the shade of the cedar trees. 'You must have been very happy, the way you were laughing.'

'I gave it up.' Shimamura felt the same senseless laugh rising again. 'I gave it up.'

'Oh?' She turned and walked slowly into the grove. Shimamura followed in silence.

It was a shrine grove. The woman sat down on a flat rock beside the moss-covered shrine dogs.

'It's always cool here. Even in the middle of the summer there's a cool wind.'

'Are all the geisha like that?'

'They're all a little like her, I suppose. Some of the older ones are very attractive, if you had wanted one of them.' Her eyes were on the ground, and she spoke coldly. The dusky green of the cedars seemed to reflect from her neck.

Shimamura looked up at the cedar branches. 'It's all over. My strength left me – really, it seems very funny.'

From behind the rock, the cedars threw up their trunks in perfectly straight lines, so high that he could see the tops only by arching his back. The dark needles blocked out the sky, and the stillness seemed to be singing quietly. The trunk against which Shimamura leaned was the oldest of all. For some reason all the branches on the north side had withered, and, their tips broken and fallen, they looked like stakes driven into the trunk with their sharp ends out, to make a terrible weapon for some god.

'I made a mistake. I saw you as soon as I came down from the mountains, and I let myself think that all the geisha here were like you,' he laughed. It occurred to him now that the thought of washing away in such short order the vigour of seven days in the mountains had perhaps first come to him when he saw the cleanness of this woman.

She gazed down at the river, distant in the afternoon sun. Shimamura was a little unsure of himself.

'I forgot,' she suddenly remarked, with forced lightness. 'I brought your tobacco. I went back up to your room a little while ago and found that you had gone out. I wondered where you could be, and then I saw you running up the mountain for all you were worth. I watched from the window. You were very funny. But you forgot your tobacco. Here.'

She took the tobacco from her kimono sleeve and lighted a match for him.

'I wasn't very nice to that poor girl.'

'But it's up to the guest, after all, when he wants to let the geisha go.'

Through the quiet, the sound of the rocky river came up to them with a rounded softness. Shadows were darkening in the mountain chasms on the other side of the valley, framed in the cedar branches.

'Unless she were as good as you, I'd feel cheated when I saw you afterwards.'

'Don't talk to me about it. You're just unwilling to admit you lost, that's all.' There was scorn in her voice, and yet an affection of quite a new sort flowed between them.

As it became clear to Shimamura that he had from the start wanted only this woman, and that he had taken his usual roundabout way of saying so, he began to see himself as rather repulsive and the woman as all the more beautiful. Something from that cool figure had swept through him after she called to him from under the cedars.

The high, thin nose was a little lonely, a little sad, but the bud of her lips opened and closed smoothly, like a beautiful little circle of leeches. Even when she was silent her lips seemed always to be moving. Had they had wrinkles or cracks, or had their colour been less fresh, they would have struck one as unwholesome, but they were never anything but smooth and shining. The line of her eyelids neither rose nor fell. As if for some special reason, it drew its way straight across her face. There was something faintly comical about the effect, but the short, thick hair of her eyebrows sloped gently down to enfold the line discreetly. There was nothing remarkable about the outlines of her round, slightly aquiline face. With her skin like white porcelain coated over a faint pink, and her throat still girlish, not yet filled out, the impression she gave was above all one of cleanness, not quite one of real beauty.

Her breasts were rather full for a woman used to the high, binding *obi* of the geisha.

'The sand flies have come out,' she said, standing up and brushing at the skirt of her kimono.

Alone in the quiet, they could think of little to say.

It was perhaps ten o'clock that night. The woman called loudly to Shimamura from the hall, and a moment later she fell into his room as if someone had thrown her. She collapsed in front of the table. Flailing with a drunken arm at everything that happened to be on it, she poured herself a glass of water and drank in great gulps.

She had gone out to meet some travellers down from the mountains that evening, men she had been friendly with during the ski-ing season the winter before. They had invited her to the inn, whereupon they had had a riotous party, complete with geisha, and had proceeded to get her drunk.

Her head waved uncertainly, and she seemed prepared to

talk on for ever. Presently she remembered herself. 'I shouldn't be here. I'll come again. They'll be looking for me. I'll come again later.' She staggered from the room.

An hour or so later, he heard uneven steps coming down the long hall. She was weaving from side to side, he could tell, running into a wall, stumbling to the floor.

'Shimamura, Shimamura,' she called in a high voice. 'I can't see. Shimamura!'

It was, with no attempt at covering itself, the naked heart of a woman calling out to her man. Shimamura was startled. That high, piercing voice must surely be echoing all through the inn. He got up hastily. Pushing her fingers through the paper panel, the woman clutched at the frame of the door, and fell heavily against him.

'You're here.' Clinging to him, she sank to the floor. She leaned against him as she spoke. 'I'm not drunk. Who says I'm drunk? Ah, it hurts, it hurts. It's just that it hurts. I know exactly what I'm doing. Give me water, I want water. I mixed my drinks, that was my mistake. That's what goes to your head. It hurts. They had a bottle of cheap whisky. How was I to know it was cheap?' She rubbed her forehead with her fists.

The sound of the rain outside was suddenly louder.

Each time he relaxed his embrace even a little, she threatened to collapse. His arm was around her neck so tight that her hair was rumpled against his cheek. He thrust a hand inside the neck of her kimono.

He added coaxing words, but she did not answer. She folded her arms like a bar over the breast he was asking for.

'What's the matter with you.' She bit savagely at her arm, as though angered by its refusal to serve her. 'Damn you, damn you. Lazy, useless. What's the matter with you.'

Shimamura drew back startled. There were deep teeth-marks on her arm.

She no longer resisted, however. Giving herself up to his hands, she began writing something with the tip of her finger. She would tell him the people she liked, she said. After she had written the names of some twenty or thirty actors, she wrote 'Shimamura, Shimamura,' over and over again.

The delicious swelling under Shimamura's hand grew warmer.

'Everything is all right.' His voice was serene. 'Everything is all right again.' He sensed something a little motherly in her.

But the headache came back. She writhed and twisted, and sank to the floor in a corner of the room.

'It won't do. It won't do. I'm going home. Going home.'

'Do you think you can walk that far? And listen to the rain.'

'I'll go home barefoot. I'll crawl home.'

'You don't think that's a little dangerous? If you have to go, I'll take you.'

The inn was on a hill, and the road was a steep one.

'Suppose you try loosening your clothes. Lie down for a little while and you'll feel well enough to go.'

'No, no. This is the way. I'm used to it.' She sat up straight and took a deep breath, but breathing was clearly painful. She felt a little sick, she said, and opened the window behind her, but she could not vomit. She seemed to be holding back the urge to fall down writhing on the floor. Now and then she came to herself. 'I'm going home, I'm going home,' she said again and again, and presently it was after two.

'Go on to bed. Go on to bed when a person tells you to.'

'But what will you do?' Shimamura asked.

'I'll just sit here like this. When I feel a little better I'll go home. I'll go home before daylight.' She crawled over on her knees and tugged at him. 'Go on to sleep. Pay no attention to me, I tell you.'

Shimamura went back to bed. The woman sprawled over the table and took another drink of water.

'Get up. Get up when a person tells you to.'

'Which do you want me to do?'

'All right, go to sleep.'

'You aren't making much sense, you know.' He pulled her into bed after him.

Her face was turned half away, hidden from him, but after a time she thrust her lips violently towards him.

Then, as if in a delirium she were trying to tell of her pain, she repeated over and over, he did not know how many times: 'No, no. Didn't you say you wanted to be friends?'

30

The almost too serious tone of it rather dulled his ardour, and as he saw her wrinkle her forehead in the effort to control herself, he thought of standing by the commitment he had made.

But then she said: 'I won't have any regrets. I'll never have any regrets. But I'm not that sort of woman. It can't last. Didn't you say so yourself?'

She was still half numb from the liquor.

'It's not my fault. It's yours. You lost. You're the weak one. Not I.' She ran on almost in a trance, and she bit at her sleeve as if to fight back the happiness.

She was quiet for a time, apparently drained of feeling. Then, as if the thought came to her from somewhere in her memory, she struck out: 'You're laughing, aren't you? You're laughing at me.'

'I'm not.'

'Deep in your heart you're laughing at me. Even if you aren't now, you will be later.' She was choked with tears. Turning away from him, she buried her face in her hands.

But a moment later she was calm again. Soft and yielding as if she were offering herself up, she was suddenly very intimate, and she began telling him all about herself. She seemed quite to have forgotten the headache. She said not a word about what had just happened.

'But I've been so busy talking I haven't noticed how late it is.' She smiled a little bashfully. She had to leave before daylight, she said. 'It's still dark. But people here get up early.' Time after time she got up to look out of the window. 'They won't be able to see my face yet. And it's raining. No one will be going out to the fields this morning.'

She seemed reluctant to go even when the lines of the mountain and of the roofs on its slopes were floating out of the rain. Finally it was time for the hotel maids to be up and about. She retouched her hair and ran, almost fled, from the room, brushing aside Shimamura's offer to see her to the door. Someone might catch a glimpse of the two of them together.

Shimamura went back to Tokyo that day.

*

'You remember what you said then? But you were wrong. Why else would anyone come to such a place in December? I wasn't laughing at you.'

The woman raised her head. Her face where it had been pressed against Shimamura's hand was red under the thick powder, from the eye across the bridge of the nose. It made him think of the snow-country cold, and yet, because of the darkness of her hair, there was a certain warmth in it.

She smiled quietly, as though dazzled by a bright light. Perhaps, as she smiled, she thought of 'them', and Shimamura's words gradually coloured her whole body. When she bowed her head, a little stiffly, he could see that even her back under her kimono was flushed a deep red. Set off by the colour of her hair, the moist sensuous skin was as if laid naked before him. Her hair could not really have been called thick. Stiff like a man's, and swept up into a high Japanese-style coiffure with not a hair out of place, it glowed like some heavy black stone.

Shimamura looked at the hair and wondered whether the coldness that had so startled him – he had never touched such cold hair, he said – might be less the cold of the snow-country winter than something in the hair itself. The woman began counting on her fingers. For some time she counted on.

'What are you counting?' he asked. Still the counting continued.

'It was the twenty-third of May.'

'You're counting the days, are you. Don't forget that July and August are two long months in a row.'

'It's the hundred-and-ninety-ninth day. It's exactly a hundred and ninety-nine days.'

'How did you remember it was the twenty-third of May?'

'All I have to do is look in my diary.'

'You keep a diary?'

'It's always fun to read an old diary. But I don't hide anything when I write in my diary, and sometimes I'm ashamed to look at it myself.'

'When did you begin?'

'Just before I went to Tokyo as a geisha. I didn't have any money, and I bought a plain notebook for two or three sen and drew in lines. I must have had a very sharp pencil. The

lines are all neat and close together, and every page is cram-
med from top to bottom. When I had enough money to buy
a diary, it wasn't the same any more. I started taking things
for granted. It's that way with my writing practice, too. I used
to practise on newspapers before I even thought of trying good
paper, but now I set it down on good paper from the start.'

'And you've kept the diary all this time?'

'Yes. The year I was sixteen and this year have been the best.
I write in my diary when I'm home from a party and ready for
bed, and when I read it over I can see places where I've gone to
sleep writing. . . . But I don't write every day. Some days I miss.
Way off here in the mountains, every party's the same. This
year I couldn't find anything except a diary with a new day on
each page. It was a mistake. When I start writing, I want to
write on and on.'

But even more than at the diary, Shimamura was surprised
at her statement that she had carefully catalogued every novel
and short story she had read since she was fifteen or sixteen.
The record already filled ten notebooks.

'You write down your criticisms, do you?'

'I could never do anything like that. I just write down the
author and the characters and how they are related to each
other. That is about all.'

'But what good does it do?'

'None at all.'

'A waste of effort.'

'A complete waste of effort,' she answered brightly, as
though the admission meant little to her. She gazed solemnly
at Shimamura, however.

A complete waste of effort. For some reason Shimamura
wanted to stress the point. But, drawn to her at that moment,
he felt a quiet like the voice of the rain flow over him. He
knew well enough that for her it was in fact no waste of effort,
but somehow the final determination that it was had the effect
of distilling and purifying the woman's existence.

Her talk of novels seemed to have little to do with 'literature' in the everyday sense of the word. The only friendly ties
she had with the people of this village had come from exchanging women's magazines, and afterwards she had gone on

with her reading by herself. She was quite indiscriminate and had little understanding of literature, and she borrowed even the novels and magazines she found lying in the guests' rooms at the inn. Not a few of the new novelists whose names came to her meant nothing to Shimamura. Her manner was as though she were talking of a distant foreign literature. There was something lonely, something sad in it, something that rather suggested a beggar who has lost all desire. It occurred to Shimamura that his own distant fantasy on the Occidental ballet, built up from words and photographs in foreign books, was not in its way dissimilar.

She talked on happily too of films and plays she had never seen. She had no doubt been starved all these months for someone who would listen to her. Had she forgotten that a hundred and ninety-nine days earlier exactly this sort of conversation had set off the impulse to throw herself at Shimamura? Again she lost herself in the talk, and again her words seemed to be warming her whole body.

But her longing for the city had become an undemanding dream, wrapped in simple resignation, and the note of wasted effort was much stronger in it than any suggestion of the exile's lofty dissatisfaction. She did not seem to find herself especially sad, but in Shimamura's eyes there was something strangely touching about her. Were he to give himself quite up to that consciousness of wasted effort, Shimamura felt, he would be drawn into a remote emotionalism that would make his own life a waste. But before him was the quick, live face of the woman, ruddy from the mountain air.

In any case, he had revised his view of her, and he had found, surprisingly, that her being a geisha made it even more difficult for him to be free and open with her.

Dead-drunk that night, she had savagely bitten her half-paralysed arm in a fit of irritation at its recalcitrance. 'What's the matter with you? Damn you, damn you. Lazy, worthless. What's the matter with you?'

And, unable to stand, she had rolled from side to side. 'I'll never have any regrets. But I'm not that sort of woman. I'm not that sort of woman.'

'The midnight for Tokyo.' The woman seemed to sense his

hesitation, and she spoke as if to push it away. At the sound of the train whistle she stood up. Roughly throwing open a paper-panelled door and the window behind it, she sat down on the sill with her body thrown back against the railing. The train moved off into the distance, its echo fading into a sound as of the night wind. Cold air flooded the room.

'Have you lost your mind?' Shimamura too went over to the window. The air was still, without a suggestion of wind.

It was a stern night landscape. The sound of the freezing of snow over the land seemed to roar deep into the earth. There was no moon. The stars, almost too many of them to be true, came forward so brightly that it was as if they were falling with the swiftness of the void. As the stars came nearer, the sky retreated deeper and deeper into the night colour. The layers of the Border Range, indistinguishable one from another, cast their heaviness at the skirt of the starry sky in a blackness grave and sombre enough to communicate their mass. The whole of the night scene came together in a clear, tranquil harmony.

As she sensed Shimamura's approach, the woman fell over with her breast against the railing. There was no hint of weakness in the pose. Rather, against the night, it was the strongest and most stubborn she could have taken. So we have to go through that again, thought Shimamura.

Black though the mountains were, they seemed at that moment brilliant with the colour of the snow. They seemed to him somehow transparent, somehow lonely. The harmony between sky and mountains was lost.

Shimamura put his hand to the woman's throat. 'You'll catch cold. See how cold it is.' He tried to pull her back, but she clung to the railing.

'I'm going home.' Her voice was choked.

'Go home, then.'

'Let me stay like this a little longer.'

'I'm going down for a bath.'

'No, stay here with me.'

'If you close the window.'

'Let me stay here like this a little longer.'

Half the village was hidden behind the cedars of the shrine

grove. The light in the railway station, not ten minutes away by taxi, flickered on and off as if crackling in the cold.

The woman's hair, the glass of the window, the sleeve of his kimono – everything he touched was cold in a way Shimamura had never known before.

Even the straw mats under his feet seemed cold. He started down to the bath.

'Wait. I'll go with you.' The woman followed meekly.

As she was rearranging the clothes he had thrown to the floor outside the bath, another guest, a man, came in. The woman crouched low in front of Shimamura and hid her face.

'Excuse me.' The other guest started to back away.

'No, please,' Shimamura said quickly. 'We'll go next door.' He scooped up his clothes and stepped over to the women's bath. The woman followed as if they were married. Shimamura plunged into the bath without looking back at her. He felt a high laugh mount to his lips now that he knew she was with him. He put his face to the hot-water tap and noisily rinsed his mouth.

Back in the room, she raised her head a little from the pillow and pushed her side hair up with her little finger.

'This makes me very sad.' She said only that. Shimamura thought for a moment that her eyes were half open, but he saw that the thick eyelashes created the illusion.

The woman, always high-strung, did not sleep the whole night.

It was apparently the sound of the *obi* being tied that awakened Shimamura.

'I'm sorry. I should have let you sleep. It's still dark. Look – can you see me?' She turned off the light. 'Can you see me? You can't?'

'I can't see you. It's still pitch dark.'

'No, no. I want you to look close. Now. Can you see me?' She threw open the window. 'It's no good. You can see me. I'm going.'

Surprised anew at the morning cold, Shimamura raised his head from the pillow. The sky was still the colour of night, but in the mountains it was already morning.

36

'But it's all right. The farmers aren't busy this time of the year, and no one will be out so early. But do you suppose someone might be going out into the mountains?' She talked on to herself, and she walked about trailing the end of the half-tied *obi*. 'There were no guests on the five-o'clock from Tokyo. None of the inn people will be up for a long while yet.'

Even when she had finished tying the *obi*, she stood up and sat down and stood up again, and wandered about the room with her eye on the window. She seemed on edge, like some restless night beast that fears the approach of the morning. It was as though a strange, magical wildness had taken her.

Presently the room was so light that he could see the red of her cheeks. His eye was fastened on that extraordinarily bright red.

'Your cheeks are flaming. That's how cold it is.'

'It's not from the cold. It's because I've taken off my powder. I only have to get into bed and in a minute I'm warm as an oven. All the way to my feet.' She knelt at the mirror by the bed.

'It's daylight. I'm going home.'

Shimamura glanced up at her, and immediately lowered his head. The white in the depths of the mirror was the snow, and floating in the middle of it were the woman's bright red cheeks. There was an indescribably fresh beauty in the contrast.

Was the sun already up? The brightness of the snow was more intense, it seemed to be burning icily. Against it, the woman's hair became a clearer black, touched with a purple sheen.

Probably to keep snow from piling up, the water from the baths was led around the walls of the inn by a makeshift ditch, and in front of the entrance it spread out like a shallow spring. A powerful black dog stood on the stones by the doorway lapping at the water. Skis for the hotel guests, probably brought out from a store-room, were lined up to dry, and the faint smell of mildew was sweetened by the steam. The snow that had fallen from the cedar branches to the roof of the public bath was breaking down into something warm and shapeless.

By the end of the year, that road would be shut off from sight by the snowstorms. She would have to go to her parties in long rubber boots with baggy 'mountain trousers' over her kimono, and she would have a cape pulled around her and a veil over her face. The snow would by then be ten feet deep – the woman had looked down on the steep road from the window of the inn, high on a hill, before daybreak this morning, and now Shimamura was walking down the same road. Napkins hung high beside the road to dry. Under them stretched the vista of the Border Range, the snow on its peaks glowing softly. The green onions in the garden patches were not yet buried in the snow.

Children of the village were ski-ing in the fields.

As he started into the part of the village that fronted on the highway, he heard a sound as of quiet rain.

Little icicles glistened daintily along the eaves.

'While you're at it, would you mind shovelling a little from ours?' Dazzled by the bright light, a woman on her way back from the bath wiped at her forehead with a damp towel as she looked up at a man shovelling snow from a roof. A waitress, probably, who had drifted into the village a little in advance of the ski-ing season. Next door was a café with a sagging roof, its painted window flaking with age.

Rows of stones held down the shingles with which most of the houses along the street were roofed. Only on the side exposed to the sun did the round stones show their back surfaces, less a moist black from the melting snow than an inkstone black, beaten away at by icy wind and storm. The houses were of a kind, with the dark stones on their roofs. The low eaves hugging the ground seemed to have in them the very essence of the north country.

Children were breaking off chunks of ice from the drains and throwing them down in the middle of the road. It was no doubt the sparkle of the ice as it went flying off into bits that enchanted them so. Shimamura, standing in the sunlight, found it hard to believe that the ice could be so thick. He stopped for a moment to watch.

A girl of twelve or thirteen stood knitting, apart from the rest, her back against a stone wall. Under the baggy 'mountain trousers', her feet were bare but for sandals, and Shimamura could see that the soles were red and cracked from the cold. A girl of perhaps two stood on a bundle of firewood beside her patiently holding a ball of yarn. Even the faded, ashen line of reclaimed yarn from the younger girl to the older seemed warmly aglow.

He could hear a carpenter's plane in a ski shop seven or eight doors down the street. Five or six geisha were talking under the eaves opposite. Among them, he was sure, would be the woman, Komako – he had just that morning learned her geisha name from a maid at the inn. And indeed, there she was. She had apparently noticed him. The deadly serious expression on her face set her off from the others. She would of course flush scarlet, but if she could at least pretend that nothing had happened – before Shimamura had time to go further with his thoughts, he saw that she had flushed to the throat. She might better have looked away, but her head turned little by little to follow him, while her eyes were fixed on the ground in acute discomfort.

Shimamura's cheeks too were aflame. He walked briskly by, and immediately Komako came after him.

'You mustn't. You embarrass me, walking by at a time like this.'

'I embarrass you – you think I'm not embarrassed myself, with all of you lined up to waylay me? I could hardly make myself walk past. Is it always this way?'

'Yes, I suppose so. In the afternoon."

'But I'd think you'd be even more embarrassed, turning bright red and then chasing after me.'

'What difference does it make?' The words were clear and definite, but she was blushing again. She stopped and put her arm around a persimmon tree beside the road. 'I ran after you because I thought I might ask you to come to my house.'

'Is your house near here?'

'Very near.'

'I'll come if you'll let me read your diary.'

'I'm going to burn my diary before I die.'

'But isn't there a sick man in your house?'

'How did you know?'

'You were at the station to meet him yesterday. You had on a dark-blue cape. I was sitting near him on the train. And there was a woman with him, looking after him, as gentle as she could be. His wife? Or someone who went from here to bring him home? Or someone from Tokyo? She was exactly like a mother. I was very much impressed.'

'Why didn't you say so last night? Why were you so quiet?' Something had upset her.

'His wife?'

Komako did not answer. 'Why didn't you say anything last night? What a strange person you are.'

Shimamura did not like this sharpness. Nothing he had done and nothing that had happened seemed to call for it, and he wondered if something basic in the woman's nature might not be coming to the surface. Still, when she came at him the second time, he had to admit that he was being hit in a vulnerable spot. This morning, as he glanced at Komako in that mirror reflecting the mountain snow, he had of course thought of the girl in the evening train window. Why then had he said nothing?

'It doesn't matter if there is a sick man. No one ever comes to my room.' Komako went in through an opening in a low stone wall.

To the right was a small field, and to the left persimmon trees stood along the wall that marked off the neighbouring plot. There seemed to be a flower garden in front of the house, and red carp were swimming in the little lotus pond. The ice had been broken away and lay piled along the bank. The house was old and decayed like the pitted trunk of a persimmon. There were patches of snow on the roof, the rafters of which sagged to draw a wavy line at the eaves.

The air in the earthen-floored hallway was still and cold. Shimamura was led up a ladder before his eyes had become accustomed to the darkness. It was a ladder in the truest sense of the word, and the room at the top was an attic.

'This is the room the silkworms used to live in. Are you surprised?'

'You're lucky you've never fallen downstairs, drinking the way you do.'

40

'I have. But generally when I've had too much to drink I crawl into the *kotatsu* downstairs and go off to sleep.' She pushed her hand tentatively into the *kotatsu*, then went below for charcoal. Shimamura looked around at the curious room. Although there was but one low window, opening to the south, the freshly changed paper on the door turned off the rays of the sun brightly. The walls had been industriously pasted over with rice paper, so that the effect was rather like the inside of an old-fashioned paper box; but overhead was only the bare roof sloping down towards the window, as if a dark loneliness had settled itself over the room. Wondering what might be on the other side of the wall, Shimamura had the uneasy feeling that he was suspended in a void. But the walls and the floor, for all their shabbiness, were spotlessly clean.

For a moment he was taken with the fancy that the light must pass through Komako, living in the silkworms' room, as it passed through the translucent silkworms.

The *kotatsu* was covered with a quilt of the same rough, striped cotton material as the standard 'mountain trousers'. The chest of drawers was old, but the grain of the wood was fine and straight – perhaps it was a relic of Komako's years in Tokyo. It was badly paired with a cheap dresser, while the vermilion sewing-box gave off the luxurious glow of good lacquer. The boxes stacked along the wall behind a thin woollen curtain apparently served as bookshelves.

The kimono of the evening before hung on the wall, open to show the brilliant red under-kimono.

Komako came spryly up the ladder with a supply of charcoal.

'It's from the sickroom. But you needn't worry. They say fire spreads no germs.' Her newly dressed hair almost brushed the *kotatsu* as she stirred away at the coals. The music teacher's son had intestinal tuberculosis, she said, and had come home to die.

But it was not entirely accurate to say that he had 'come home'. He had as a matter of fact not been born here. This was his mother's home. His mother had taught dancing down on the coast even when she was no longer a geisha, but she had had a stroke while she was still in her forties, and had

come back to this hot spring to recover. The son, fond of ma-
chinery since he was a child, had stayed behind to work in a
watch-shop. Presently he moved to Tokyo and started going
to night school, and the strain was evidently too much for
him. He was only twenty-five.

All this Komako told him with no hesitation, but she said
nothing about the girl who had brought the man home, and
nothing about why she herself was in this house.

Shimamura felt most uncomfortable at what she did say,
however. Suspended there in the void, she seemed to be broad-
casting to the four directions.

As he stepped from the hall-way, he saw something faintly
white through the corner of his eye. It was a samisen box, and
it struck him as larger and longer than it should be. He found
it hard to imagine her carrying so unwieldy an object to parties. The darkened door inside the hall-way slid open.

'Do you mind if I step over this, Komako?' It was that clear
voice, so beautiful that it was almost sad. Shimamura waited
for an echo to come back.

It was Yoko's voice, the voice that had called out over the
snow to the station-master the night before.

'No, please go ahead.' Yoko stepped lightly over the samisen
box, a glass chamber-pot in her hand.

It was clear, from the familiar way she had talked to the
station-master the evening before and from the way she wore
'mountain trousers', that she was a native of this snow country, but the bold pattern of her *obi*, half visible over the trousers, made the rough russet and black stripes of the latter seem
fresh and cheerful, and for the same reason the long sleeves
of her woollen kimono took on a certain voluptuous charm.
The trousers, split just below the knees, filled out towards the
hips, and the heavy cotton, for all its natural stiffness, was
somehow supple and gentle.

Yoko darted one quick, piercing glance at Shimamura and
went silently out over the earthen floor.

Even when he had left the house, Shimamura was haunted
by that glance, burning just in front of his forehead. It was
cold as a very distant light, for the inexpressible beauty of it
had made his heart rise when, the night before, that light off

in the mountains had passed across the girl's face in the train window and lighted her eye for a moment. The impression came back to Shimamura, and with it the memory of the mirror filled with snow, and Komako's red cheeks floating in the middle of it.

He walked faster. His legs were round and plump, but he was seized with a certain abandon as he walked along gazing at the mountains he was so fond of, and his pace quickened, though he hardly knew it. Always ready to give himself up to reverie, he could not believe that the mirror floating over the evening scenery and the other snowy mirror were really works of man. They were part of nature, and part of some distant world.

And the room he had only this moment left had become part of that same distant world.

Startled at himself, in need of something to cling to, he stopped a blind masseuse at the top of the hill.

'Could you give me a massage?'

'Let me see. What time will it be?' She tucked her cane under her arm and, taking a covered pocket watch from her *obi*, felt at the face with her left hand. 'Two thirty-five. I have an appointment over beyond the station at three-thirty. But I suppose it won't matter if I'm a little late.'

'You're very clever to be able to tell the time.'

'It has no glass, and I can feel the hands.'

'You can feel the figures?'

'Not the figures.' She took the watch out again, a silver one, large for a woman, and flicked open the lid. She laid her fingers across the face with one at twelve and one at six, and a third halfway between at three. 'I can tell the time fairly well. I may be a minute off one way or the other, but I never miss by as much as two minutes.'

'You don't find the road a little slippery?'

'When it rains my daughter comes to call for me. At night I take care of the people in the village, and never come up this far. The maids at the inn are always joking and saying it's because my husband won't let me go out at night.'

'Your children are growing up?'

'The oldest girl is twelve.' They had reached Shimamura's

room, and they were silent for a time as the massaging began. The sound of a samisen came to them from the distance.

'Who would that be, I wonder?'

'You can always tell which geisha it is by the tone?'

'I can tell some of them. Some I can't. You must not have to work. Feel how nice and soft you are.'

'No stiff muscles on me.'

'A little stiff here at the base of the neck. But you're just right, not too fat and not too thin. And you don't drink, do you?'

'You can tell that?'

'I have three other customers with physiques exactly like yours.'

'A common sort of physique.'

'But when you don't drink, you don't know what it is really to enjoy yourself – to forget everything that happens.'

'Your husband drinks, does he?'

'Much too much.'

'But whoever it is, she's not much of a musician.'

'Very poor indeed.'

'Do you play yourself?'

'I did when I was young. From the time I was eight till I was nineteen. I haven't played for fifteen years now. Not since I was married.'

Did all blind people look younger than they were? Shimamura wondered.

'But if you learn when you're young, you never forget.'

'My hands have changed from doing this sort of work, but my ear is still good. It makes me very impatient to hear them playing. But then I suppose I felt impatient at my own playing when I was young.' She listened for a time. 'Fumi at the Izutsuya, maybe. The best ones and the worst are the easiest to tell.'

'There are good ones?'

'Komako is very good. She's young, but she's improved a great deal lately.'

'Really?'

'You know her, don't you? I say she's good, but you have to

remember that our standards here in the mountains are not very high.'

'I don't really know her. I was on the train with the music teacher's son last night, though.'

'He's well again?'

'Apparently not.'

'Oh? He's been sick for a long time in Tokyo, and they say it was to help pay the doctors' bills that Komako became a geisha last summer. I wonder if it did any good.'

'Komako, you say?'

'They were only engaged. But I suppose you feel better afterwards if you've done everything you can.'

'She was engaged to him?'

'So they say. I don't really know, but that's the rumour.'

It was almost too ordinary a thing to hear gossip about geisha from the hot-spring masseuse, and that fact had the perverse effect of making the news the more startling; and Komako's having become a geisha to help her fiancé was so ordinary a bit of melodrama that he found himself almost refusing to accept it. Perhaps certain moral considerations – questions of the propriety of selling oneself as a geisha – helped the refusal.

Shimamura was beginning to think he would like to go deeper into the story, but the masseuse was silent.

If Komako was the man's fiancée, and Yoko was his new lover, and the man was going to die – the expression 'wasted effort' again came into Shimamura's mind. For Komako thus to guard her promise to the end, for her even to sell herself to pay doctors' bills – what was it if not wasted effort?

He would accost her with this fact, he would drive it home, when he saw her again, he said to himself; and yet her existence seemed to have become purer and cleaner for this new bit of knowledge.

Aware of a shameful danger lurking in his numbed sense of the false and empty, he lay concentrating on it, trying to feel it, for some time after the masseuse left. He was chilled to the pit of his stomach – but someone had left the windows wide open.

The colour of evening had already fallen on the mountain valley, early buried in shadows. Out of the dusk the distant mountains, still reflecting the light of the evening sun, seemed to have come much nearer.

Presently, as the mountain chasms were far and near, high and low, the shadows in them began to deepen, and the sky was red over the snowy mountains, bathed now in but a wan light.

Cedar groves stood out darkly by the river bank, at the ground, around the shrine.

Like a warm light, Komako poured in on the empty wretchedness that had assailed Shimamura.

There was a meeting at the inn to discuss plans for the ski season. She had been called in for the party afterwards. She put her hands into the *kotatsu*, then quickly reached up and stroked Shimamura's cheek.

'You're pale this evening. Very strange.' She clutched at the soft flesh of his cheek as if to tear it away. 'Aren't you a foolish one, though.'

She already seemed a little drunk. When she came back from the party she collapsed before the mirror, and drunkenness came out on her face to almost comic effect. 'I know nothing about it. Nothing. My head aches. I feel terrible. Terrible. I want a drink. Give me water.'

She pressed both hands to her face and tumbled over with little concern for her carefully dressed hair. Presently she brought herself up again and began cleaning away the thick powder with cold cream. The face underneath was a brilliant red. She was quite delighted with herself. To Shimamura it was astonishing that drunkenness could pass so quickly. Her shoulders were shaking from the cold.

All through August she had been near nervous collapse, she told him quietly.

'I thought I'd go mad. I kept brooding over something, and I didn't know myself what it was. It was terrifying. I couldn't sleep. I kept myself under control only when I went out to a party. I had all sorts of dreams, and I lost my appetite. I would sit there jabbing at the floor for hours on end, all through the hottest part of the day.'

'When did you first go out as a geisha?'

'In June. I thought for a while I might go to Hamamatsu.'

'Get married?'

She nodded. The man had been after her to marry him, but she couldn't like him. She had had great trouble deciding what to do.

'But if you didn't like him, what were you so undecided about?'

'It's not that simple.'

'Marriage has so much charm?'

'Don't be nasty. It's more that I want to have everything around me tidy and in order.'

Shimamura grunted.

'You're not a very satisfying person, you know.'

'Was there something between you and the man from Hamamatsu?'

She flung out her answer: 'If there had been, do you think I would have hesitated? But he said that as long as I stayed here, he wouldn't let me marry anyone else. He said he would do everything possible to stand in the way.'

'But what could he do from as far away as Hamamatsu? You worried about that?'

Komako stretched out for a time, enjoying the warmth of her body. When she spoke again, her tone was quite casual. 'I thought I was pregnant.' She giggled. 'It seems ridiculous when I look back on it now.'

She curled up like a little child, and grabbed at the neck of his kimono with her two fists.

The rich eyelashes again made him think that her eyes were half open.

Her elbow against the brazier, Komako was scribbling something on the back of an old magazine when Shimamura awoke the next morning.

'I can't go home. I jumped up when the maid came to bring charcoal, but it was already broad daylight. The sun was shining in on the door. I was a little drunk last night, and I slept too well.'

'What time is it?'

'It's already eight.'

'Let's go and have a bath.' Shimamura got out of bed.

'I can't. Someone might see me in the hall.' She was completely tamed. When Shimamura came back from the bath, he found her industriously cleaning the room, a kerchief draped artistically over her head.

She had polished the legs of the table and the edge of the brazier almost too carefully, and she stirred up the charcoal with a practised hand.

Shimamura sat idly smoking, his feet in the *kotatsu*. When the ashes dropped from his cigarette Komako took them up in a handkerchief and brought him an ashtray. He laughed, a bright morning laugh. Komako laughed too.

'If you had a husband, you'd spend all your time scolding him.'

'I would not. But I'd be laughed at for folding up even my dirty clothes. I can't help it. That's the way I am.'

'They say you can tell everything about a woman by looking inside her dresser drawers.'

'What a beautiful day.' They were having breakfast, and the morning sun flooded the room. 'I should have gone home early to practise the samisen. The sound is different on a day like this.' She looked up at the crystal-clear sky.

The snow on the distant mountains was soft and creamy, as if veiled in a faint smoke.

Shimamura, remembering what the masseuse had said, suggested that she practise here instead. Immediately she telephoned her house to ask for music and a change of clothes.

So the house he had seen the day before had a telephone, thought Shimamura. The eyes of the other girl, Yoko, floated into his mind.

'That girl will bring your music?'

'She might.'

'You're engaged to the son, are you?'

'Well! When did you hear that?'

'Yesterday.'

'Aren't you strange? If you heard it yesterday, why didn't you tell me?' But her tone showed none of the sharpness of the day before. Today there was only a clean smile on her face.

'That sort of thing would be easier to talk about if I had less respect for you.'

'What are you really thinking, I wonder? That's why I don't like Tokyo people.'

'You're trying to change the subject. You haven't answered my question, you know.'

'I'm not trying to change the subject. You really believed it?'

'I did.'

'You're lying again. You didn't really.'

'I couldn't quite believe all of it, as a matter of fact. But they said you went to work as a geisha to help pay doctors' bills.'

'It sounds like something out of a cheap magazine. But it's not true. I was never engaged to him. People seem to think I was, though. It wasn't to help anyone in particular that I became a geisha. But I owe a great deal to his mother, and I had to do what I could.'

'You're talking in riddles.'

'I'll tell you everything. Very clearly. There does seem to have been a time when his mother thought it would be a good idea for us to get married. But she only thought it. She never said a word. Both of us knew in a vague sort of way what was on her mind, but it went no farther. And that's all there is to tell.'

'Childhood friends.'

'That's right. But we've lived most of our lives apart. When they sent me to Tokyo to be a geisha, he was the only one who saw me off. I have that written down on the very first page of my very oldest diary.'

'If the two of you had stayed together, you'd probably be married by now.'

'I doubt it.'

'You would be, though.'

'You needn't worry about him. He'll be dead before long.'

'But is it right for you to be spending your nights away from home?'

'It's not right for you to ask. How can a dying man keep me from doing as I like?'

Shimamura could think of no answer.

Why was it that Komako said not a word about the girl Yoko?

And Yoko, who had taken care of the sick man on the train, quite as his mother must have when he was very young – how would she feel coming to an inn with a change of kimono for Komako, who was something, Shimamura could not know what, to the man Yoko had come home with?

Shimamura found himself off in his usual distant fantasies.

'Komako, Komako.' Yoko's beautiful voice was low but clear.

'Thank you very much.' Komako went out to the dressing-room. 'You brought it yourself, did you? It must have been heavy.'

Yoko left immediately.

The top string snapped as Komako plucked tentatively at the samisen. Shimamura could tell even while she was changing the string and tuning the instrument that she had a firm, confident touch. She took up a bulky bundle and undid it on the *kotatsu*. Inside were an ordinary book of lyrics and some twenty scores. Shimamura glanced curiously at the latter.

'You practise from these?'

'I have to. There's no one here who can teach me.'

'What about the woman you live with?'

'She's paralysed.'

'If she can talk she ought to be able to help you.'

'But she can't talk. She can still use her left hand to correct mistakes in dancing, but it only annoys her to have to listen to the samisen and not be able to do anything about it.'

'Can you really understand the music from only a score?'

'I understand it very well.'

'The publishing gentleman would be happy if he knew he had a real geisha – not just an ordinary amateur – practising from his scores way off here in the mountains.'

'In Tokyo I was expected to dance, and they gave me dancing lessons. But I got only the faintest idea of how to play the samisen. If I were to lose that there would be no one here to teach me again. So I use scores.'

'And singing?'

'I don't like singing. I did learn a few songs from my dancing, and I manage to get through them, but newer things I've had to pick up from the radio. I've no idea how near right I am. My own private style – you'd laugh at it, I know. And then my voice gives out when I'm singing for someone I know well. It's always loud and brave for strangers.' She looked a little bashful for a moment, then brought herself up and glanced at Shimamura as though signalling that she was ready for him to begin.

He was embarrassed. He was unfortunately no singer.

He was generally familiar with the Nagauta music of the Tokyo theatre and dance, and he knew the words to most of the repertoire. He had had no formal training, however. Indeed he associated the Nagauta less with the parlour performance of the geisha than with the actor on the stage.

'The customer is being difficult.' Giving her lower lip a quick little bite, Komako brought the samisen to her knee, and, as if that made her a different person, turned earnestly to the lyrics before her.

'I've been practising this one since last autumn.'

A chill swept over Shimamura. The goose flesh seemed to rise even to his cheeks. The first notes opened a transparent emptiness deep in his entrails, and in the emptiness the sound of the samisen reverberated. He was startled – or, better, he fell back as under a well-aimed blow. Taken with a feeling almost of reverence, washed by waves of remorse, defenceless, quite deprived of strength – there was nothing for him to do but give himself up to the current, to the pleasure of being swept off wherever Komako would take him.

She was a mountain geisha, not yet twenty, and she could hardly be as good as all that, he told himself. And in spite of the fact that she was in a small room, was she not slamming away at the instrument as though she were on the stage? He was being carried away by his own mountain emotionalism. Komako purposely read the words in a monotone, now slowing down and now jumping over a passage that was too much trouble; but gradually she seemed to fall into a spell. As her voice rose higher, Shimamura began to feel a little frightened. How far would that strong, sure touch take him? He rolled over and pillowed his head on an arm, as if in bored indifference.

The end of the song released him. Ah, this woman is in love with me – but he was annoyed with himself for the thought.

Komako looked up at the clear sky over the snow. 'The tone is different on a day like this.' The tone had been as rich and vibrant as her remark suggested. The air was different. There were no theatre walls, there was no audience, there was none of the city dust. The notes went out crystalline into the clean winter morning, to sound on the far, snowy peaks.

Practising alone, not aware herself of what was happening, perhaps, but with all the wideness of nature in this mountain valley for her companion, she had come quite as a part of nature to take on this special power. Her very loneliness beat down sorrow and fostered a wild strength of will. There was no doubt that it had been a great victory of the will, even granted that she had had an amount of preparatory training, for her to learn complicated airs from only a score, and presently go through them from memory.

To Shimamura it was wasted effort, this way of living. He sensed in it too a longing that called out to him for sympathy. But the life and way of living no doubt flowed thus grandly from the samisen with a new worth for Komako herself.

Shimamura, untrained in the niceties of samisen technique and conscious only of the emotion in the tone, was perhaps an ideal audience for Komako.

By the time she had begun her third song – the voluptuous softness of the music itself may have been responsible – the chill and the goose flesh had disappeared, and Shimamura, relaxed and warm, was gazing into Komako's face. A feeling of intense physical nearness came over him.

The high, thin nose was usually a little lonely, a little sad, but today, with the healthy, vital flush on her cheeks, it was rather whispering: I am here too. The smooth lips seemed to reflect back a dancing light even when they were drawn into a tight bud; and when for a moment they were stretched wide, as the singing demanded, they were quick to contract again into that engaging little bud. Their charm was exactly like the charm of her body itself. Her eyes, moist and shining, made her look like a very young girl. She wore no powder, and the polish of the city geisha had over it a layer of mountain colour. Her skin, suggesting the newness of a freshly peeled onion or perhaps a lily bulb, was flushed faintly, even to the throat. More than anything, it was clean.

Seated rigidly upright, she seemed more demure and maidenly than usual.

This time using a score, she sang a song she had not yet finished memorizing. At the end she silently pushed the plectrum under the strings and let herself fall into an easier posture.

Her manner quickly took on a touch of the seductive and alluring.

Shimamura could think of nothing to say. Komako did not seem to care particularly what he thought of her playing, however. She was quite unaffectedly pleased with herself.

'Can you always tell which geisha it is from the tone of the samisen?'

'That's easy. There aren't twenty of us all together. It depends a little on the style, though. The individual comes out more in some styles than in others.'

She took up the samisen again and shifted her weight so that her feet were a little to one side and the instrument rested on the calf of one leg.

'This is the way you hold it when you're small.' She leaned towards the samisen as though it were too large for her. 'Da-a-ark hair....' Her voice was deliberately childish and she picked out the notes uncertainly.

'"Dark Hair" was the first one you learned?'

'Uh uh.' She shook her head girlishly, as no doubt she did in the days when she was still too small to hold the samisen properly.

Komako no longer tried to leave before daybreak when she stayed the night.

'Komako,' the two-year-old daughter of the innkeeper would call from far down the hall, her voice rising in the mountain-country lilt. The two of them would play happily in the *kotatsu* until nearly noon, when they would go for a bath.

Back from the bath, Komako was combing her hair. 'Whenever the child sees a geisha, she calls out "Komako" in that funny accent, and when she sees a picture of someone with her hair done in the old way, that's "Komako" too. Children can tell when you like them. Come, Kimi. Let's go and play at Komako's.' She stood up to leave, then sat down lazily on the veranda. 'Eager people from Tokyo already out ski-ing.'

The room looked from high ground directly south over the ski runs at the base of the mountain.

Shimamura glanced up from the *kotatsu*. There were patches of snow on the mountain, and five or six figures in black ski clothes were moving about in the terraced fields. It seemed a trifle silly. The slope was a gentle one, and the walls between the fields were not yet covered with snow.

'They look like students. Is today Sunday? Do you suppose that's fun?'

'They're good, though,' Komako said, as if to herself. 'Guests are always surprised when a geisha says hello to them on the ski grounds. They don't recognize her for the snowburn. At night the powder hides it.'

'You wear ski clothes?'

She wore 'mountain trousers', she said. 'But what a nuisance the ski season is. It's all coming again. You see them in the evening at the inn, and they say they'll see you again the next day ski-ing. Maybe I should give up ski-ing this year. Good-bye. Come along, Kimi. We'll have snow this evening. It's always cold the night before it snows.'

Shimamura went out to the veranda. Komako was leading Kimi down the steep road below the ski grounds.

The sky was clouding over. Mountains still in the sunlight stood out against shadowed mountains. The play of light and shade changed from moment to moment, sketching a chilly landscape. Presently the ski grounds too were in shadow. Below the window Shimamura could see little needles of frost like isinglass among the withered chrysanthemums, though water was still dripping from the snow on the roof.

It did not snow that evening. A hailstorm turned to rain.

Shimamura called Komako again the night before he was to leave. It was a clear, moonlit night. At eleven o'clock the air was bitterly cold, but Komako insisted on going for a walk. She pulled him roughly from the *kotatsu*.

The road was frozen. The village lay quiet under the cold sky. Komako hitched up the skirt of her kimono and tucked it into her *obi*. The moon shone like a blade frozen in blue ice.

'We'll go to the station,' said Komako.

'You're insane. It's more than a mile each way.'

'You'll be going back to Tokyo soon. We'll go and look at the station.'

Shimamura was numb from his shoulders to his thighs.

Back in his room, Komako sank disconsolately to the floor. Her head was bowed and her arms were deep in the *kotatsu*. Strangely, she refused to go with him to the bath.

Bedding had been laid out with the foot of the mattress inside the *kotatsu*. Komako was sitting forlornly beside it when Shimamura came back from the bath. She said nothing.

'What's the matter?'

'I'm going home.'

'Don't be foolish.'

'Go on to bed. Just let me sit here for a little while.'

'Why do you want to go home?'

'I'm not going home. I'll sit here till morning.'

'Don't be difficult.'

'I'm not being difficult. I'm not being difficult.'

'Then ...?'

'I ... don't feel well.'

'Is that all?' Shimamura laughed. 'I'll leave you quite to yourself.'

'No.'

'And why did you have to go out and run all over town?'

'I'm going home.'

'There's no need to go home.'

'But it's not easy for me. Go on back to Tokyo. It's not easy for me.' Her face was low over the *kotatsu*.

Was it sorrow at finding herself about to sink into too deep a relationship with a traveller? Or at having to keep herself under control at so dear a moment? She has come that far, then, Shimamura said to himself. He too was silent for a time.

'Please go back to Tokyo.'

'As a matter of fact, I was thinking of going back tomorrow.'

'No! Why are you going back?' She looked up, startled, as though aroused from sleep.

'What can I do for you, no matter how long I stay?'

She gazed at him for a moment, then burst out violently: 'You don't have to say that. What reason have you to say that?' She stood up irritably, and threw herself at his neck. 'It's wrong of you to say such things. Get up. Get up, I tell you.' The words poured out deliriously, and she fell down beside him, quite forgetting in her derangement the physical difficulty she had spoken of earlier.

Some time later, she opened warm, moist eyes.

She picked up the hair ornament that had fallen to the floor.

'You really must go back tomorrow,' she said quietly.

As Shimamura was changing clothes to leave on the three-o'clock train the next afternoon, the manager of the inn beckoned Komako into the hall. 'Let's see. Suppose we make it about eleven hours,' he could hear Komako's answer. They were evidently discussing the bill for her services as a geisha, and the manager perhaps thought it would be unreasonable to charge for the whole sixteen or seventeen hours.

The bill as a matter of fact was computed by the hour – 'Left at five,' or 'Left at twelve' – without the usual charge for overnight services.

Komako, in an overcoat and a white scarf, saw him to the station.

Even when he had finished buying presents to take back to Tokyo, he had some twenty minutes to kill. Walking with Komako in the slightly raised station yard, he thought what a narrow little valley it was, crowded in among the snowy mountains. Komako's too-black hair was a little touching, a little sad, in the loneliness of the shadowed mountain pocket.

The sun shone dimly on a spot in the mountains far down the river.

'It's melted a good deal since I came.'

'Two days of snow, though, and we'll have six feet. Then it snows again, and before long the lights on those poles are out of sight. I'll walk along thinking of you, and I'll find myself strung up on a wire.'

'The snow is that deep?'

'They say that in the next town up the line the schoolchildren jump naked from the second floor of the dormitory. They sink out of sight in the snow, and they move around under it as though they were swimming. Look, a snowplough.'

'I'd like to see it that deep. But I suppose the inn will be crowded. And there might be danger of slides along the way.'

'With you it's not a question of money, is it? Have you always had so much to spend?' She turned to look up at his face. 'Why don't you grow a moustache?'

'I've thought of it.' Shimamura, freshly shaven, stroked the blue-black traces of his beard. A deep line from the corner of his mouth set off the softness of his cheek. Was that, he wondered, what Komako found attractive? 'You always look a little as though you'd just shaved too when you take off that powder.'

'Listen! The crows. That frightening way they sometimes have. Where are they, I wonder? And isn't it cold!' Komako hugged herself as she looked up at the sky.

'Shall we go in by the stove?'

A figure in 'mountain trousers' came running up the wide road from the main highway into the station yard. It was Yoko.

'Komako. Yukio – Komako,' she panted, clinging to Komako like a child that has run frightened to its mother, 'come home. Right away. Yukio's worse. Right away.'

Komako closed her eyes, as if from the pain of the assault on her shoulder. Her face was white, but she shook her head with surprising firmness.

'I can't go home. I'm seeing off a guest.'

Shimamura was startled. 'You needn't see me off.'

'It's not right to leave. How do I know you'll come again?'

'I'll come, I'll come.'

Yoko seemed not to hear the exchange. 'I just rang the inn,' she went on feverishly, 'and they said you were at the station. So I came here. I ran all the way. Yukio is asking for you.' She pulled at Komako, but Komako shook her off impatiently.

'Leave me alone.'

It was Komako who reeled back, however. She retched violently, but nothing came from her mouth. The rims of her eyes were moist. There was goose flesh on her cheeks.

Yoko stood rigid, gazing at Komako. Her face, like a mask, wore an expression of such utter earnestness that it was impossible to tell whether she was angry or surprised or grieved. It seemed an extraordinarily pure and simple face to Shimamura.

She turned quickly and, without the slightest change of expression, clutched at Shimamura's hand. 'I'm sorry, but would you let her go home?' A tense high-pitched voice assailed him. 'Let her go home.'

'Of course I'll let her go home. Go on home,' he called out to Komako. 'Don't be a fool.'

'And what say do you have in the matter?' Komako pushed Yoko roughly away from him.

Shimamura tried to signal the taxi waiting in front of the station. Yoko clutched at his arm so tightly that his fingers were numbed. 'I'll send her home in a taxi,' he said. 'Why don't you go on ahead? People will be watching us.'

Yoko nodded quickly, and turned away with almost unbelievable alacrity. Why was the girl always so earnest, so sober, Shimamura wondered. But such musings did not seem entirely in keeping with the occasion.

That voice, so beautiful it was almost lonely, lingered in Shimamura's ears as if it were echoing back from somewhere in the snowy mountains.

'Where are you going?' Komako pulled at Shimamura. He had signalled the taxi and was walking toward it. 'I won't. I'm not going home.'

For an instant Shimamura felt something very near physical revulsion.

'I don't know what there is between the three of you, but the man may be dying even now. She came for you, didn't she, because he wants to see you. Go home like a good girl. You'll regret it all your life if you don't. What if he dies even while you're standing here? Don't be stubborn. Forgive and forget.'

'Forgive and forget? You don't understand. You don't understand at all.'

'And when they sent you to Tokyo, he was the only one who saw you off, didn't you say? Do you think it's right not to say good-bye to the man you yourself said was on the very first page of the very first volume of your diary? This is the very last page of his.'

'But I don't want to. I don't want to see a man die.'

It could have been the coldest heartlessness or too warm a passion – Shimamura did not know which.

'I'll not be able to write in my diary any more. I'll burn it,' she said softly, almost to herself. Her cheeks were flushed. 'You're a good, simple person at heart, aren't you? If you really are, I won't mind sending my whole diary to you. You won't laugh at me? You're a good, honest person at heart, I'm sure.'

Shimamura was moved by a wave of feeling he could not define himself. He thought he must indeed be the plainest, most honest person in the world. He no longer worried about sending Komako home. She said nothing more.

A porter from the inn came to tell them that the gate to the tracks was open.

Four or five villagers in sombre winter dress got on and off the train.

'I'll not go to the platform with you. Good-bye.' Komako stood inside the closed window of the waiting-room. From the train window it was as though one strange piece of fruit had been left behind in the grimy glass case of a shabby mountain grocery.

The window of the waiting-room was clear for an instant as the train started to move. Komako's face glowed forth, and as quickly disappeared. It was the bright red it had been in the mirror that snowy morning, and for Shimamura that colour again seemed to be the point at which he parted with reality.

The train climbed the north slope of the Border Range into the long tunnel. On the far side it moved down a mountain valley. The colour of evening was descending from chasms between the peaks. The dim brightness of the winter afternoon seemed to have been sucked into the earth, and the

59

battered old train had shed its bright shell in the tunnel. There was no snow on the south slope.

Following a stream, the train came out on the plain. A mountain, cut at the top in curious notches and spires, fell off in a graceful sweep to the far skirts. Over it the moon was rising. The solid, integral shape of the mountain, taking up the whole of the evening landscape there at the end of the plain, was set off in a deep purple against the pale light of the sky. The moon was no longer an afternoon white, but, faintly coloured, it had not yet taken on the clear coldness of the winter night. There was not a bird in the sky. Nothing broke the lines of the wide skirts to the right and the left. Where the mountain swept down to meet the river, a stark white building, a hydro-electric plant perhaps, stood out sharply from the withered scene the train window framed, one last spot saved from the night.

The window began to steam over. The landscape outside was dusky, and the figures of the passengers floated up half-transparent. It was the play of that evening mirror again. The train, probably no more than three or four worn-out, faded, old-fashioned coaches strung together, was not from the same world as the trains one finds on the main lines. The light inside was dim.

Shimamura abandoned himself to the fancy that he had stepped into some unreal conveyance, that he was being borne away in emptiness, cut off from time and place. The monotonous sound of the wheels became the woman's voice.

Her words, though short and broken, were a sign that she was alive in all her vital intensity, and he knew he had not forgotten her from the fact that listening was a trial. But to the Shimamura of that moment, moving away from the woman, the voice was already a distant one that could do no more than sharpen the poignancy of travel.

Would Yukio be breathing his last even now? Komako had for reasons of her own refused to go home; and had she then failed to reach his bedside in time?

There were so few passengers that Shimamura felt a little uneasy.

Besides Shimamura himself, there were only a man, probably in his fifties, and opposite him a red-faced girl. A black shawl was thrown over the full flesh of her shoulders, and her cheeks were a wonderful, fiery red. She leaned slightly forward to catch every word the man said, and she answered him happily. A pair off on a long journey together, Shimamura concluded.

As the train pulled into a station behind which rose the chimneys of spinning-factories, however, the man hastily got up, took a wicker trunk from the baggage rack, and threw it out of the window to the platform. 'Maybe we'll meet again sometime,' he called back to the girl as he hurried from the train.

Shimamura suddenly wanted to weep. He had been caught quite off guard, and it struck him afresh that he had said good-bye to the woman and was on his way home.

He had not considered the possibility that the two had simply met on the train. The man was perhaps a travelling salesman.

Part Two

It was the egg-laying season for moths, Shimamura's wife told him as he left Tokyo, and he was not to leave his clothes hanging in the open. There were indeed moths at the inn. Five or six large corn-coloured moths clung to the decorative lantern under the eaves, and in the little dressing-room was a moth whose body was large out of all proportion to its wings.

The windows were still screened from the summer. A moth so still that it might have been glued there clung to one of the screens. Its feelers stood out like delicate wool, the colour of cedar bark, and its wings, the length of a woman's finger, were a pale, almost diaphanous green. The ranges of mountains beyond were already autumn-red in the evening sun. That one spot of pale green struck him as oddly like the colour of death. The fore and after wings overlapped to make a deeper green, and the wings fluttered like thin pieces of paper in the autumn wind.

Wondering if the moth was alive, Shimamura went over to the window and rubbed his finger over the inside of the screen. The moth did not move. He struck at it with his fist, and it fell like a leaf from a tree, floating lightly up midway to the ground.

In front of the cedar grove opposite, dragonflies were bobbing about in countless swarms, like dandelion floss in the wind.

The river seemed to flow from the tips of the cedar branches.

He thought he would never tire of looking at the autumn flowers that spread a blanket of silver up the side of the mountain.

A White Russian woman, a peddler, was sitting in the hallway when he came out of the bath. So you find them even in these mountains – he went for a closer look.

She appeared to be in her forties. Her face was wrinkled and dirty, but her skin, where it showed at the full throat and beyond, was a pure, glowing white.

'Where are you from?' Shimamura asked.

'Where am I from? Where am I from?' The woman seemed troubled for an answer. She began to put away her wares, the most ordinary Japanese cosmetics and hair ornaments.

Her skirt, like a dirty sheet wrapped around her, had quite lost the feel of Occidental dress, and had taken on instead something of the air of Japan. She carried her wares on her back in a large Japanese-style kerchief. But for all that, she still wore foreign shoes.

The innkeeper's wife stood beside Shimamura watching the Russian leave. The two of them went into the office, where a large woman was seated at the hearth with her back to them. She took her long skirts in her hand as she stood up to go. Her cloak was a formal black.

She was a geisha Shimamura remembered having seen with Komako in an advertising photograph, the two of them on skis with cotton 'mountain trousers' pulled over party kimonos. She seemed to be well on in years, plump and to all appearances good-natured.

The innkeeper was warming thick, oblong cakes over the embers.

'Won't you have one?' he asked Shimamura. 'You really must have one. The geisha you saw brought them to celebrate the end of her term.'

'She's leaving, is she?'

'Yes.'

'She looks like a good sort.'

'She was very popular. Today she's going the rounds to say good-bye.'

Shimamura blew on the cake and bit into it. The hard crust, a little sour, gave off a musty smell.

Outside the window, the bright red of ripe persimmons was bathed in the evening sun. It seemed to send out a red glow even to the bamboo of the pot-hook over the hearth.

'See how long they are.' Shimamura looked out in astonishment at the steep path, down which old women were trudging with bundles of autumn grass on their backs. The grass looked to be twice the height of the women, and the tassels were long and powerful.

'It's *kaya* grass.'

'*Kaya*, is it?'

'The government railways built a sort of rest-room, I suppose you would call it, for their hot-spring exhibit, and they thatched the teahouse with *kaya* from these mountains. Someone in Tokyo bought it exactly as it was.'

'*Kaya*, is it,' Shimamura repeated, half to himself. 'It's *kaya* then on the mountain? I thought it must be a flower of some sort.'

The first thing that had struck Shimamura's eye as he got off the train was that array of silver-white. High up the mountain, the *kaya* spread out silver in the sun, like the autumn sunlight itself pouring over the face of the mountain. Ah, I am here, something in Shimamura called out as he looked up at it.

But the great strands he saw here seemed quite different in nature from the grasses that had so moved him. The large bundles hid the women carrying them, and rustled against the rocks that flanked the path. And the plumes were long and powerful.

Under the dim light in the dressing-room, Shimamura could see that the large-bodied moth was laying eggs along the black lacquer of the clothes-frame. Moths were beating at the lantern under the eaves.

There was a steady humming of autumn insects, as there had been from before sundown.

Komako was a little late.

She gazed in at him from the hall.

'Why have you come here? Why have you come to a place like this?'

'I've come to see you.'

'You don't mean that. I dislike people from Tokyo because they're always lying.' She sat down, and her voice was softer. 'I'm never going to see anyone off again. I can't describe how it felt to see you off.'

'This time I'll go without telling you.'

'No. I mean I won't go to the station again.'

'What happened to him?'

'He died, of course.'

'While you were seeing me off?'

'But that's not the reason. I had no idea I could hate so to see someone off.'

Shimamura nodded.

'Where were you on the fourteenth of February? I was waiting for you. But I'll know better than to believe you next time.'

The fourteenth of February was the 'bird-chasing festival', a children's festival that had in it the spirit of this snow country. For ten days before the festival the children of the village tramped down the snow with straw boots, and presently, cutting the now boardlike snow into two-foot cubes, they built a snow palace some six yards square and more than ten feet high. Since the New Year was celebrated here early in February, the traditional straw ropes were still strung up over the village doorways. On the fourteenth the children gathered the ropes and burned them in a red bonfire before the snow palace. They pushed and jostled one another on the roof and sang the bird-chasing song, and afterwards, setting out lights, they spent the night in the palace. At dawn on the fifteenth they again climbed to the roof to sing bird-chasing song.

It was then that the snow was deepest, and Shimamura had told Komako he would come for the festival.

'I was at home in February. I took a holiday. I was sure you would be here on the fourteenth, and I came back especially. I could have stayed to take care of her longer if I had known.'

'Was someone ill?'

'The music teacher. She had pneumonia down on the coast. The telegram came when I was at home, and I went down to take care of her.'

'Did she get better?'

'No.'

'I'm sorry.' Shimamura's words could have been either an expression of sympathy or an apology for the broken promise.

Komako shook her head mildly, and wiped at the table with

66

her handkerchief. 'The place is alive with insects.' A swarm of tiny winged insects fell from the table to the floor. Several small moths were circling the light.

Moths, how many kinds he could not tell, dotted the screen, floating on the clear moonlight.

'My stomach aches.' Komako thrust both hands tight inside her *obi*, and her head fell to Shimamura's knee. 'My stomach aches.'

Insects smaller than moths gathered on the thick white powder at her neck. Some of them died there as Shimamura watched.

The flesh on her neck and shoulders was richer than it had been the year before. She is just twenty, he told himself.

He felt something warm and damp on his knee.

' "Komako, go on up and look in the Camellia Room," they said in the office, very pleased with themselves. I don't like that way they have. I'd been to see Kikuyu off, and I was just ready for a good nap when someone said there had been a call from here. I didn't feel like coming. I had too much to drink last night at Kikuyu's farewell party. They only laughed down in the office and wouldn't tell me who was here. And it was you. It's been a whole year. You're the sort that comes only once a year?'

'I had one of the cakes she left.'

'You did?' Komako sat up. Her face was red where it had been pressed against his knee. She seemed very young.

She had seen the old geisha Kikuyu to the second station down the line, she said.

'It's very sad. We used to be able to work things out together, but now it's every geisha for herself. The place has changed. New geisha come in and no one gets along with anyone else. I'll be lonely without Kikuyu. She was at the centre of everything. And she made more money than any of the rest of us. Her people took very good care of her.'

Kikuyu had worked out her contract, and she was going home. Would she get married or would she open an inn or restaurant of her own? Shimamura asked.

'Kikuyu is a very sad case. She made a bad marriage, and she came here afterwards.' Komako was silent for a time, evidently unsure how much she should tell. She looked out towards the slope below the terraced fields, bright in the moonlight. 'You know the new house halfway up the hill?'

'The restaurant – the Kikumura, is it called?'

'That's the one. Kikuyu was supposed to manage the Kikumura, but at the last minute she had a change of heart. It caused all sorts of excitement. She had a patron build the place for her, and then, when she was all ready to move in, she threw it over. She found someone she liked and was going to marry him, but he ran off and left her. Is that what happens when you lose your head over a man? I wonder. She can't very well go back to her old work, and she can't take over the restaurant now that she's turned it down, and she's ashamed to stay here after all that's happened. There's nothing for her to do but start again somewhere else. It makes me very sad to think about Kikuyu. There were all sorts of people – but of course we don't really know the details.'

'Men? How many? Five or so?'

'I wonder.' Komako laughed softly and turned away. 'Kikuyu was weak. A weakling.'

'Maybe there was nothing else she could do.'

'But isn't it so? You can't go losing your head over every man that likes you.' Her eyes were on the floor, and she was stroking her hair meditatively with a hair ornament. 'It wasn't easy, seeing her off.'

'And what happened to the restaurant?'

'The wife of the man who built it has taken it over.'

'An interesting situation. The wife managing the mistress's restaurant.'

'But what else could they do? The place was ready to open, and the wife moved in with all her children.'

'What about her own house?'

'They left the old woman to take care of it, I hear. The man's a farmer, but he likes to have his fun. He's a very interesting fellow.'

'So it would seem. Is he well on in years?'

'He's young. No more than thirty-one or thirty-two.'

'The mistress must be older than the wife, then.'

'They're both twenty-six.'

'The "Kiku" of "Kikumura" would be from "Kikuyu."
And the wife took over the name even?'

'But they couldn't change the name once it was advertised.'

Shimamura straightened the collar of his kimono. Komako
got up to close the window.

'Kikuyu knew all about you. She told me today you were
here.'

'I saw her down in the office when she came to say good-
bye.'

'Did she say anything to you?'

'Not a thing.'

'Do you know how I feel?' Komako threw open the window she had just shut, and sat down on the sill as if she meant
to throw herself out.

'The stars here are different from the stars in Tokyo,' Shimamura said after a time. 'They seem to float up from the sky.'

'Not tonight, though. The moon is too bright. . . . The snow
was dreadful this year.'

'I understand there were times when the trains couldn't get
through.'

'I was almost afraid. The roads weren't open until May, a
month later than usual. You know the shop up at the ski
grounds? An avalanche went through the second floor of it.
The people below heard a strange noise and thought the rats
were tearing up the kitchen. There were no rats, though, and
when they looked upstairs the place was full of snow and the
shutters and all had been carried off. It was just a surface slide,
but there was a great deal of talk on the radio. The skiers
were frightened away. I said I wouldn't ski any more and I
gave my skis away at the end of last year, but I went out again
after all. Twice, three times maybe. Have I changed?'

'What have you been doing since the music teacher died?'

'Don't you worry about other people's problems. I came
back and I was waiting for you in February.'

'But if you were down on the coast you could have written
me a letter.'

'I couldn't. I really couldn't. I couldn't possibly write the
sort of letter your wife would see. I couldn't bring myself to.
I don't tell lies just because people might be listening.' The

words came at him in a sudden torrent. He only nodded. 'Why don't you turn out the light? You don't have to sit in this swarm of insects.'

The moonlight, so bright that the furrows in the woman's ear were clearly shadowed, struck deep into the room and seemed to turn the mats on the floor a chilly green.

'No. Let me go home.'

'I see you haven't changed.' Shimamura raised his head. There was something strange in her manner. He peered into the slightly aquiline face.

'People say I haven't changed since I came here. I was six-teen then. But life goes on the same, year after year.'

Her cheeks still carried the ruddiness of her north-country girlhood. In the moonlight the fine geisha-like skin took on the lustre of a sea shell.

'But did you hear I'd moved?'

'Since the teacher died? You're not in the silkworms' room any more, then? This time it's a real geisha house?'

'A real geisha house? I suppose it is. They sell tobacco and sweets in the shop, and I'm the only geisha they have. I have a real contract, and when I read late in the night I always use a candle to save electricity.'

Shimamura let out a loud guffaw.

'The meter, you know. Shouldn't use too much electricity.'

'I see, I see.'

'But they're very good to me, so good that I sometimes find it hard to believe I'm really hired out as a geisha. When one of the children cries, the mother takes it outside so that I won't be bothered. I have nothing to complain about. Only sometimes the bedding is crooked. When I come home late at night, everything is laid out for me, but the mattresses aren't square one on the other, and the sheet is wrong. I hate it. After they've been so kind, though, I feel guilty making the bed over again.'

'You'd wear yourself out if you had a house of your own.'

'So everyone says. There are four little children, and the place is a terrible clutter. I spend the whole day picking things up. I know everything will be thrown down again as soon as my back is turned, but somehow I can't help myself. I want to

70

be as clean and neat as the place will let me.... Do you understand how I feel?'

'I understand.'

'If you understand, then tell me. Tell me, if you see how I feel.' Again that tense, urgent note came into her voice. 'See, you can't. Lying again. You have plenty of money, and you're not much of a person. You don't understand at all.' She lowered her voice. 'I'm very lonely sometimes. But I'm a fool. Go back to Tokyo, tomorrow.'

'It's all very well for you to condemn me, but how can you expect me to tell you exactly what I mean?'

'Why can't you? It's wrong of you.' Her voice was almost desperate. Then she closed her eyes, and began again as if she had asked herself whether Shimamura knew her, felt her for what she was, and had answered that he did. 'Once a year is enough. You'll come once a year, won't you, while I'm here?'

Her contract was for four years, she said.

'When I was at home, I didn't dream I would ever be a geisha again. I even gave away my skis before I left. And so all I've accomplished, I suppose, has been to give up smoking.'

'I remember how much you used to smoke, now that you mention it.'

'When guests at parties give me cigarettes, I tuck them away in my sleeve, and I have a fine collection by the time I'm ready to go home.'

'But four years – that's a long time.'

'It will pass in a hurry.'

'Aren't you warm, though.' Shimamura took her in his arms as she came to him.

'I've always been warm.'

'I suppose the nights will be getting chilly.'

'It's five years now since I came here. At first I wondered how I could live in such a place – especially before the railway came through. And it's going on for two years since you first came.'

He had come three times in less than two years, and on each visit he had found Komako's life changed.

Crickets were chirping outside in a noisy chorus.

'I wish they'd be a little quieter.' Komako pulled away from Shimamura.

The moths at the window started up as the wind came from the north.

Shimamura knew well enough that the thick eyelashes made her eyes seem half open, and yet he found himself looking again to be sure.

'I'm fatter now that I've stopped smoking.'

The fat on her abdomen was heavier, he had noticed.

They had long been apart, but what eluded his grasp when he was away from her was immediately near and familiar when he was beside her again.

'One is bigger than the other.' She cupped her breasts lightly in her hands.

'I suppose that's a habit of his – one side only.'

'What a nasty thing to say!' Here she was – this was it, he remembered.

'Next time tell him to treat them both alike.'

'Alike? Shall I tell him to treat them both alike?' She brought her face gently towards his.

It was a second-floor room, but it seemed to be surrounded by croaking toads. Two and three of them were moving from spot to spot, remarkably long-winded croakers.

Back from the bath, Komako began talking to herself. Her voice was quiet and her manner was completely serene.

The first physical examination she had had here – she thought it would be as when she was an apprentice geisha, and she bared her chest for a tuberculosis check. The doctor laughed, and she burst into tears – such were the intimate details she went into. She talked on as Shimamura encouraged her with questions.

'I'm always exactly on the calendar. Two days less than a month each time.'

'I don't suppose it keeps you from your parties?'

'You understand such things, do you?'

Every day she had a bath in the hot spring, famous for its lingering warmth. She walked two miles and more between parties at the old spring and the new, and here in the mountains there were few parties that kept her up late. She was therefore healthy and full-bodied, though she did have a suggestion of the low, bunched-up hips so common with geisha, narrow from side to side and wide from back to front. To Shimamura there was something touching about the fact that such a woman could call him back from afar.

'I wonder if I can have children.' And she wondered too if being generally faithful to one man was not the same thing as being married.

That was the first Shimamura had heard of the 'one man' in Komako's life. She had known him since she was sixteen, she said. Shimamura thought he understood now the lack of caution that had at first so puzzled him.

She had never liked the man, Komako continued, and had never felt near him, perhaps because the affair had begun when she was down on the coast just after the death of the man who had paid her debts.

'But it's certainly better than average if it's lasted five years.'

'I've had two chances to leave him. When I went to work as a geisha here, and when I moved after the music teacher died. But I've never had the will power to do it. I don't have much will power.'

The man was still down on the coast. It had not been convenient to keep her there, and when the music teacher came back to these mountains he had left Komako with her. He had been very kind, Komako said, and it made her sad to think that she could not give her whole self to him. He was considerably older than she, and he came but rarely to see her.

'I sometimes think it would be easiest to break away from him if I were to be really bad. I honestly think so sometimes.'

'That would never do.'

'But I wouldn't be up to it. It's not in my nature. I'm fond of this body I live in. If I tried, I could cut my four years down to two, but I don't strain myself. I take care of myself. Think of all the money I could make if I really tried. But it's enough if the man I have my contract with hasn't lost money at the end of four years. I know about how much it takes each month for an instalment on the loan, and interest, and taxes, and my own keep, and I don't strain myself to make more. If it's a party that doesn't seem worth the trouble, I slip off and go home, and they don't call me late at night even from the inn unless an old guest had asked especially for me. If I wanted to be extravagant, I could go on and on, but I work as the mood takes me. That's enough. I've already paid back more than half the money, and it's not a year yet. But even so I manage to spend thirty yen or so on myself every month.'

It was enough if she made a hundred yen a month, she said. The month before, the least busy of the year, she had made sixty yen. She had had some ninety parties, more than any other geisha. She received a fixed amount for herself from each party, and the large number of parties therefore meant relatively more for her and less for the man to whom she was indentured. But she moved busily from one to another as the spirit took her. There was not a single geisha at this hot spring who lost money and had to extend her contract.

Komako was up early the next morning. 'I dreamed I was cleaning house for the woman who teaches flower-arranging, and I woke up.'

She had moved the little dresser over to the window. In the mirror the mountains were red with autumn leaves, and the autumn sun was bright.

This time it was not Yoko he heard. Yoko calling through the door in that voice so clear he found it a little sad. Komako's clothes were brought rather by the little daughter of the man with whom she had her contract.

'What happened to the girl?' Shimamura asked.

Komako darted a quick glance at him. 'She spends all her time at the cemetery. Over there at the foot of the ski course. See the buckwheat field – the white flowers? And the cemetery to the left of it?'

Shimamura went for a walk in the village when Komako had left.

Before a white wall, shaded by eaves, a little girl in 'mountain trousers' and an orange-red flannel kimono, clearly brand-new, was bouncing a rubber ball. For Shimamura, there was autumn in the little scene.

The houses were built in the style of the old régime. No doubt they were there when provincial lords passed down this north-country road. The eaves and the verandas were deep, while the latticed, paper-covered windows on the second floor were long and low, no more than a foot or so high. There were reed blinds hanging from the eaves.

Slender autumn grasses grew along the top of an earthen wall. The pale-yellow plumes were at their most graceful, and below each plume narrow leaves spread out in a delicate fountain.

Yoko knelt on a straw mat beside the road, flailing at beans spread out before her in the sunlight.

The beans jumped from their dry pods like little drops of light.

Perhaps she could not see him because of the scarf around her head. She knelt, flailing away at the beans, her knees spread apart in their 'mountain trousers', and she sang in that voice so clear it was almost sad, the voice that seemed to be echoing back from somewhere.

> 'The butterfly, the dragonfly, the cricket.
> The pine cricket, bell cricket, horse cricket
> Are singing in the hills.'

How large the crow is, starting up from the cedar in the evening breeze – so says the poet. Again there were swarms of dragonflies by the cedar grove Shimamura could see from the window. As the evening approached, they seemed to swim about faster, more restlessly.

Shimamura had bought a new guide to these mountains while he was waiting for his train in Tokyo. Thumbing through it, he learned that near the top of one of the Border Range peaks a path threaded its way through beautiful lakes and marshes, and in this watery belt Alpine plants grew in the wildest profusion. In the summer red dragonflies flew calmly about, lighting on a hat or a hand, or the rim of a pair of spectacles, as different from the persecuted city dragonfly as a cloud from a mud puddle.

But the dragonflies here before him seemed to be driven by something. It was as though they wanted desperately to avoid being pulled in with the cedar grove as it darkened before the sunset.

The western sun fell on distant mountains, and in the

evening light he could see how the red leaves were working their way down from the summits.

'People are delicate, aren't they?' Komako had said that morning. 'Broken into a pulp, they say, skull and bones and all. And a bear could fall from a higher ledge and not be hurt in the least.' There had been another accident up among the rocks, and she had pointed out the mountain on which it had happened.

If man had a tough, hairy hide like a bear, his world would be different indeed, Shimamura thought. It was through a thin, smooth skin that man loved. Looking out at the evening mountains, Shimamura felt a sentimental longing for the human skin.

'The butterfly, the dragonfly, the cricket.' A geisha had been singing the song to a clumsy samisen accompaniment as he sat down to an early dinner.

The guide-book gave only the most essential information on routes, schedules, lodgings, costs, and left the rest to the imagination. Shimamura had come down from these mountains, as the new green was making its way through the last of the snow, to meet Komako for the first time; and now, in the autumn climbing season, he found himself drawn again to the mountains he had left his tracks in. Though he was an idler who might as well spend his time in the mountains as anywhere, he looked upon mountain climbing as almost a model of wasted effort. For that very reason it pulled at him with the attraction of the unreal.

When he was far away, he thought incessantly of Komako; but now that he was near her, this sighing for the human skin took on a dreamy quality like the spell of the mountains. Perhaps he felt a certain security, perhaps he was at the moment too intimate, too familiar with her body. She had stayed with him the night before. Sitting alone in the quiet, he could only wait for her. He was sure she would come without his calling. As he listened to the noisy chatter of a group of schoolgirls out on the hiking trip, however, he began to feel a little sleepy. He went to bed early.

Rain fell during the night, one of those quick showers that come in the autumn.

When he awoke the next morning, Komako was sitting primly beside the table, a book open before her. She wore an everyday kimono and cloak.

'Are you awake?' Her voice was soft as she turned to him.

'What are you doing here?'

'Are you awake?'

Shimamura glanced around the room, wondering if she had come in the night without his knowing it. He picked up the watch beside his pillow. It was only six-thirty.

'You're early.'

'But the maid has already brought charcoal.'

A morning-like steam was rising from the tea-kettle.

'It's time to get up.' She sat beside his pillow, the picture of the proper housewife. Shimamura stretched and yawned. He took the hand on her knee and caressed the small fingers, calloused from playing the samisen.

'But it's barely sunrise.'

'Did you sleep well by yourself?'

'Very well.'

'You didn't grow a moustache after all.'

'You did tell me to grow a moustache, didn't you?'

'It's all right. I knew you wouldn't. You always shave yourself nice and blue.'

'And you always look as if you'd just shaved when you wash away that powder.'

'Isn't your face a little fatter, though? You were very funny asleep, all round and plump with your white skin and no moustache.'

'Sweet and gentle?'

'But unreliable.'

'You were staring at me, then? I'm not sure I like having people stare at me when I'm asleep.'

Komako smiled and nodded. Then, like a glow that breaks into a flame, the smile became a laugh. There was strength in the fingers that took his.

'I hid in the cupboard. The maid didn't suspect a thing.'

'When? How long were you hidden?'

'Just now, of course. When the maid came to bring charcoal.' She laughed happily at the prank, and suddenly she was red to the ears. As if to hide her confusion, she began fanning herself with the edge of his quilt. 'Get up. Get up, please.'

'It's cold.' Shimamura pulled the quilt away from her. 'Are the inn people up yet?'

'I have no idea. I came in from the back.'

'The back?'

'I fought my way up from the cedar grove.'

'Is there a path at the back?'

'No. But it's shorter.'

Shimamura looked at her in surprise.

'No one knows I'm here. I heard someone in the kitchen, but the front door must still be locked.'

'You seem to be an early riser.'

'I couldn't sleep.'

'Did you hear the rain?'

'It rained? That's why the underbush was wet, then. I'm going home. Go on back to sleep.'

But Shimamura jumped vigorously out of bed, the woman's hand still in his. He went over to the window and looked down at the hill she said she had come up. Below the shrubbery, halfway down towards the cedar grove, dwarf bamboo was growing in a wild tangle. Directly below the window were rows of taro and sweet potatoes, onions and radishes. It was a most ordinary garden patch, and yet the varied colours of the leaves in the morning sun made him feel that he was seeing them for the first time.

The porter was throwing feed to the carp from the corridor that led to the bath.

'It's colder, and they aren't eating well,' he said as Shimamura passed. Shimamura stood for a moment looking at the feed on the water, dried and crumbled silkworms.

Komako was waiting for him, clean and prim as before, when he came back from the bath.

'It would be good to work on my sewing in a quiet place like this,' she said.

The room had evidently been cleaned, and the sun poured in on the deepest corners of the slightly worn matting.

'You sew, do you?'

'What an insulting question. I had to work harder than anyone else in the family. I see now, looking back, that the years when I was growing up were the worst ones of all.' She spoke almost to herself, but her voice was tense as she continued: 'The maid saw me. She gave me a strange look and asked when I had come. It was very embarrassing – but I couldn't go on hiding in the cupboard for ever. I'm going home. I'm very busy. I couldn't sleep, and I thought I'd wash my hair. I have to wait for it to dry, and then go to the hairdresser's, and if I don't wash it early in the morning I'm never ready for an afternoon party. There's a party here too, but they only told me about it last night. I won't come. I've made other promises. And I won't be able to see you tonight – it's Saturday and I'll be very busy.'

She showed no sign of leaving, however.

She decided not to wash her hair after all. She took Shimamura down to the back garden. Her damp sandals and stockings were hidden under the veranda where she had come in.

The dwarf bamboo she said she had fought her way through seemed impassable. Starting down along the garden path towards the sound of the water, they came out on the high river bank. There were children's voices in the chestnut trees. A number of burrs lay in the grass at their feet. Komako stamped them open and took out the fruit. The kernels were small.

Kaya plumes waved on the steep slope of the mountain opposite, a dazzling silver in the morning sun. Dazzling, and yet rather like the fleeting translucence that moved across the autumn sky.

'Shall we cross over? We can see your fiancé's grave.'

Komako brought herself to her full height and glared at him. A handful of chestnuts came at his face.

'You're making fun of me.'

Shimamura had no time to dodge. The chestnuts lashed at his forehead.

'What possible reason could you have for going to the cemetery?'

'But there's no need to lose your temper.'

'I was completely in earnest. I'm not like people who can do exactly as they want and think of no one else.'

'And who can do that?' Shimamura muttered weakly.

'Why do you have to call him my fiancé? Didn't I tell you very carefully he wasn't? But you've forgotten, of course.'

Shimamura had not forgotten. Indeed, the memory gave the man Yukio a certain weight in his thoughts.

Komako seemed to dislike talking about Yukio. She was not his fiancée, perhaps, but she had become a geisha to help pay doctors' bills. There was no doubt that she had been 'completely in earnest'.

Shimamura showed no anger even under the barrage of chestnuts. Komako looked curiously at him, and her resistance seemed to collapse. She took his arm. 'You're a simple, honest person at heart, aren't you? Something must be making you sad.'

'They're watching us from the trees.'

'What of it? Tokyo people are complicated. They live in such noise and confusion that their feelings are broken to little bits.'

'Everything is broken to little bits.'

'Even life, before long. . . . Shall we go to the cemetery?'

'Well . . .'

'See? You don't really want to go at all.'

'But you made such an issue of it.'

'Because I've never once gone to the cemetery. I really haven't gone once. I feel guilty sometimes, now that the teacher's buried there too. But I can't very well start going now. I'd only be pretending.'

'You're more complicated than I am.'

'Why? I'm never able to be completely open with living people, and I want at least to be honest with him now that he's dead.'

They came out of the cedar grove, where the quiet seemed to fall in chilly drops. Following the railway along the foot of the ski grounds, they were soon at the cemetery. Some ten weathered old tombstones and a forlorn statue of Jizo, guardian of children, stood on a tiny island of high ground among the paddies. There were no flowers.

Quite without warning, Yoko's head and shoulders rose from the bushes behind the Jizo. Her face wore the usual solemn, mask-like expression. She darted a burning glance at the two of them, and nodded a quick greeting to Shimamura. She said nothing.

'Aren't you early, though, Yoko? I thought of going to the hairdresser's ...' As Komako spoke, a black squall came upon them and threatened to sweep them from their feet.

A goods train roared past.

'Yoko, Yoko....' A boy was waving his hat in the door of a black goods truck.

'Saichiro, Saichiro,' Yoko called back.

It was the voice that had called to the station master at the snowy signal stop, a voice so beautiful it was almost lonely, calling out as if to someone who could not hear, on a ship far away.

The train passed, and the buckwheat across the tracks emerged fresh and clean as the blind was lifted. The field of white flowers on red stems was quietness itself.

The two of them had been so startled at seeing Yoko that they had not noticed the approach of the goods train; but the first shock was dispelled by the train.

They seemed still to hear Yoko's voice, and not the dying mumble of the goods train. It seemed to come back like an echo of distilled love.

'My brother,' said Yoko, looking after the train. 'I wonder if I should go to the station.'

'But the train won't wait for you at the station,' Komako laughed.

'I suppose not.'

'I didn't come to see Yukio's grave.'

Yoko nodded. She seemed to hesitate a moment, then knelt down before the grave.

Komako watched stiffly.

Shimamura looked away, towards the Jizo. It had three long faces, and, besides the hands clasped at its breast, a pair each to the left and to the right.

'I'm going to wash my hair,' Komako said to Yoko. She turned and started back along a ridge between the paddies.

It was the practice in the snow country to string wooden or bamboo poles on a number of levels from tree trunk to tree trunk, and to hang rice sheaves head down from them to dry.

At the height of the harvest the frames presented a solid screen of rice. Farmers were hanging out rice along the path Shimamura and Komako took back to the village.

A farm girl threw up a sheaf of rice with a twist of her trousered hips, and a man high above her caught it expertly and in one deft sweep of his hand spread it to hang from the frame. The unconscious, practised motions were repeated over and over.

Komako took one of the dangling sheaves in her hand and shook it gently up and down, as though she were feeling the weight of a jewel.

'See how it's headed. And how nice it is to the touch. Entirely different from last year's rice.' She half-closed her eyes from the pleasure. A disorderly flock of sparrows flew low over her head.

An old notice was pasted to a wall beside the road: 'Pay for field hands. Ninety sen a day, meals included. Women forty per cent less.'

There were rice frames in front of Yoko's house too, beyond the slightly depressed field that separated the house from the road. One set of frames was strung up high in a row of persimmon trees, along the white wall between the garden and the house next door, while another, at right angles to it, followed the line between the field and the garden. With an opening for a doorway at one end, the frames suggested a make-shift little theatre covered not with the usual straw mats but with unthreshed rice. The taro in the field still sent out powerful stems and leaves, but the dahlias and roses beyond were withered. The lotus pond with its red carp was hidden behind the screen of rice, as was the window of the silkworm room, where Komako had lived.

Bowing her head sharply, almost angrily, Yoko went in through the opening in the headed rice.

'Does she live alone?' Shimamura asked, looking after the bowed figure.

'I imagine not.' Komako's answer was a little tart. 'But what a nuisance. I'll not go to the hairdresser's after all. You say things you have no business saying, and we ruin her visit to the cemetery.'

'You're only being difficult – is it really so terrible to run into her at the cemetery?'

'You have no idea how I feel. . . . If I have time later, I'll stop by to wash my hair. I may be late, but I'll stop by.'

It was three in the morning.

Shimamura was awakened by a slamming as though someone were knocking the doors loose. Komako lay stretched out on top of him.

'I said I would come and I've come. Haven't I? I said I'd come and I've come, haven't I?' Her chest, even her abdomen, rose and fell violently.

'You're dead-drunk.'

'Haven't I? I said I'd come and I've come, haven't I?'

'You have indeed.'

'Couldn't see a thing on the way. Not a thing. My head aches.'

'How did you manage to get up the hill?'

'I have no idea. Not the slightest.' She lay heavily across his chest. He found it a little oppressive, especially when she turned over and arched her back, but, too suddenly awakened, he fell back as he tried to get up. It was an astonishingly hot object that his head came to rest on.

'You're on fire.'

'Oh? Fire for a pillow. See that you don't burn yourself.'

'I might very well.' He closed his eyes and the warmth sank into his head, bringing an immediate sense of life. Reality came through the violent breathing, and with it a sort of nostalgic remorse. He felt as though he were waiting tranquilly for some undefined revenge.

'I said I'd come, and I've come.' She spoke with the utmost concentration. 'I've come, and now I'm going home. I'm going to wash my hair.'

She got to her knees and took a drink of water in great swallows.

'I can't let you go home like this.'

'I'm going home. I have some people waiting. Where did I leave my towel?'

Shimamura got up and turned on the light. 'Don't!' She

hid her face in her hands, then buried it, hands and all, in the quilt.

She had on a bold informal kimono with a narrow undress *obi*, and under it a nightgown. Her under-kimono had slipped down out of sight. She was flushed from drink even to the soles of her bare feet, and there was something very engaging about the way she tried to tuck them out of sight.

Evidently she had thrown down her towel and bath utensils when she came in. Soap and combs were scattered over the floor.

'Cut. I brought scissors.'

'What do you want me to cut?'

'This.' She pointed at the strings that held her Japanese coiffure in place. 'I tried to do it myself, but my hands wouldn't work. I thought maybe I could ask you.'

Shimamura separated the hair and cut at the strings, as he cut she shook the long hair loose. She was somewhat calmer.

'What time is it?'

'Three o'clock.'

'Not really. You'll be careful not to cut the hair, won't you?'

'I've never seen so many strings.'

The false hair that filled out the coiffure was hot where it touched her head.

'Is it really three o'clock? I must have fallen asleep when I got home. I promised to come for a bath with some people, and they stopped by to call me. They'll be wondering what's happened.'

'They're waiting for you?'

'In the public bath. Three of them. There were six parties, but I only got to four. Next week we'll be very busy with people coming to see the maple leaves. Thanks very much.' She raised her head to comb her hair, now long and flowing, and she laughed uncertainly. 'Funny, isn't it.' Unsure what to do with herself, she reached to pick up the false hair. 'I have to go. It's not right to keep them waiting. I'll not come again tonight.'

'Can you see your way home?'

'Yes.'

84

But she tripped over the skirt of her kimono on the way out.

At seven and again at three in the morning – twice in one short day she had chosen unconventional hours to come calling. There was something far from ordinary in all this, Shimamura told himself.

Guests would soon be coming for the autumn leaves. The door of the inn was being decorated with maple branches to welcome them.

The porter who was somewhat arrogantly directing operations was fond of calling himself a 'migrant bird'. He and his kind worked the mountain resorts from spring through to the autumn leaves, and moved down to the coast for the winter. He did not much care whether or not he came to the same inn each year. Proud of his experience in the prosperous coast resorts, he had no praise for the way the inn treated its guests. He reminded one of a not-too-sincere beggar as he rubbed his hands together and hovered about prospective guests at the station.

'Have you ever tasted one of these?' he asked Shimamura, picking up a pomegranate-like *akebi*. 'I can bring some in from the mountains if you like.' Shimamura, back from a walk, watched him tie the *akebi*, stem and all, to a maple branch.

The freshly cut branches were so long that they brushed against the eaves. The hallway glowed a bright, fresh scarlet. The leaves were extraordinarily large.

As Shimamura took the cool *akebi* in his hand, he noticed that Yoko was sitting by the hearth in the office.

The innkeeper's wife was heating *saké* in a brass boiler. Yoko, seated opposite her, nodded quickly in answer to each remark. She was dressed informally, though she did not have on the everyday 'mountain trousers'. Her plain woollen kimono was freshly washed.

'That girl is working here?' Shimamura asked the porter nonchalantly.

'Yes, sir. Thanks to all of you, we've had to take on extra help.'

'You, for instance.'

'That's right. She's an unusual type, though, for a girl from these parts.'

Yoko worked only in the kitchen, apparently. She was not yet serving at parties. As the inn filled, the voices of the maids in the kitchen became louder, but he did not remember having heard Yoko's clear voice among them. The maid who took care of his room said that Yoko liked to sing in the bath before she went to bed, but that, too, Shimamura had missed.

Now that he knew Yoko was in the house, he felt strangely reluctant to call Komako. He was conscious of an emptiness that made him see Komako's life as beautiful but wasted, even though he himself was the object of her love; and yet the woman's existence, her straining to live, came touching him like naked skin. He pitied her, and he pitied himself.

He was sure that Yoko's eyes, for all their innocence, could send a probing light to the heart of these matters, and he somehow felt drawn to her too.

Komako came often enough without being called.

When he went to see the maple leaves up the valley, he passed her house. Hearing the car and thinking it must be he, she ran out to look – and he did not even glance back, she complained. That was most unfeeling of him. She of course called in whenever she came to the inn, and she called in too on her way to the bath. When she was to go to a party, she came an hour or so early and waited in his room for the maid to call her. Often she would slip away from a party for a few minutes. After retouching her face in the mirror, she would stand up to leave. 'Back to work. I'm all business. Business, business.'

She was in the habit of forgetting something she had brought with her, a cloak, perhaps, or the cover to a samisen plectrum.

'Last night when I got home there was no hot water for tea. I hunted through the kitchen and found the left-overs from breakfast. Co-o-old .... They didn't call me this morning. When I woke up it was already ten-thirty. I meant to come and see you at seven, but it was no good.'

Such were the things she talked of. Or she told him of the

inn she had gone to first, and the next and the next, and the parties she had been to at each.

'I'll come again later.' She had a glass of water before she left. 'Or maybe I won't. Thirty guests and only three of us. I'll be much too busy.'

But almost immediately she was back.

'It's hard work. Thirty of them and only three of us. And the other two are the very oldest and the very youngest in town, and that leaves all the hard work for me. Stingy people. A travel club of some sort, I suppose. With thirty guests you need at least six geisha. I'll go and have a drink and pick a fight with them.'

So it was every day. Komako must have wanted to crawl away and hide at the thought of where it was leading. But that indefinable air of loneliness only made her the more seductive.

'The floor always creaks when I come down the hall. I walk very softly, but they hear me just the same. "Off to the Camellia Room again, Komako?" they say as I go by the kitchen. I never thought I'd have to worry so about my reputation.'

'The town's really too small.'

'Everyone has heard about us, of course.'

'That will never do.'

'You begin to have a bad name, and you're ruined in a little place like this.' But she looked up and smiled. 'It makes no difference. My kind can find work anywhere.'

That straightforward manner, so replete with direct, immediate feeling, was quite foreign to Shimamura, the idler who had inherited his money.

'It will be the same, wherever I go. There's nothing to be upset about.'

But he caught an echo of the woman underneath the surface nonchalance.

'And I can't complain. After all, only women are able really to love.' She flushed a little and looked at the floor.

Her kimono stood out from her neck, and her back and shoulders were like a white fan spread under it. There was something sad about the full flesh under that white powder. It suggested a woollen cloth, and again it suggested the pelt of some animal.

'In the world as it is,' he murmured, chilled at the sterility of the words even as he spoke.

But Komako only replied: 'As it always has been.' She raised her head and added absent-mindedly: 'You didn't know that?'

The red under-kimono clinging to her skin disappeared as she looked up.

Shimamura was translating Valéry and Alain, and French treatises on the dance from the golden age of the Russian ballet. He meant to bring them out in a small luxury edition at his own expense. The book would in all likelihood contribute nothing to the Japanese dancing world. One could nonetheless say, if pressed, that it would bring aid and comfort to Shimamura. He pampered himself with the somewhat whimsical pleasure of sneering at himself through his work, and it may well have been from such a pleasure that his sad little dream world sprang. Off on a trip, he saw no need to hurry himself.

He spent much of his time watching insects in their death agonies.

Each day, as the autumn grew colder, insects died on the floor of his room. Stiff-winged insects fell on their backs and were unable to get to their feet again. A bee walked a little and collapsed, walked a little and collapsed. It was a quiet death that came with the change of seasons. Looking closely, however, Shimamura could see that the legs and feelers were trembling in the struggle to live. For such a tiny death, the empty eight-mat room* seemed enormous.

As he picked up a dead insect to throw it out, he sometimes thought for an instant of the children he had left in Tokyo.

A moth on the screen was still for a very long time. It too was dead, and it fell to the earth like a dead leaf. Occasionally a moth fell from the wall. Taking it up in his hand, Shimamura would wonder how to account for such beauty.

The screens were removed, and the singing of the insects was more subdued and lonely day by day.

The russet deepened on the Border Range. In the evening sun the mountains lighted up sharply, like a rather chilly stone. The inn was filled with maple-viewing guests.

*About four yards square.

'I don't think I'll come again tonight. Some people from the village are having a party.' Komako left, and presently he heard a drum in the large banquet-room, and strident women's voices. At the very height of the festivities he was startled by a clear voice almost at his elbow.

'May I come in?' It was Yoko. 'Komako asked me to bring this.'

She thrust her hand out like a postman. Then, remembering her manners, she knelt down awkwardly before him. Shimamura opened the knotted bit of paper, and Yoko was gone. He had not had time to speak to her.

'Having a fine, noisy time. And drinking.' That was the whole of the message, written in a drunken hand on a paper napkin.

Not ten minutes later Komako staggered in.

'Did she bring something to you?'

'She did.'

'Oh?' Komako cocked an eye at him in wonderfully high spirits. 'I do feel good. I said I'd go and order more *saké*, and I ran away. The porter caught me. But *saké* is wonderful. I don't care a bit if the floor creaks. I don't care if they scold me. As soon as I come here I start feeling drunk, though. Damn. Well, back to work.'

'You're rosy down to the tips of your fingers.'

'Business is waiting. Business, business. Did she say anything? Terribly jealous. Do you know how jealous?'

'Who?'

'Someone will be murdered one of these days.'

'She's working here?'

'She brings *saké*, and then stands there staring in at us, with her eyes flashing. I suppose you like her sort of eyes.'

'She probably thinks you're a disgrace.'

'That's why I gave her a note to bring to you. I want water. Give me water. Who's a disgrace? Try seducing her too before you answer my question. Am I drunk?' She peered into the mirror, bracing both hands against the stand. A moment later, kicking aside the long skirts, she swept from the room.

The party was over. The inn was soon quiet, and Shimamura

could hear a distant clatter of dishes. Komako must have been taken off by a guest to a second party, he concluded, but just then Yoko came in with another bit of paper.

'Decided not to go to Sampukan go from here to the Plum Room may call in on way home good night.'

Shimamura smiled wryly, a little uncomfortable before Yoko. 'Thank you very much. You've come to help here?'

She darted a glance at him with those beautiful eyes, so bright that he felt impaled on them. His discomfort was growing.

The girl left a deep impression each time he saw her, and now she was sitting before him – a strange uneasiness swept over him. Her too-serious manner made her seem always at the very centre of some remarkable occurrence.

'They're keeping you busy, I suppose.'

'But there's very little I can do.'

'It's strange how often I see you. The first time was when you were bringing that man home. You talked to the station master about your brother. Do you remember?'

'Yes.'

'They say you sing in the bath before you go to bed.'

'Really! They accuse me of having such bad manners?' The voice was astonishingly beautiful.

'I feel I know everything about you.'

'Oh? And have you asked Komako, then?'

'She won't say a thing. She seems to dislike talking about you.'

'I see.' Yoko turned quickly away. 'Komako is a fine person, but she's not been lucky. Be good to her.' She spoke rapidly, and her voice trembled very slightly on the last words.

'But there's nothing I can do for her.'

It seemed that the girl's whole body must soon be trembling. Shimamura looked away, fearful that a dangerous light would be breaking out on the too-earnest face.

He laughed. 'I think I'd best go back to Tokyo soon.'

'I'm going to Tokyo myself.'

'When?'

'It doesn't matter.'

'Shall I see you to Tokyo when I go back?'

'Please do.' The seriousness was intense, and at the same time her tone suggested that the matter was after all trivial. Shimamura was startled.

'If it will be all right with your family.'

'The brother who works on the railway is all the family I have. I can decide for myself.'

'Have you made arrangements in Tokyo?'

'No.'

'Have you talked to Komako, then?'

'To Komako? I don't like Komako. I haven't talked to her.'

She looked up at him with moist eyes – a sign perhaps that her defences were breaking down – and he found in them an uncanny sort of beauty. But at that moment his affection for Komako welled up violently. To run off to Tokyo, as if eloping, with a nondescript woman would somehow be in the nature of an intense apology to Komako, and a penance for Shimamura himself.

'It doesn't frighten you to go off alone with a man?'

'Why should it?'

'It doesn't seem dangerous to go to Tokyo without at least deciding where you will stay and what you might want to do?'

'A woman by herself can always get by.' There was a delicious lilt in her speech. Her eyes were fixed on his as she spoke again: 'You won't hire me as a maid?'

'Really, now. Hire you as a maid?'

'But I won't want to be a maid.'

'What were you in Tokyo before?'

'A nurse.'

'You were in a hospital? Or in nursing school?'

'I just thought I'd like to be a nurse.'

Shimamura smiled. This perhaps explained the earnestness with which she had taken care of the music teacher's son on the train.

'And you still want to be a nurse?'

'I won't be a nurse now.'

'But you'll have to make up your mind. This indecisiveness will never do.'

'Indecisiveness? It has nothing to do with indecisiveness.' Her laugh threw back the accusation.

Her laugh, like her voice, was so high and clear that it was almost lonely. There was not a suggestion in it of the dull or the simple-minded; but it struck emptily at the shell of Shimamura's heart, and fell away in silence.

'What's funny?'

'But there has only been one man I could possibly nurse.'

Again Shimamura was startled.

'I could never again.'

'I see.' His answer was quiet. He had been caught off guard. 'They say you spend all your time at the cemetery.'

'I do.'

'And for the rest of your life you can never nurse anyone else, or visit anyone else's grave?'

'Never again.'

'How can you leave the grave and go off to Tokyo, then?'

'I'm sorry. Do take me with you.'

'Komako says you're frightfully jealous. Wasn't the man her fiancé?'

'Yukio? It's a lie. It's a lie.'

'Why do you dislike Komako, then?'

'Komako.' She spoke as if calling to someone in the same room, and she gazed hotly at Shimamura. 'Be good to Komako.'

'But I can do nothing for her.'

There were tears in the corners of Yoko's eyes. She sniffled as she slapped at a small moth on the matting. 'Komako says I'll go crazy.' With that she slipped from the room.

Shimamura felt a chill come over him.

As he opened the window to throw out the moth, he caught a glimpse of the drunken Komako playing parlour games with a guest. She leaned forward half from her seat, as though to push her advantage home by force. The sky had clouded over. Shimamura went down for a bath.

In the women's bath next door, Yoko was bathing the innkeeper's little daughter.

Her voice was gentle as she undressed the child and bathed it – soothing and agreeable, like the voice of a young mother.

Presently she was singing in that same voice:

> 'See, out at the back,
> Three pears, three cedars,
> Six trees in all.
> Crows' nests below,
> Sparrows' nests above.
> And what is it they're singing?
> *"Hakarmairi itchō, itchō, itchō ya"*'*

It was a song little girls sang as they bounced rubber balls. The quick, lively manner in which Yoko rolled off the nonsense-words made Shimamura wonder if he might not have seen the earlier Yoko in a dream.

She chatted on as she dressed the child and led it from the bath, and even when she was gone her voice seemed to echo on like a flute. On the worn floor of the hallway, polished to a dark glow, a geisha had left behind a samisen box, the very embodiment of quiet in the late autumn night. As Shimamura was looking for the owner's name, Komako came out from the direction of the clattering dishes.

'What are you looking at?'

'Is she staying the night?'

'Who? Oh, her. Don't be foolish. You think we carry these with us wherever we go, do you? Sometimes we leave them at an inn for days on end.' She laughed, but almost immediately she was breathing painfully and her eyes were screwed tightly shut. Dropping her long skirts, she fell against Shimamura. 'Take me home, please.'

'You don't have to go, do you?'

'It's no good. I have to go. The rest went on to other parties and left me behind. No one will say anything if I don't stay too long – I had business here. But if they call at my house on their way to the bath and find me away, they'll start talking.'

Drunk though she was, she walked briskly down the steep hill.

'You made that girl weep.'

'She does seem a trifle crazy.'

'And do you enjoy making such remarks?'

'But didn't you say it yourself? She remembered how you said she would go crazy, and it was then that she broke down – mostly out of resentment, I suspect.'

*In imitation of the birds. Literally: "To the cemetery, a hundred yards, a hundred yards, a hundred yards again."

'Oh? It's all right, then.'

'And not ten minutes later she was in the bath, singing in fine voice.'

'She's always liked to sing in the bath.'

'She said very seriously that I must be good to you.'

'Isn't she foolish, though? But you didn't have to tell me.'

'Tell you? Why is it that you always seem so touchy when the girl is mentioned?'

'Would you like to have her?'

'See? What call is there for a remark like that?'

'I'm not joking. Whenever I look at her, I feel as though I have a heavy load and can't get rid of it. Somehow I always feel that way. If you're really fond of her, take a good look at her. You'll see what I mean.' She laid her hand on his shoulder and leaned towards him. Then, abruptly, she shook her head. 'No, that's not what I want. If she were to fall into the hands of someone like you, she might not go crazy after all. Why don't you take my load for me?'

'You're going a little too far.'

'You think I'm drunk and talking nonsense? I'm not. I would know she was being well taken care of, and I could go pleasantly to seed here in the mountains. It would be a fine, quiet feeling.'

'That's enough.'

'Just leave me alone.' In her flight, she ran into the closed door of the house she lived in.

'They've decided you're not coming home.'

'But I can open it.' The door sounded old and dry as she lifted it from the groove and pushed it back.

'Come on in.'

'But think of the hour.'

'Everyone will be asleep.'

Shimamura hesitated.

'I'll see you back to the inn, then.'

'I can go by myself.'

'But you haven't seen my room.'

They stepped through the kitchen door, and the sleeping figures of the family lay sprawled before them. The thin mattresses on the floor were covered with cheap striped cloth, now faded, of the sort often used for 'mountain trousers'. The mother and father and five or six children, the oldest a girl perhaps sixteen, lay under a scorched lampshade. Heads faced in every direction. There was drab poverty in the scene, and yet under it there lay an urgent, powerful vitality.

As if thrown back by the warm breath of all the sleepers, Shimamura started towards the door. Komako noisily closed it in his face, however, and went in through the kitchen. She made no attempt to soften her footsteps. Shimamura followed stealthily past the children's pillows, a strange thrill rising in his chest.

'Wait here. I'll turn on the light upstairs.'

'It's all right.' Shimamura climbed the stairs in the dark. As he looked back, he saw the sweetshop beyond the homely sleeping faces.

The matting was worn in the four rustic rooms on the second floor.

'It's a little large, I have to admit, for just one person.' The partitions between the rooms had been taken down, and Komako's bedding lay small and solitary inside the sliding doors, their paper panels yellowed with age, that separated the rooms from the skirting corridor. Old furniture and tools, evidently the property of the family she lived with, were piled in the far room. Party kimonos hung from pegs along the wall. The whole suggested a fox's or badger's lair to Shimamura.

Komako sat down solidly in the slightly raised alcove and offered him the only cushion.

'Bright red.' She peered into the mirror. 'Am I really so drunk?' She fumbled through the top drawer of the dresser. 'Here. My diary.'

'As long as this, is it?'

She took up a small figured-paper box, filled to the top with assorted cigarettes.

'I push them up my sleeve or inside my *obi* when a guest gives them to me, and some of them are a little smashed. They're clean, though. I make up for wrinkles by having every variety to offer.' She stirred up the contents to demonstrate that he could have his choice.

'But I haven't a match. I don't need matches now that I've stopped smoking.'

'It's all right. How is the sewing?'

'I try to work at it, but the guests for the maple leaves keep me busy.' She turned to put away the sewing that lay in front of the dresser.

The fine-grained chest of drawers and the expensive vermilion-lacquered sewing-box, relics perhaps of her years in Tokyo, were as they had been in the attic that so resembled an old paper box; but they seemed sadly out of place in these dilapidated second-floor rooms.

A thin string ran from Komako's pillow to the ceiling.

'I turn the light out with this when I'm reading.' She tugged at the string. Gentle and subdued, the proper housewife again, she was not quite able even so to hide her discomposure.

'Lonely as the fox's lady out at night, aren't you.'

'I really am.'

'And do you mean to live here four years?'

'But it's going on for a year already. It won't be long.'

Shimamura was nervous. He thought he could hear the breathing of the family below, and he had run out of things to talk about. He stood up to leave.

Komako slid the door half shut behind him. She glanced up at the sky. 'It's beginning to look like snow. The end of the maple leaves.' She recited a line of poetry* as she stepped outside: 'Here in our mountains, the snow falls even on the maple leaves.'

'Well, good night.'

'Wait. I'll see you back to the hotel. As far as the door, no farther.'

But she followed him inside.

'Go on to bed.' She slipped away, and a few minutes later she was back with two glasses filled to the brim with *saké*.

'Drink,' she ordered as she stepped into the room. 'We're going to have a drink.'

'But aren't they asleep? Where did you find it?'

'I know where they kept it.' She had quite obviously had a

*The line is from a Kabuki play.

96

drink herself as she poured from the vat. The earlier drunkenness had come back. With narrowed eyes, she watched the *saké* spill over on her hand. 'It's no fun, though, swallowing the stuff down in the dark.'

Shimamura drank meekly from the cup that was thrust at him.

It was not usual for him to get drunk on so little; but perhaps he was chilled from the walk. He began to feel sick. His head was whirling, and he could almost see himself going pale. He closed his eyes and fell back on the quilt. Komako put her arms around him in alarm. A child-like feeling of security came to him from the warmth of her body.

She seemed ill at ease, like a young woman, still childless, who takes a baby up in her arms. She raised her head and looked down, as at the sleeping child.

'You're a good girl.'

'Why? Why am I good? What's good about me?'

'You're a good girl.'

'Don't tease me. It's wrong of you.' She looked aside, and she spoke in broken phrases, like little blows, as she rocked him back and forth.

She laughed softly to herself.

'I'm not good at all. It's not easy having you here. You'd best go home. Each time I come to see you I want to put on a new kimono, and now I have none left. This one is borrowed. So you see I'm not really good at all.'

Shimamura did not answer.

'And what do you find good in me?' Her voice was a little husky. 'The first day I met you I thought I had never seen anyone I disliked more. People just don't say the sort of things you said. I hated you.'

Shimamura nodded.

'Oh? You understand then why I've not mentioned it before? When a woman has to say these things, she has gone as far as she can, you know.'

'But it's all right.'

'Is it?' They were silent for some moments. Komako seemed to be looking back on herself, and the awareness of a woman's being alive came to Shimamura in her warmth.

'You're a good woman.'

'How am I good?'

'A good woman.'

'What an odd person.' Her face was hidden from him, as though she were rubbing her jaw against an itching shoulder. Then suddenly, Shimamura had no idea why, she raised herself angrily to an elbow.

'A good woman – what do you mean by that? What do you mean?'

He only stared at her.

'Admit it. That's why you came to see me. You were laughing at me. You were laughing at me after all.'

She glared at him, scarlet with anger. Her shoulders were shaking. But the flush receded as quickly as it had come, and tears were falling over her blanched face.

'I hate you. How I hate you.' She rolled out of bed and sat with her back to him.

Shimamura felt a stabbing in his chest as he saw what the mistake had been. He lay silent, his eyes closed.

'It makes me very sad,' she murmured to herself. Her head was on her knees, and her body was bent into a tight ball.

When she had wept herself out, she sat jabbing at the floor mat with a silver hair-ornament. Presently she slipped from the room.

Shimamura could not bring himself to follow her. She had reason to feel hurt.

But soon she was back, her bare feet quiet in the corridor. 'Are you going for a bath?' she called from outside the door. It was a high, thin little voice.

'If you want to.'

'I'm sorry. I've reconsidered.'

She showed no sign of coming in. Shimamura picked up his towel and stepped into the hall. She walked ahead of him with her eyes on the floor, like a criminal being led away. As the bath warmed her, however, she became strangely gay and winsome, and sleep was out of the question.

The next morning Shimamura awoke to a voice reciting a Nō play.

He lay for a time listening. Komako turned and smiled from the mirror.

'The guests in the Plum Room. I was called there after my first party. Remember?'

'A Nō club out on a trip?'

'Yes.'

'It snowed?'

'Yes.' She got up and threw open the sliding door in front of the window. 'No more maple leaves.'

From the grey sky, framed by the window, the snow floated towards them in great flakes, like white peonies. There was something quietly unreal about it. Shimamura stared with the vacantness that comes from lack of sleep.

The Nō reciters had taken out a drum.

He remembered the snowy morning towards the end of the year before, and glanced at the mirror. The cold peonies floated up yet larger, cutting a white outline around Komako. Her kimono was open at the neck, and she was wiping at her throat with a towel.

Her skin was as clean as if it had just been laundered. He had not dreamed that she was a woman who would find it necessary to take offence at such a trivial remark, and that very fact lent her an irresistible sadness.

The mountains, more distant each day as the russet of the autumn leaves had darkened, came brightly back to life with the snow.

The cedars, under a thin coating of snow, rose sheer from the white ground to the sky, each cut off sharply from the rest.

The thread was spun in the snow, and the cloth woven in the snow, washed in the snow, and bleached in the snow. Everything, from the first spinning of the thread to the last finishing touches, was done in the snow. 'There is Chijimi linen because there is snow,' someone wrote long ago. 'Snow is the mother of Chijimi.'

The Chijimi grass-linen of this snow country was the handwork of the mountain maiden through the long, snowbound winters. Shimamura searched for the cloth in old-clothes shops to use for summer kimonos. Through acquaintances in the dance world, he had found a shop that specialized in old Nō robes, and he had a standing order that when a good piece of Chijimi came in he was to see it.

In the old days, it is said, the early Chijimi fair was held in the spring, when the snow had melted and the snow blinds were taken down from the houses. People came from far and near to buy Chijimi, even wholesalers from the great commercial cities, Edo, Nagoya, and Osaka; and the inns at which they stayed were fixed by tradition. Since the labours of half a year were on display, youths and maidens gathered from all the mountain villages. Sellers' booths and buyers' booths were lined up side by side, and the market took on the air of a festival. With prizes awarded for the best pieces of weaving, it came also to be sort of competition for husbands. The girls learned to weave as children, and they turned out their best work between the ages of perhaps fourteen and twenty-four. As they grew older they lost the touch that gave tone to the finest Chijimi. In their desire to be numbered among the few outstanding weavers, they put their whole labour and love into this product of the long snowbound months – the months of seclusion and boredom, between October, under the old lunar calendar, when the spinning began, and mid-February of the following year, when the last bleaching was finished.

There may have been among Shimamura's kimonos one or more woven by these mountain maidens towards the middle of the last century.

He still sent his kimonos back for 'snow-bleaching'. It was a great deal of trouble to return old kimonos – that had touched the skin of he could not know whom – for rebleaching each year to the country that had produced them; but when he considered the labours of those mountain maidens, he wanted the bleaching to be done properly in the country where the maidens had lived. The thought of the white linen, spread out on the deep snow, the cloth and the snow glowing scarlet in the rising sun, was enough to make him feel that the dirt of the summer had been washed away, even that he himself had been bleached clean. It must be added, however, that a Tokyo shop took care of the details for him, and he had no way of knowing that the bleaching had really been done in the old manner.

From ancient times there were houses that specialized in bleaching. The weavers for the most part did not do their own. White Chijimi was spread out on the snow after it was woven, coloured Chijimi bleached on frames while still in thread. The bleaching season came in January and February under the lunar calendar, and snow-covered fields and gardens were the bleaching grounds.

The cloth or thread was soaked overnight in ash water. The next morning it was washed over and over again, wrung, and put out to bleach. The process was repeated day after day, and the sight when, as the bleaching came to an end, the rays of the rising sun turned the white Chijimi blood-red was quite beyond description, Shimamura had read in an old book. It was something to be shown to natives of warmer provinces. And the end of the bleaching was a sign that spring was coming to the snow country.

The land of the Chijimi was very near this hot spring, just down the river, where the valley began to widen out. Indeed it must almost have been visible from Shimamura's window. All of the Chijimi market towns now had railway stations, and the region was still a well-known weaving centre.

Since Shimamura had never come to the snow country in midsummer, when he wore Chijimi, or in the snowy season, when it was woven, he had never had occasion to talk of it to Komako; and she hardly seemed the person to ask about the fate of an old folk art.

When he heard the song Yoko sang in the bath, it had come to him that, had she been born long ago, she might have sung thus as she worked over her spools and looms, so exactly suited to the fancy was her voice.

The thread of the grass-linen, finer than animal hair, is difficult to work except in the humidity of the snow, it is said, and the dark, cold season is therefore ideal for weaving. The ancients used to add that the way this product of the cold has of feeling cool to the skin in the hottest weather is a play of the principles of light and darkness. This Komako too, who had so fastened herself to him, seemed at centre cool, and the remarkable, concentrated warmth was for that fact all the more touching.

But this love would leave behind it nothing so definite as a piece of Chijimi. Though cloth to be worn is among the most short-lived of craftworks, a good piece of Chijimi, if it has been taken care of, can be worn quite unfaded a half-century and more after weaving. As Shimamura thought absently how human intimacies have not even so long a life, the image of Komako as the mother of another man's children suddenly floated into his mind. He looked around, startled. Possibly he was tired.

He had stayed so long that one might wonder whether he had forgotten his wife and children. He stayed not because he could not leave Komako nor because he did not want to. He had simply fallen into the habit of waiting for those frequent visits. And the more continuous the assault became, the more he began to wonder what was lacking in him, what kept him from living as completely. He stood gazing at his own cold-ness, so to speak. He could not understand how she had so lost herself. All of Komako came to him, but it seemed that noth-ing went out from him to her. He heard in his chest, like snow piling up, the sound of Komako, an echo beating against empty walls. And he knew that he could not go on pampering him-self for ever.

He leaned against the brazier, provided against the coming of the snowy season, and thought how unlikely it was that he would come again once he had left. The innkeeper had lent him an old Kyoto tea-kettle, skilfully inlaid in silver with flowers and birds, and from it came the sound of wind in the pines. He could make out two pine breezes, as a matter of fact, a near one and a far one. Just beyond the far breeze he heard faintly the tinkling of a bell. He put his ear to the kettle and listened. Far away, where the bell tinkled on, he suddenly saw Komako's feet, tripping in time with the bell. He drew back. The time had come to leave.

He thought of going to see the Chijimi country. That excur-sion might set him on his way towards breaking away from this hot spring.

He did not know at which of the towns downstream he

should get off the train. Not interested in modern weaving centres, he chose a station that looked suitably lonely and backward. After walking for a time he came out on what seemed to be the main street of an old post town.

The eaves pushing out far beyond the houses were supported by pillars along both sides of the street, and in their shade were passages for communication when the snow was deep, rather like the open lean-to the old Edo shopkeeper used for displaying his wares. With deep eaves on one side of each house, the passages stretched on down the street.

Since the houses were joined in a solid block, the snow from the roofs could only be thrown down into the street. One might more accurately say that at its deepest the snow was thrown not down but up, to a high bank of snow in the middle of the street. Tunnels were cut through for passage from one side to the other.

The houses in Komako's hot-spring village, for all of its being a part of this same snow country, were separated by open spaces, and this was therefore the first time Shimamura had seen the snow passages. He tried walking in one of them. The shade under the old eaves was dark, and the leaning pillars were beginning to rot at their bases. He walked along looking into the houses as into the gloom where generation after generation of his ancestors had endured the long snows.

He saw that the weaver maidens, giving themselves up to their work here under the snow, had lived lives far from as bright and fresh as the Chijimi they made. With an allusion to a Chinese poem, Shimamura's old book had pointed out that in harsh economic terms the making of Chijimi was quite impractical, so great was the expenditure of effort that went into even one piece. It followed that none of the Chijimi houses had been able to hire weavers from outside.

The nameless workers, so diligent while they lived, had presently died, and only the Chijimi remained, the plaything of men like Shimamura, cool and fresh against the skin in the summer. This rather unremarkable thought struck him as most remarkable. The labour into which a heart has poured its whole love – where will it have its say, to excite and inspire, and when?

Like the old post road that was its ancestor, the main street ran without a curve through the straggling village, and no doubt on through Kamoko's hot spring. The roofs, with rows of stones to weigh down their shingles, were very much like the ones he already knew.

The pillars supporting the deep eaves cast dim shadows across the ground. With his hardly having noticed, afternoon had drawn on towards evening.

There was nothing more to see. He took a train to another village, very much like the first. Again he walked about for a time. Feeling a little chilly, he stopped for a bowl of noodles.

The noodle shop stood beside a river, probably the river that flowed past the hot spring. Shaven-headed Buddhist nuns were crossing a bridge in twos and threes to the far side. All wore rough straw sandals, and some had dome-shaped straw hats tied to their backs. Evidently on their way from a service, they looked like crows hurrying home to their nests.

'Quite a procession of them,' Shimamura said to the woman who kept the shop.

'There's a nunnery up in the hills. I suppose they're getting everything done now. It will be next to impossible for them to go out once the heavy snows begin.'

The mountain beyond the bridge, growing dark in the twilight, was already covered with snow.

In this snow country, cold, cloudy days succeed one another as the leaves fall and the winds grow chilly. Snow is in the air. The high mountains near and far become white in what the people of the country call 'the round of the peaks'. Along the coast the sea roars, and inland the mountains roar – 'the roaring at the centre', like a distant clap of thunder. The round of the peaks and the roaring at the centre announce that the snows are not far away. This too Shimamura had read in his old book.

The first snow had fallen the morning he lay in bed listening to the Nō recital. Had the roaring already been heard, then, in the sea and the mountains? Perhaps his senses were sharper, off on a trip with only the company of the woman Komako: even now he seemed to catch an echo of a distant roaring.

'They'll be snowbound too, will they? How many are there?'

'A great many.'

'What do they do with themselves, do you suppose, shut up together through the snows? Maybe we could set them to making Chijimi.'

The woman smiled vaguely at the inquisitive stranger.

Shimamura went back to the station and waited two hours for a train. The wintry sun set, and the air was so clear that it seemed to burnish the stars. Shimamura's feet were cold.

He arrived back at the hot spring not knowing what he had gone out looking for. The taxi crossed the tracks into the village as usual. A brightly lighted house stood before them as they skirted the cedar grove. Shimamura felt warm and safe again. It was the restaurant Kikumura, and three or four geisha were talking in the doorway.

Komako will be among them – but almost before he had time to frame the thought he saw only Komako.

The driver put on the brakes. Apparently he had heard rumours about the two.

Shimamura turned away from her to look out of the rear window. In the light of the stars, the tracks were clear against the snow, surprisingly far into the distance.

Komako closed her eyes and jumped at the taxi. It moved slowly up the hill without stopping. She stood on the running-board, hunched over the door handle.

She had leaped at the car as if to devour it, but for Shimamura something warm had suddenly come near. The impulsive act struck him as neither rash nor unnatural. Komako raised one arm, half-embracing the closed window. Her kimono sleeve fell back from her wrist, and the warm red of the under-kimono, spilling through the thick glass, sank its way into the half-frozen Shimamura.

She pressed her forehead to the window. 'Where have you been? Tell me where you've been,' she called in a high voice.

'Don't be a fool. You'll get hurt,' he shouted back, but they both knew it was only a gentle game.

She opened the door and fell inside the taxi. It had already stopped, however. They were at the foot of the path up the mountain.

'Where have you been?'

'Well ...'

'Where?'

'Nowhere in particular.'

He noticed with surprise that she had the geisha's way of arranging her skirts.

The driver waited silently. It was a bit odd, Shimamura had to admit, for them to be sitting in a taxi that had gone as far as it could.

'Let's get out.' Komako put her hand on his. 'Cold. See how cold. Why didn't you take me with you?'

'You think I should have?'

'What a strange person.' She laughed happily as she hurried up the stone steps. 'I saw you leave. About two ... a little before three?'

'That's right.'

'I ran out when I heard the car. I ran out in front. And you didn't look round.'

'Look round?'

'You didn't. Why didn't you look round?'

Shimamura was a little surprised at this insistence.

'You didn't know I was seeing you off, did you?'

'I didn't.'

'See?' Laughing happily to herself, she came very near him. 'Why didn't you take me along? You leave me behind and you come back cold – I don't like it at all.'

Suddenly a fire-alarm was ringing, with the special fury that told of an emergency.

They looked back.

'Fire, fire!'

'A fire!'

A column of sparks was rising in the village below.

Komako cried out two or three times, and clutched at Shimamura's hand.

A tongue of flames shot up intermittently in the spiral of smoke, dipping down to lick at the roofs about it.

'Where is it? Fairly near the music teacher's?'

'No.'

'Where, then?'

106

'Farther up towards the station.'

The tongue of flame sprang high over the roofs.

'It's the cocoon-warehouse. The warehouse. Look, look!' The cocoon-warehouse is on fire.' She pressed her face to his shoulder. 'The warehouse, the warehouse!'

The fire blazed higher. From the mountain, however, it was as quiet under the starry sky as a little make-believe fire. Still the terror of it came across to them. They could almost hear the roar of the flames. Shimamura put his arm around Komako's shoulders.

'What is there to be afraid of?'

'No, no, no!' Komako shook her head and burst into tears. Her face seemed smaller than usual in Shimamura's hand. The hard forehead was trembling.

She had burst out weeping at the sight of the fire, and Shimamura held her to him without thinking to wonder what had so upset her.

She stopped weeping as quickly as she had begun, and pulled away from him.

'There's a film show in the warehouse. Tonight. The place will be full of people. . . . People will be hurt. People will burn to death.'

They hurried up towards the inn. There was shouting above them. Guests stood on the second- and third-floor verandas, flooded with light from the open doors. At the edge of the garden, withering chrysanthemums were silhouetted against the light from the inn – or the starlight. For an instant he almost thought it was the light from the fire. Several figures stood beyond the chrysanthemums. The porter and two or three others came bounding down the steps.

'Is it the cocoon-warehouse?' Komako called after them.

'That's right.'

'Is anyone hurt? Has anyone been hurt?'

'They're getting everyone out. The film caught fire, and in no time the whole place was on fire. Heard it over the telephone. Look!' The porter raised one arm as he ran off. 'Throwing children over one after another from the balcony, they say.'

'What shall we do?' Komako started off down the stairs

after the porter. Several others overtook her, and she too broke into a run. Shimamura followed.

At the foot of the stairs, their uneasiness increased. Only the very tip of the flames showed over the roofs, and the fire-alarm was nearer and more urgent.

'Careful. It's frozen, and you might slip.' She stopped as she turned to look back at him. 'But it's all right. You don't need to go any farther. I ought to go on myself to see if anyone has been hurt.'

There was indeed no reason for him to go on. His excitement fell away. He looked down at his feet and saw that they had come to the crossing.

'The Milky Way. Beautiful, isn't it,' Komako murmured. She looked up at the sky as she ran off ahead of him.

The Milky Way. Shimamura too looked up, and he felt himself floating into the Milky Way. Its radiance was so near that it seemed to take him up into it. Was this the bright vastness the poet Bashō saw when he wrote of the Milky Way arched over a stormy sea? The Milky Way came down just over there, to wrap the night earth in its naked embrace. There was a terrible voluptuousness about it. Shimamura fancied that his own small shadow was being cast up against it from the earth. Each individual star stood apart from the rest, and even the particles of silver dust in the luminous clouds could be picked out, so clear was the night. The limitless depth of the Milky Way pulled his gaze up into it.

'Wait, wait,' Shimamura called.

'Come on.' Komako ran towards the dark mountain on which the Milky Way was falling.

She seemed to have her long skirts in her hands, and as her arms waved the skirts rose and fell a little. He could feel the red over the starlit snow.

He ran after her as fast as he could.

She slowed down and took his hand, and the long skirts fell to the ground. 'You're going too?'

'Yes.'

'Always looking for excitement.' She clutched at her skirts, now trailing over the snow. 'But people will laugh. Please go back.'

'Just a little farther.'

'But it's wrong. People won't like it if I take you to a fire.'

He nodded and stopped. Her hand still rested lightly on his sleeve, however, as she walked on.

'Wait for me somewhere. I'll be right back. Where will you wait?'

'Wherever you say.'

'Let's see. A little farther.' She peered into his face, and abruptly shook her head. 'No. I don't want you to.'

She threw herself against him. He reeled back a step or two. A row of onions was growing in the thin snow beside the road.

'I hated it.' That sudden torrent of words came at him again. 'You said I was a good woman, didn't you? You're going away. Why did you have to say that to me?'

He could see her stabbing at the mat with that silver hair-ornament.

'I cried about it. I cried again after I got home. I'm afraid to leave you. But please go away. I won't forget that you made me cry.'

A feeling of nagging, hopeless impotence came over Shimamura at the thought that a simple misunderstanding had worked its way so deep into the woman's being. But just then they heard shouts from the direction of the fire, and a new burst of flames sent up its column of sparks.

'Look. See how it's flaming up again.'

They ran on, released.

Komako ran well. Her sandals skimmed the frozen snow, and her arms, close to her sides, seemed hardly to move. She was as one whose whole strength is concentrated in the breast – a strangely small figure, Shimamura thought. Too plump for running himself, he was exhausted the more quickly from watching her. But Komako too was soon out of breath. She fell against him.

'My eyes are watering,' she said. 'That's how cold it is.'

Shimamura's eyes too were moist. His cheeks were flushed, and only his eyes were cold. He blinked, and the Milky Way came to fill them. He tried to keep the ears from spilling over.

'Is the Milky Way like this every night?'

109

'The Milky Way? Beautiful, isn't it? But it's not like this every night. It's not usually so clear.'

The Milky Way flowed over them in the direction they were running, and seemed to bathe Komako's head in its light.

The shape of her slightly aquiline nose was not clear, and the colour was gone from her small lips. Was it so dim, then, the light that cut across the sky and overflowed it? Shimamura found that hard to believe. The light was dimmer even than on the night of the new moon, and yet the Milky Way was brighter than the brightest full moon. In the faint light that left no shadows on the earth, Komako's face floated up like an old mask. It was strange that even in the mask there should be the scent of the woman.

He looked up, and again the Milky Way came down to wrap itself around the earth.

And the Milky Way, like a great aurora, flowed through his body to stand at the edges of the earth. There was a quiet, chilly loneliness in it, and a sort of voluptuous astonishment.

'If you leave, I'll lead an honest life,' Komako said, walking on again. She put her hand to her disordered hair. When she had gone five or six steps she turned to look back at him. 'What's the matter? You don't have to stand there, do you?'

But Shimamura stood looking at her.

'Oh? You'll wait, then? And afterwards you'll take me to your room with you.'

She raised her left hand a little and ran off. Her retreating figure was drawn up into the mountain. The Milky Way spread its skirts to be broken by the waves of the mountain, and, fanning out again in all its brilliant vastness higher in the sky, it left the mountain in a deeper darkness.

Komako turned into the main street and disappeared. Shima-mura started after her.

Several men were pulling a fire-pump down the street to a rhythmical chant. Floods of people poured after them. Shima-mura joined the crowd from the side-road he and Komako had taken.

Another pump came down the street. He let it pass, and fell in behind it.

It was an old wooden hand-pump, ridiculously small, with

swarms of men at the long rope pulling it and other swarms to man it.

Komako too had stopped to let it pass. She spotted Shimamura and ran along beside him. All down the road people who had stood aside fell in again as if sucked up by the pump. The two of them were now no more than part of a mob running to a fire.

'So you came. Always looking for excitement.'

'That's right. It's a sad little pump, though, isn't it. The better part of a hundred years old.'

'At least. Careful you don't fall.'

'It is slippery.'

'Come sometime when we have a real blizzard, and the snow drives along the ground all night long. But you won't, of course. Rabbits and pheasants come running inside the house to get out of the storm.' Komako's voice was bright and eager. She seemed to take her beat from the chanting voices and the tramping feet around her. Shimamura too was buoyed up by the crowd.

They could hear the sound of the flames now, and tongues of flame leaped up before them. Komako clutched at Shimamura's arm. The low, dark houses along the street seemed to be breathing as they floated up in the light of the fire and faded away again. Water from the pumps flowed along the street. They came against a wall of people. Mixed in with the smoke was a smell like boiling cocoons.

The same standard remarks were taken up in loud voices through the crowd: the fire had started at the projector; children had been thrown one after another from the balcony; no one was hurt; it was lucky there had been no rice or cocoons in the warehouse. And yet a sort of quiet unified the whole fiery scene, as though everyone were voiceless before the flames, as though the heart, the point of reference, had been torn away from each individual. Everyone seemed to be listening to the sound of the fire and the pumps.

Now and then a villager came running up late, and called out the name of a relative. There would be an answer, and the two would call happily back and forth. Only those voices seemed alive and present. The fire-alarm no longer sounded.

111

Afraid people would be watching, Shimamura slipped away from Komako and stood behind a group of children. The children moved back from the heat. The snow at their feet was melting, while farther on it had already turned to slush from the fire and water, a muddy confusion of footprints.

They were standing in the field beside the cocoon-warehouse. Most of the crowd in the main street had poured into that same open space.

The fire had apparently started near the entrance, and the walls and roof of half the building had burned away. The pillars and beams were still smouldering. It was a wide barn of a building, only shingles and boarded walls and floors, and the inside was fairly free of smoke. Though the roof, soaked from the pumps, did not seem to be burning, the fire continued to spread. A tongue would shoot up from a quite unexpected spot, the three pumps would turn hastily towards it, and a shower of sparks would fly up in a cloud of black smoke.

The sparks spread off into the Milky Way, and Shimamura was pulled up with them. As the smoke drifted away, the Milky Way seemed to dip and flow in the opposite direction. Occasionally a pump missed the roof, and the end of its line of water wavered and turned to a faint white mist, as though lighted by the Milky Way.

Komako had come up to him, he did not know when. She took his hand. He looked around at her, but said nothing. She gazed at the fire, the pulse of the fire beating on her intent, slightly flushed face. Shimamura felt a violent rising in his chest. Komako's hair was coming undone, and her throat was bare and arched. His fingers trembled from the urge to touch it. His hand was warm, but Komako's was still warmer. He did not know why he should feel that a separation was forcing itself upon them.

Flames shot up again from the pillars and beams at the entrance. A line of water was turned on them. Hissing clouds of steam arose as the framework began to give way.

The crowd gasped as one person. A woman's body had fallen through the flames.

The cocoon-warehouse had a balcony that was little more than a perfunctory recognition of its duties as an auditorium.

Since it fell from the balcony, low for a second floor, the body could have taken but a fraction of a second to reach the ground; but the eye had somehow been able to trace its passage in detail. Perhaps the strange, puppet-like deadness of the fall was what made that fraction of a second seem so long. One knew immediately that the figure was unconscious. It made no noise as it struck the ground between the fire that had newly blazed up and the fire that still smouldered beyond. Water had collected inside the building, and no dust arose from the fall.

A line of water from one of the pumps arched down on the smouldering fire, and a woman's body suddenly floated up before it: such had been the fall. The body was quite horizontal as it passed through the air. Shimamura started back – not from fear, however. He saw the figure as a phantasm from an unreal world. That stiff figure, flung out into the air, became soft and pliant. With a doll-like passiveness, and the freedom of the lifeless, it seemed to hold both life and death in abeyance. If Shimamura felt even a flicker of uneasiness, it was lest the head drop, or a knee or a hip bend to disturb that perfectly horizontal line. Something of the sort must surely happen; but the body was still horizontal when it struck the ground.

Komako screamed and brought her hands to her eyes. Shimamura gazed at the still form.

When did he realize that it was Yoko? The gasp from the crowd and Komako's scream seemed to come at the same instant; and that instant too there was a suggestion of a spasm in the calf of Yoko's leg, stretched out on the ground.

The scream stabbed him through. At the spasm in Yoko's leg, a chill passed down his spine to his very feet. His heart was pounding in an indefinable anguish.

Yoko's leg moved very slightly, hardly enough to catch the eye.

Even before the spasm passed, Shimamura was looking at the face and the kimono, an arrow figure against a red ground. Yoko had fallen face up. The skirt of her kimono was pulled just over one knee. There was but that slight movement in her leg after she struck the earth. She lay unconscious. For some

113

reason Shimamura did not see death in the still form. He felt rather that Yoko had undergone some shift, some metamorphosis.

Two or three beams from the collapsing balcony were burning over her head. The beautiful eyes that so pierced their object were closed. Her jaw was thrust slightly out, and her throat was arched. The fire flickered over the white face.

Shimamura felt a rising in his chest again as the memory came to him of the night he had been on his way to visit Komako, and he had seen that mountain light shine in Yoko's face. The years and months with Komako seemed to be lighted up in that instant; and there, he knew, was the anguish.

Komako put her hands to her eyes and screamed, and even as the ground held its breath in that first gasp she broke away from Shimamura and ran toward the fire.

The long geisha's skirts trailing behind her, she staggered through the pools of water and the charred bits of wood that lay scattered over the ground. She turned and struggled back with Yoko at her breast. Her face was strained and desperate, and beneath it Yoko's face hung vacantly, as at the moment of the soul's flight. Komako struggled forward as if she bore her sacrifice, or her punishment.

The crowd found its various voices again. It surged forward to envelop the two.

'Keep back. Keep back, please.' He heard Komako's cry. 'This girl is insane. She's insane.'

He tried to move toward that half-mad voice, but he was pushed aside by the men who had come up to take Yoko from her. As he caught his footing, his head fell back, and the Milky Way flowed down inside him with a roar.

Thousand Cranes

A Note on the Tea Ceremony, the Backdrop for this Novel

The beginnings of the tea cult can be traced to the thirteenth century and the beginnings of Zen Buddhism in Japan. Early Zen masters recommended tea as the beverage most excellent for cultivating the spirit, and in the centuries that followed, an elaborate symbolism and a carefully contrived ritual encouraged the Zen disciple in his aim to achieve imperturbability. Rustic utensils and surroundings were brought into harmony to remind him of the Buddhahood in a clod of earth, and the withdrawn repose of the cottage and its garden turned his mind to the permanent behind the ephemeral – to the intersection of time and eternity. If the quiet and restraint of the ideal tea ceremony are somewhat lacking in ceremonies described in this novel, Mr Kawabata's characters nonetheless seem to pause at the intersection, marked for them by the permanence of the old tea vessels and the impermanence of the owners.

The tea ceremony is a stylized way of preparing tea from water heated over a charcoal hearth. The smallest detail, from the charcoal to the receptacle for left-over water, must be carefully planned. The host pours water from an iron kettle into a handleless cup – here translated 'bowl' because it is considerably larger than an ordinary teacup – adds powdered tea, and stirs with a bamboo whisk until an appropriate layer of foam has accumulated. The guest drinks according to a prescribed form and returns the bowl. That, on the surface, is all; but to the initiated the details of the cottage, the utensils, and the performance have given something more – perhaps only an impression of affluence, perhaps a sense of timelessness.

Thousand Cranes

Even when he reached Kamakura and the Engakuji Temple, Kikuji did not know whether or not he would go to the tea ceremony. He was already late.

He received an announcement whenever Kurimoto Chikako offered tea at the inner cottage of the Engakuji. He had not once gone since his father's death, however. He thought of the announcements as no more than formal gestures in memory of his father.

This time there had been a postscript: she wanted him to meet a young lady to whom she was giving tea lessons.

As he read it, Kikuji thought of Chikako's birthmark.

Had he been eight, perhaps, or nine? He had been taken by his father to visit Chikako, and they had found her in the breakfast room. Her kimono was open. She was cutting the hair on her birthmark with a small pair of scissors. It covered half the left breast and ran down into the hollow between her breasts, as large as the palm of one's hand. Hair seemed to be growing on the purple-black mark, and Chikako was in the process of cutting it.

'You brought the boy with you?'

In surprise, she snatched at the neck of her kimono. Then, perhaps because haste only complicated her efforts to cover herself, she turned slightly away and carefully tucked kimono into obi.

The surprise must have been less at Kikuji's father than at Kikuji. Since a maid had met them at the door, Chikako must have known at least that Kikuji's father had come.

Kikuji's father did not go into the breakfast room. He sat down in the next room instead, the room where Chikako gave lessons.

119

'Do you suppose I could have a cup of tea?' Kikuji's father asked absently. He looked up at the hanging in the alcove.

'Yes.' But Chikako did not move.

On the newspaper at her knee, Kikuji had seen hairs like whiskers.

Though it was broad daylight, rats were scurrying about in the hollow ceiling. A peach tree was in bloom near the veranda.

When at length she took her place by the tea hearth, Chikako seemed preoccupied.

Some ten days later, Kikuji heard his mother telling his father, as if it were an extraordinary secret of which he could not have known, that Chikako was unmarried because of the birthmark. There was compassion in her eyes.

'Oh?' Kikuji's father nodded in apparent surprise. 'But it wouldn't matter, would it, if her husband were to see it? Especially if he knew of it before he married her?'

'That's exactly what I said to her. But after all a woman is a woman. I don't think I would ever be able to tell a man that I had a big mark on my breast.'

'But she's hardly young any more.'

'Still it wouldn't be easy. A man with a birthmark could probably get married and just laugh when he was found out.'

'Did you see the mark?'

'Don't be silly. Of course not.'

'You just talked about it?'

'She came for my lesson, and we talked about all sorts of things. I suppose she felt like confessing.'

Kikuji's father was silent.

'Suppose she were to marry. What would the man think?'

'He'd probably be disgusted by it. But he might find something attractive in it, in having it for a secret. And then again the defect might bring out good points. Anyway, it's hardly a problem worth worrying about.'

'I told her it was no problem at all. But it's on the breast, she says.'

'Oh?'

'The hardest thing would be having a child to nurse. The husband might be all right, but the child.'

'The birthmark would keep milk from coming?'

'Not that. No, the trouble would be having the child look at the birthmark while it was nursing. I hadn't seen quite so far myself, but a person who actually has a birthmark thinks of these things. From the day it was born it would drink there; and from the day it began to see, it would see that ugly mark on its mother's breast. Its first impression of the world, its first impression of its mother, would be that ugly birthmark, and there the impression would be, through the child's whole life.'

'Oh? But isn't that inventing worries?'

'You could nurse it on cow's milk, I suppose, or hire a wet nurse.'

'I should think the important thing would be whether or not there was milk, not whether or not there was a birthmark.'

'I'm afraid not. I actually wept when I heard. So that's how it is, I thought. I wouldn't want our Kikuji nursing at a breast with a birthmark on it.'

'Oh?'

At this show of ingenuousness, a wave of indignation came over Kikuji, and a wave of resentment at his father, who could ignore him even though he too had seen the mark.

Now, however, almost twenty years later, Kikuji was able to smile at the thought of his father's confusion.

From the time he was ten or so, he often thought of his mother's words and started with uneasiness at the idea of a half-brother or half-sister sucking at the birthmark.

It was not just fear of having a brother or sister born away from home, a stranger to him. It was rather fear of that brother or sister in particular. Kikuji was obsessed with the idea that a child who sucked at that breast, with its birthmark and its hair, must be a monster.

Chikako appeared to have had no children. One could, if one wished, suspect that his father had not allowed her to. The association of birthmark and baby that had saddened his mother might have been his father's device for convincing Chikako that she did not want children. In any case, Chikako produced none, either while Kikuji's father lived or after his death.

Perhaps Chikako had made her confession so soon after

Kikuji had seen the birthmark because she feared that Kikuji himself would tell of it.

Chikako did not marry. Had the birthmark then governed her whole life?

Kikuji never forgot the mark. He could sometimes imagine even that his own destinies were enmeshed in it.

When he received the note saying that Chikako meant to make the tea ceremony her excuse for introducing him to a young lady, the birthmark once more floated before him; and, since the introduction would be made by Chikako, he wondered if the young lady herself would have a perfect skin, a skin unmarred by so much as a dot.

Had his father occasionally squeezed the birthmark between his fingers? Had he even bitten at it? Such were Kikuji's fantasies.

Even now, as he walked through the temple grounds and heard the chirping of birds, those were the fantasies that came to him.

Some two or three years after the incident, Chikako had somehow turned masculine in manner. Now she was quite sexless.

At the ceremony today she would be bustling about energetically. Perhaps that breast with its birthmark would have withered. Kikuji felt a smile of relief come to his lips; and just then two young women hurried up behind him.

He stopped to let them pass.

'Do you know whether the cottage Miss Kurimoto has taken might be in this direction?' he asked.

'Yes, it is,' the two answered in unison.

Kikuji already knew, and he could have told from their dress that they were on their way to a tea ceremony. He had asked because he had to make it clear to himself that he was going.

One of the girls was beautiful. She carried a bundle wrapped in a kerchief, the thousand-crane pattern in white on a pink crêpe background.

The two girls were changing to fresh *tabi** when Kikuji arrived.

*Short split-toed socks.

He looked in from behind them. The main room was a large one, some eight mats in area.*

Even so, the guests presented a solid row of knees. There seemed to be only women, women in bright kimonos.

Chikako saw him immediately. As if in surprise, she stood up to greet him.

'Come in, come in. What a prize! Please, it will be quite all right to come in from there.' She pointed to the sliding door at the upper end of the room, before the alcove.

Kikuji flushed. He felt the eyes of all those women.

'Ladies only, is it?'

'We did have a gentleman earlier, but he left. You are the one bright spot.'

'Hardly bright.'

'Oh, certainly, you have all the qualifications. The one spot of scarlet.'

Kikuji waved his hand to indicate that he would prefer a less conspicuous door.

The young lady was wrapping her discarded *tabi* in the thousand-crane kerchief. She stood aside to let him pass.

The anteroom was cluttered with boxes of sweets, tea utensils brought by Chikako, and bundles that belonged to the guests. In the far corner a maid was washing something.

Chikako came in.

'Well, what do you think of her? A nice girl, isn't she?'

'The one with the thousand-crane kerchief?'

'Kerchief? How would I know about kerchiefs? The one who was standing here, the pretty one. She's the Inamura girl.'

Kikuji nodded vaguely.

'Kerchief. What odd things you notice. A person can't be too careful. I thought you had come together. I was delighted.'

'What are you talking about?'

'You met on the way. It's a sign of a bond between you. And your father knew Mr Inamura.'

'Oh?'

'The family had a raw-silk business in Yokohama. She

*A mat is about one yard by two.

123

knows nothing about today. You can look her over at your leisure.'

Chikako's voice was no small one, and Kikuji was in an agony of apprehension lest she be heard through the paper-panelled door that separated them from the main party. Suddenly she brought her face close to his.

'But there's a complication.' She lowered her voice. 'Mrs Ota is here, and her daughter with her.' She studied Kikuji's expression. 'I didn't invite her. But it's been the rule that anyone who happens to be in the neighbourhood can drop in. The other day I even had some Americans. I'm sorry, but what am I to do when she gets wind of an affair? Of course she doesn't know about you and the Inamura girl.'

'About me and the Inamura girl? But I ...' Kikuji wanted to say that he had not come prepared for a *miai*, a meeting the announced purpose of which was to view a prospective bride. Somehow the words would not come. His throat muscles stiffened.

'But Mrs Ota is the one who should be uncomfortable. You can pretend that nothing is wrong.'

Chikako's way of dismissing the matter annoyed him.

Her intimacy with his father had evidently been of short duration. For the rest of his father's life, however, Chikako made herself useful in his house. She would come to help in the kitchen when there was to be a tea ceremony and even when ordinary guests were expected.

The idea that Kikuji's mother should begin feeling jealous of a sexless Chikako seemed funny, worth only a wry smile. No doubt his mother came to sense that his father had seen the birthmark, but the storm had passed; and Chikako, as if she too had quite forgotten, became his mother's companion.

In the course of time Kikuji too came to treat her lightly. As he turned his childish tantrums on her, the suffocating revulsion of his younger days seemed to fade.

It was perhaps an appropriate life for Chikako, that she had lapsed into sexlessness and been made a convenient fixture.

With Kikuji's family her base, she was modestly successful as an instructor in the tea ceremony.

Kikuji even felt a certain faint sympathy for her when,

upon his father's death, it came to him that she had repressed the woman in her after that one brief, fleeting affair.

The hostility of Kikuji's mother, moreover, was held in check by the question of Mrs Ota.

After the death of Ota, who had been a companion in the pursuit of tea, Kikuji's father had undertaken to dispose of Ota's tea utensils, and he had thus been drawn to the widow.

Chikako hastened to inform Kikuji's mother.

Chikako of course became his mother's ally – indeed a too hard-working ally. She prowled after his father, she frequently went to threaten Mrs Ota. All her own latent jealousy seemed to explode.

Kikuji's quiet, introspective mother, taken aback at this flaming intervention, worried rather about what people might think.

Even in front of Kikuji, Chikako would berate Mrs Ota, and when his mother showed signs of displeasure, Chikako would say that it did Kikuji no harm to hear.

'And the time before, too, when I went to have it out with her, there was the child, listening to everything. I ask you, didn't I all of a sudden hear sniffling in the next room?'

'A girl?' Kikuji's mother frowned.

'Yes. Eleven years old, I believe Mrs Ota said. Really, there is something wrong with that woman. I thought she would scold the girl for eavesdropping, and what did she do but get up and bring her in, and sit holding her, right there in front of me. I suppose she needed a supporting actor to help with the sobbing.'

'But don't you think it's a little sad for the child?'

'That's exactly why we should use the child to get back at her. The child knows everything. I must say that it's a pretty child, though. A round little face.' Chikako looked at Kikuji. 'Suppose we have Kikuji here speak to his father.'

'Try not to spread the poison too far, if you don't mind.' Even Kikuji's mother had to protest.

'You keep the poison dammed up inside you, that's the whole trouble. Pull yourself together; spit it all out. See how thin you are, and she all plump and glowing. There really is something not right about her – she thinks that if she weeps pathetically enough, everyone will understand. And right there in the room where she sees Mr Mitani, she has a picture of her own husband on exhibit. I'm surprised Mr Mitani hasn't spoken to her about it.'

And, after the death of Kikuji's father, this Mrs Ota came to Chikako's tea ceremony and even brought her daughter.

Kikuji felt the touch of something cold.

Chikako said that she had not invited Mrs Ota today. Still it was astonishing: the two women had been seeing each other since his father's death. Perhaps even the daughter was taking tea lessons.

'If it bothers you, I might ask her to leave.' Chikako looked into his eyes.

'It makes no difference to me. Of course, if she wants to go . . .'

'If she were a person who thought of such things, she wouldn't have brought so much unhappiness to your father and mother.'

'The daughter is with her?' Kikuji had never seen the daughter.

It seemed wrong to meet the girl of the thousand cranes here before Mrs Ota. And he was even more repelled at the thought of meeting the daughter today.

But Chikako's voice clawed at his ear and scraped at his nerves. 'Well, she will know I'm here. I can't run away now.' He stood up.

He went in through the door by the alcove, and took his place at the upper end of the room.

Chikako followed close after him. 'This is Mr Mitani. Old Mr Mitani's son.' Her tone was most formal.

Kikuji made his bow, and as he raised his head he had a clear view of the daughter. Somewhat flustered, he had at first not distinguished one lady from another in the bright flood of kimonos. He saw now that Mrs Ota was directly opposite him.

'Kikuji.' It was Mrs Ota. Her voice, audible throughout the room, was frankly affectionate. 'I haven't written in so long. And it's been so very long since I last saw you.' She tugged at the daughter's sleeve, urging her to be quick with her greetings. The daughter flushed and looked at the floor.

To Kikuji this was indeed odd. He could not detect the faintest suggestion of hostility in Mrs Ota's manner. She seemed wholly warm, tender, overcome with pleasure at an unexpected meeting. One could only conclude that she was wholly unaware of her place in the assembly.

The daughter sat stiffly, with bowed head.

At length noticing, Mrs Ota, too, flushed. She still looked at Kikuji, however, as if she wanted to rush to his side, or as if there were things she must say to him. 'You are studying tea, then, are you?'

'I know nothing at all about it.'

'Really? But you have it in your blood.' Her emotions seemed too much for her. Her eyes were moist.

Kikuji had not seen her since his father's funeral.

She had hardly changed in four years.

The white neck, rather long, was as it had been, and the full shoulders that strangely matched the slender neck – it was a figure young for her years. The mouth and nose were small in proportion to the eyes. The little nose, if one bothered to notice, was cleanly modelled and most engaging. When she spoke, her lower lip was thrust forward a little, as if in a pout.

The daughter had inherited the long neck and the full shoulders. Her mouth was larger, however, and tightly closed. There was something almost funny about the mother's tiny lips beside the daughter's.

Sadness clouded the girl's eyes, darker than her mother's.

Chikako poked at the embers in the hearth. 'Miss Inamura, suppose you make tea for Mr Mitani. I don't believe you've had your turn yet.'

The girl of the thousand cranes stood up.

Kikuji had noticed her beside Mrs Ota.

He had avoided looking at her, however, once he had seen Mrs Ota and the daughter.

Chikako was of course showing the girl off for his inspection.

When she had taken her place at the hearth, she turned to Chikako.

'And which bowl shall I use?'

'Let me see. The Oribe* should do,' Chikako answered. 'It belonged to Mr Mitani's father. He was very fond of it, and he gave it to me.'

Kikuji remembered the tea bowl Chikako had placed before the girl. It had indeed belonged to his father, and his father had received it from Mrs Ota.

And what of Mrs Ota seeing at the ceremony today a bowl that had been treasured by her dead husband and passed from Kikuji's father to Chikako?

Kikuji was astounded at Chikako's tactlessness.

But one could not avoid concluding that Mrs Ota, too, showed a certain want of tact.

Here, making tea for him, clean against the rankling histories of the middle-aged women, the Inamura girl seemed beautiful to him.

Unaware that she was on display, she went through the ceremony without hesitation, and she herself set the tea before Kikuji.

After drinking, Kikuji looked at the bowl. It was black Oribe, splashed with white on one side, and there decorated, also in black, with crook-shaped bracken shoots.

"You must remember it,' said Chikako from across the room.

Kikuji gave an evasive answer and put the bowl down.

'The pattern has the feel of the mountains in it,' said Chikako. 'One of the best bowls I know for early spring – your father often used it. We're just a little out of season, but then I thought that for Kikuji . . .'

'But what difference does it make that my father owned it for a little while? It's four hundred years old, after all – its history† goes back to Momoyana and Rikyū† himself. Tea masters have looked after it and passed it down through the centuries. My father is of very little importance.' So Kikuji tried to forget the associations the bowl called up.

It had passed from Ota to his wife, from the wife to Kikuji's father, from Kikuji's father to Chikako; and the two men,

---

*A Seto ware dating from the sixteenth century.
†Sen Rikyū (1521–91), an early tea master.

Ota and Kikuji's father, were dead, and here were the two women. There was something almost weird about the bowl's career.

Here, again, Ota's widow and daughter, and Chikako, and the Inamura girl, and other young girls too, were holding the old tea bowl in their hands, and bringing it to their lips.

'Might I have tea from the Oribe myself?' asked Mrs Ota suddenly. 'You gave me a different one last time.'

Kikuji was startled afresh. Was the woman foolish, or shameless?

He was overcome with pity for the daughter, still sitting with bowed head.

For Mrs Ota, the Inamura girl once more went through the ceremony. Everyone was watching her. She probably did not know the history of the black Oribe. She went through the practised motions.

It was a straightforward performance, quite without personal quirks. Her bearing, from shoulders to knees, suggested breeding and refinement.

The shadow of young leaves fell on the paper-panelled door. One noted a soft reflection from the shoulders and the long sleeves of the gay kimono. The hair seemed luminous.

The light was really too bright for a tea cottage, but it made the girl's youth glow. The tea napkin, as became a young girl, was red, and it impressed one less with its softness than with its freshness, as if the girl's hand were bringing a red flower into bloom.

And one saw a thousand cranes, small and white, start up in flight around her.

Mrs Ota took the black Oribe in the palm of her hand. 'The green tea against the black, like traces of green in early spring.' But not even she mentioned that the bowl had belonged to her husband.

Afterwards there was a perfunctory inspection of the tea utensils. The girls knew little about them, and were for the most part satisfied with Chikako's explanation.

The water jar and the tea measure had belonged to Kikuji's father. Neither he nor Chikako mentioned the fact.

As Kikuji sat watching the girls leave, Mrs Ota came towards him.

'I'm afraid I was very rude. I may have annoyed you, but when I saw you it seemed that the old days came before everything.'

'Oh?'

'But see what a gentleman you've become.' She looked as if she might weep. 'Oh, yes. Your mother. I meant to go to the funeral, and then somehow couldn't.'

Kikuji looked uncomfortable.

'Your father and then your mother. You must be very lonely.'

'Yes, perhaps I am.'

'You're not leaving yet?'

'Well, as a matter of fact . . .

'There are so many things we must talk about, sometime.'

'Kikuji.' Chikako called from the next room.

Mrs Ota stood up regretfully. Her daughter had gone out and was waiting in the garden.

The two of them left after nodding their farewell to Kikuji. There was a look of appeal in the girl's eyes.

Chikako, with a maid and two or three favourite pupils, was cleaning the other room.

'And what did Mrs Ota have to say?'

'Nothing in particular. Nothing at all.'

'You must be careful with her. So meek and gentle – she always manages to make it look as if she could do no one the least harm. But you can never tell what she's thinking.'

'I suppose she comes to your parties often?' Kikuji asked with a touch of sarcasm. 'When did she begin?'

To escape Chikako's poison, he started into the garden.

Chikako followed him. 'And did you like her? A nice girl, didn't you think?'

'A very nice girl. And she would have seemed even nicer if I'd met her without the rest of you hovering around, you and Mrs Ota and Father's ghost.'

'Why should that bother you? Mrs Ota has nothing to do with the Inamura girl.'

'It just seemed the wrong thing to do to the girl.'

'Why? If it bothered you to have Mrs Ota here, I apologize, but you must remember that I didn't invite her. And you're to think of the Inamura girl separately.'

'I'm afraid I have to go.' He stopped. If he went on walking with Chikako, there was no telling when she would leave him.

By himself again, he noted that the azaleas up the side of the mountain were in bud. He heaved a deep sigh.

He was disgusted with himself for having let Chikako's note lure him out; but the impression of the girl with the thousand-crane kerchief was fresh and clean.

It was perhaps because of her that the meeting with two of his father's women had upset him no more than it had.

The two women were still here to talk of his father, and his mother was dead. He felt a surge of something like anger. The ugly birthmark came to him again.

An evening breeze was rustling the new leaves. Kikuji walked slowly, hat in hand.

From a distance he saw Mrs Ota standing in the shadow of the main gate.

He looked for a way of avoiding her. If he climbed to the right or left, he could probably leave the temple by another exit.

Nevertheless, he walked toward the gate. A suggestion of grimness came over his face.

Mrs Ota saw him, and came toward him. Her cheeks were flushed.

'I waited for you. I wanted to see you again. I must seem brazen, but I had to say something more. If we had said good-bye there, I would have had no way of knowing when I might see you again.'

'What happened to your daughter?'

'Fumiko went on ahead. She was with a friend.'

'She knew, then, that you would be waiting for me?'

'Yes.' She looked into his eyes.

'I doubt if she approves. I felt very sorry for her back there. It was clear that she did not want to see me.' The words may have been blunt, and again they may have been circumspect; but her answer was quite straightforward.

'It was a trial for Fumiko to see you.'

'Because my father caused her a great deal of pain.'

Kikuji meant to suggest that Mrs Ota had caused him a great deal of pain.

'Not at all. Your father was very good to her. Sometime I must tell you all about it. At first she would not be friendly, no matter how kind he was to her; but then, towards the end of the war, when the air raids were bad, she changed. I had no idea why. In her own way, she did her very best for him. Her very best, I say, but she was only a girl. Her best was going out to buy chicken and fish and the like for him. She was very determined, and she didn't mind taking risks. She went out into the country for rice, even during the raids. Your father was astonished, the change was so sudden. I found it very touching myself, so touching that it almost hurt. And at the same time I felt that I was being scolded.'

Kikuji wondered if he and his mother might also have had favours from the Ota girl. The remarkable gifts his father brought home from time to time – were they among her purchases?

'I don't know why Fumiko changed so. Maybe it was because we didn't know from one day to the next whether we would still be alive. I suppose she was feeling sorry for me, and she went to work for your father too.'

In the confusion of defeat, the girl must have known how desperately her mother clung to Kikuji's father. In the violent reality of those days, she must have left behind the past that was her own father, and seen only the present reality of her mother.

'Did you notice the ring Fumiko was wearing?'

'No.'

'Your father gave it to her. Even when he was with me, your father would go home if there was an air-raid warning. Fumiko would see him home, and no one could talk her out of it. There was no telling what would happen if he went alone, she would say. One night she didn't come back. I hoped she had stayed at your house, but I was afraid the two of them had been killed. Then in the morning she came home and said that she had seen him as far as your gate and spent the rest of the night in an air-raid shelter. He thanked her the next time he came, and gave her that ring. I'm sure she was embarrassed to have you see it.'

Kikuji was most uncomfortable. And it was odd that the woman seemed to expect sympathy as a matter of course.

His mood was not clearly one of dislike or distrust, however. There was a warmth in her that put him off guard.

When the girl had desperately been doing everything she could for his father, had she been watching her mother, and yet unable to watch?

Kikuji sensed that Mrs Ota was talking of her own love as she talked of the girl.

She seemed to be pleading something with all the passion she had, and in its final implications the plea did not seem to make a distinction between Kikuji's father and Kikuji himself. There was a deep, affectionate nostalgia in it, as if she meant to be talking to Kikuji's father.

The hostility which Kikuji, with his mother, had felt for Mrs Ota had lost some of its strength, though it had not entirely disappeared. He even feared that unless he was careful he might find in himself the father loved by Mrs Ota. He was tempted to imagine that he had known this woman's body long ago.

His father had soon left Chikako, Kikuji knew, but he had stayed with Mrs Ota until his death. Still it seemed probable that Chikako had treated Mrs Ota with derision. Kikuji saw signs of much the same cruelty in himself, and he found something seductive in the thought that he could do her injury with a light heart.

'Do you often go to Kurimoto's affairs?' he asked. 'Didn't you have enough of her in the old days?'

'I had a letter from her after your father died. I missed your father a great deal. I was feeling very lonely.' She spoke with bowed head.

'And does your daughter go too?'

'Fumiko? Fumiko just keeps me company.'

They had crossed the tracks and passed the North Kamakura Station, and were climbing the hill opposite the Engakuji.

Mrs Ota was at least forty-five, some twenty years older than Kikuji, but she had made him forget her age when they made love. He felt that he had had a woman younger than he in his arms.

Sharing a happiness that came from the woman's experience, Kikuji felt none of the embarrassed reticence of inexperience.

He felt as if he had for the first time known woman, and as if for the first time he had known himself as a man. It was an extraordinary awakening. He had not guessed that a woman could be so wholly pliant and receptive, the receptive one who followed after and at the same time lured him on, the receptive one who engulfed him in her own warm scent.

Kikuji, the bachelor, usually felt soiled after such encounters; but now, when the sense of defilement should have been keenest, he was conscious only of warm repose.

He usually wanted to make his departure roughly; but today it was as though for the first time someone was warmly near him and he was drifting willingly along. He had not until then seen how the wave of woman followed after. Giving his body to the wave, he even felt a satisfaction as if drowsing off in triumph, the conqueror whose feet were being washed by a slave.

And there was a feeling of the maternal about her.

'Kurimoto has a big birthmark. Did you know it?' He bobbed his head as he spoke. Without forethought, he had introduced the unpleasant. Possibly because the fibres of his consciousness had slackened, however, he did not feel that he was wronging Chikako. He put out his hand. 'Here, on the breast, like this.'

Something had risen inside him to make him say it. Something itchy that wanted to rise against Kikuji himself and injure the woman. Or perhaps it only hid a sweet shyness in wanting to see her body, to see where the mark should be.

'How repulsive!' She quickly brought her kimono together. But there seemed to be something she could not quite accept. 'I hadn't known,' she said quietly. 'You can't see it under the kimono, can you?'

'It's not impossible.'

'No! How could you possibly?'

'You could see it if it were here, I should imagine.'

'Stop. Are you looking to see if I have a mark too?'

'No. But I wonder how you'd feel at a time like this if you did have a mark.'

'Here?' Mrs Ota looked at her own breast. 'But why do you have to speak of it? Does it make any difference?' In spite of the protest, her manner was unresisting. The poison disseminated by Kikuji seemed to have had no effect. It flowed back to Kikuji himself.

'But it does make a difference. I only saw it once, when I was eight or nine years old, and I can see it even now.'

'Why?'

'You were under the curse of that birthmark yourself. Didn't Kurimoto come at you as if she were fighting for Mother and me?'

Mrs Ota nodded, and pulled away. Kikuji put strength into his embrace.

'She was always conscious of that birthmark. It made her more and more spiteful.'

'What a frightening idea.'

'And maybe too she was out for revenge against my father.'

'For what?'

'She thought he was belittling her because of the birthmark. She may even have persuaded herself that he left her because of it.'

'Let's not talk about the repulsive thing.' But she seemed to be drawing no clear picture of the birthmark in her mind. 'I don't suppose Miss Kurimoto worries about it any more. The pain must have gone long ago.'

'Does pain go away and leave no trace, then?'

'You sometimes even feel sentimental for it.' She spoke as if still half in a dream.

Then Kikuji said what he had meant at all costs not to say.

'You remember the girl on your left this afternoon?'

'Yes, Yukiko. The Inamura girl.'

'Kurimoto invited me today so that I could inspect her.'

'No!' She gazed at him with wide, unblinking eyes. 'It was a *miai*, was it? I never suspected.'

'Not a *miai*, really.'

'So that was it. On the way home from a *miai*.' A tear drew a line from her eye down to the pillow. Her shoulders were quivering. 'It was wrong. Wrong. Why didn't you tell me?'

She pressed her face to the pillow.

Kikuji had not expected so violent a response.

'If it's wrong it's wrong, whether I'm on the way home from a *miai* or not.' He was being quite honest. 'I don't see the relationship between the two.'

But the figure of the Inamura girl at the tea hearth came before him. He could see the pink kerchief and the thousand cranes.

The figure of the weeping woman had become ugly.

'Oh, it was wrong. How could I have done it? The things I'm guilty of.' Her full shoulders were shaking.

If Kikuji had regretted the encounter, he would have had the usual sense of defilement. Quite aside from the question of the *miai,* she was his father's woman.

But he had until then felt neither regret nor revulsion.

He did not understand how it had happened, it had happened so naturally. Perhaps she was apologizing for having seduced him, and yet she had probably not meant to seduce him, nor did Kikuji feel that he had been seduced. There had been no suggestion of resistance, on his part or the woman's. There had been no qualms, he might have said.

They had gone to an inn on the hill opposite the Engakuji, and they had had dinner, because she was still talking of Kikuji's father. Kikuji did not have to listen. Indeed it was in a sense strange that he listened so quietly; but Mrs Ota, evidently with no thought for the strangeness, seemed to plead her yearning for the past. Listening, Kikuji felt expansively benevolent. A soft affection enveloped him.

It came to him that his father had been happy.

Here, perhaps, was the source of the mistake. The moment for sending her away had passed, and, in the sweet slackening of his heart, Kikuji gave himself up.

But deep in his heart there remained a dark shadow. Venomously, he spoke of Chikako and the Inamura girl.

The venom was only too effective. With regret came defilement and revulsion, and a violent wave of self-loathing swept over him, pressing him to say something even crueller.

'Let's forget about it. It was nothing,' she said. 'It was nothing at all.'

'You were remembering my father?'

'What!' She looked up in surprise. She had been weeping, and her eyelids were red. The eyes were muddied, and in the wide pupils Kikuji still saw the lassitude of woman. 'If you say so, I have no answer. But I'm a very unhappy person.'

'You needn't lie to me.' Kikuji roughly pulled her kimono open. 'If there were even a birthmark, you'd never forget. The impression . . . He was taken aback at his own words.

'You aren't to stare at me. I'm not young any more.'

Kikuji came at her as if to bite.

The earlier wave returned, the wave of woman.

He fell asleep in security.

Half awake and half asleep, he heard birds chirping. It was as if he were awakening for the first time to the call of birds.

A morning mist wet the trees at the veranda. Kikuji felt that the recesses of his mind had been washed clean. He thought of nothing.

Mrs Ota was sleeping with her back to him. He wondered when she had turned away. Raising himself to an elbow, he looked into her face in the semi-darkness.

Some two weeks later, the Ota girl called on Kikuji.

He had the maid show her into the parlour. In an effort to quiet the beating of his heart, he opened the tea cupboard and took out sweets. Had the girl come alone, or was her mother waiting outside, unable to come in?

The girl stood up as he opened the door. Her head was bowed, and Kikuji saw that the out-thrust lower lip was firmly closed.

'I've kept you waiting.' Kikuji opened the glass doors to the garden. As he passed behind the girl, he caught a faint scent from the white peony in the vase. Her full shoulders were thrown slightly forward.

'Please sit down.' Kikuji took a seat himself. He was

strangely composed, seeing the image of the mother in the daughter.

'I really should have telephoned first.' Her head was still bowed.

'Not at all. But I'm surprised that you were able to find the place.'

She nodded.

Then Kikuji remembered: during the air raids, she had seen his father as far as the gate. He had heard the story from Mrs Ota at the Engakuji.

On the point of mentioning it, he stopped himself. He looked at the girl.

Mrs Ota's warmth came over him like warm water. She had gently surrendered everything, he remembered, and he had felt secure.

Because of that security, he now felt his wariness fade. The girl did not return his gaze.

'I . . .' She broke off and looked up. 'I have a request to make. About my mother.'

Kikuji caught his breath.

'I want you to forgive her.'

'To forgive her?' Kikuji sensed that the mother had told the daughter of him. 'I'm the one to be forgiven if anyone is.'

'I'd like you to forgive her for your father too.'

'And isn't he the one to be forgiven? But my mother is no longer alive in any case, and who would do the forgiving?'

'It is Mother's fault that your father died so soon. And your mother. I told Mother so.'

'You are imagining things. You mustn't be unkind to her.'

'Mother should have died first.' She spoke as if she found the shame intolerable.

Kikuji saw that she was speaking of his own relations with her mother. How deeply they must have wounded and shamed her!

'I want you to forgive her,' the girl said once more, an urgent plea in her voice.

'It's not a question of forgiving or not forgiving.' Kikuji spoke with precision. 'I am grateful to your mother.'

'She is bad. She is no good, and you must have nothing more

138

to do with her. You are not to worry yourself about her.' The words poured out, and her voice was trembling. 'Please.'

Kikuji understood what she meant by forgive. She included a request that he see no more of Mrs Ota.

'Don't telephone her.' The girl flushed as she spoke. She raised her head and looked at him, as if in an effort to master the shyness. There were tears in the wide, near-black eyes, and there was no trace of malice. The eyes were submitting a desperate petition.

'I understand,' said Kikuji. 'I'm sorry.'

'Please, I beg you.' As the shyness deepened, the flush spread to her long, white throat. She was in European dress, and a necklace set off the beauty of the throat. 'She made an appointment over the telephone and then didn't keep it. I stopped her. When she tried to go out, I hung on her and wouldn't let her.' The voice now carried a note of relief.

Kikuji had telephoned Mrs Ota the third day after their meeting. She had seemed overjoyed, and yet she had not come to the appointed tea room.

Besides the one telephone call, Kikuji had had no communication with her.

'Afterwards I felt sorry for her, but at the time it was so wretched – I was so desperate to keep her from going. She told me to refuse for her, then, and I got as far as the telephone and couldn't say anything. Mother was staring at the telephone, and tears were streaming over her face. She felt you there in the telephone, I know she did. That is the sort of person she is.'

The two were silent for a time. Then Kikuji spoke. 'Why did you leave your mother to wait for me after Kurimoto's party?'

'Because I wanted you to know that she was not as bad as you might have thought.'

'She is too much the reverse of bad.'

The girl looked down. Below the well-shaped nose he could see the small mouth and the lower lip, thrust out as if in a pout. The softly rounded face reminded him of her mother.

'I knew that Mrs Ota had a daughter, and I used to wish I could talk to the girl about my father.'

She nodded. 'I used to wish very much the same thing.'

Kikuji thought how good it would be to talk freely of his father and take no account of Mrs Ota.

But it was because he could no longer 'take no account' that he was able to forgive her, and at the same time to feel that he was forgiving what she and his father had been. Must he find that fact strange?

Perhaps suspecting that she had stayed too long, the girl hastily stood up.

Kikuji saw her to the gate.

'I hope we will have a chance sometime to talk about my father. And about your mother, and all the beauty there is in her.' Kikuji feared that he had chosen a somewhat exaggerated way to express himself. Still, he meant what he had said.

'But you will be getting married soon.'

'I will?'

'Yes. Mother said so. It was a *miai* with Inamura Yukiko, she said.'

'It was not.'

A hill fell away from outside the gate. Halfway down the slope the street curved, and, looking back, one saw only the trees in Kikuji's garden.

The image of the girl with the thousand-crane kerchief came to him. Fumiko stopped and said good-bye.

Kikuji started back towards the house.

The Grove in the Evening Sun

Chikako telephoned Kikuji's office.

'Are you going straight home?'

He would be going home, but he frowned. 'Well ...'

'You go straight home. For your father's sake. This is the day he had his tea ceremony every year. I could hardly sit still, thinking about it.'

Kikuji said nothing.

'The tea cottage ... Hello? ... I was cleaning the tea cottage, and all of a sudden I wanted to do some cooking.'

'Where are you calling from?'

'Your house. I'm at your house. I'm sorry – I should have said so.'

Kikuji was startled.

'I just couldn't sit still. I thought I'd feel better if you would let me clean the cottage. I should have telephoned first, I know, but you would have been sure to refuse me.'

Kikuji had not used the tea cottage since his father's death.

In the months before she died, his mother had gone out to sit in the cottage from time to time. She did not put embers in the hearth, however, but carried hot water with her. Kikuji would wait uneasily for her to come back. It troubled him to imagine what she might be thinking, alone in the stillness.

He had sometimes wanted to look in on her, but to the end he had kept his distance.

Chikako rather than his mother had taken care of the cottage while his father was alive. His mother had but rarely gone into it.

It had been closed since his mother's death. A maid who had been with the family from his father's time would air it several times a year.

'How long has it been since you last cleaned the place? I can-

141

not get rid of the mildew, no matter how hard I rub.' Her voice was brassy. 'And while I was about the housecleaning, I wanted to do some cooking. The idea just came to me. I don't have everything I need, but I hope you'll come right home.'

'You don't think you're being a little forward?'

'You'll be lonely by yourself. Suppose you bring a few friends from the office.'

'Very unlikely. Not one of them is interested in tea.'

'All the better. They won't expect too much, and the preparations have been very inadequate. We can all relax.'

'Not the slightest chance.' Kikuji flung the words into the telephone.

'A pity. What shall we do? Do you suppose – someone who shared the hobby with your father? But we couldn't, at this hour. Shall I call the Inamura girl?'

'You're joking.'

'Why shouldn't I call her? The Inamuras are very interested in you, and this will be your chance to see the girl again, and have a good look at her and talk to her. I'll just call her up. If she comes it will be a sign that as far as she's concerned everything is settled.'

'I don't like anything about the idea.' Kikuji's chest tightened painfully. 'And I won't be coming home anyway.'

'This isn't the sort of question you settle over the telephone. We'll talk about it later. Well, that's how things are. Come right home, now.'

'How things are – what are you talking about?'

'Oh, don't worry. I'm just being bold.' The venomous persistence came at him over the wire.

He thought of the birthmark that covered half her breast. The sound of her broom became the sound of a broom sweeping the contents from his skull, and her cloth polishing the veranda a cloth rubbing at his skull.

Revulsion came first. But it was a remarkable story, this marching into a house with the master out, and taking over the kitchen.

She would have been easier to forgive if she had limited herself to cleaning the cottage and arranging flowers in memory of his father.

142

Into his revulsion flashed the image of the Inamura girl, a vein of light.

Chikako had drifted away after his father's death. Did she mean to use the Inamura girl as bait to draw him near again? Was he again to become entangled with her?

As always, she had made herself interesting, however – one smiled ruefully at her, and one's defences fell. Yet her obstinacy seemed to carry a threat.

Kikuji feared that the threat came from his own weakness. Weak and quivering, he could not really be angry at the importunate woman.

Had she sensed the weakness, and was she hastening to take advantage of it?

Kikuji went to the Ginza, and into a dirty little bar.

Chikako was right: he should go home. But the weakness was an oppressive burden to have to take with him.

Chikako could hardly know that Kikuji had spent the night in that Kamakura inn. Or had she seen Mrs Ota afterwards?

It seemed to him that there was more than Chikako's usual brazenness in this persistence.

Yet perhaps, in the way most natural for her, she was pushing the Inamura girl's suit.

He fidgeted for a time in the bar, then started home.

As the train approached Tokyo Central Station, he looked down upon a tree-lined avenue.

It ran east and west, almost at right angles to the railroad. The western sun poured into it, and the street glittered like a sheet of metal. The trees, with the sun behind them, were darkened almost to black. The shadows were cool, the branches wide, the leaves thick. Solid Occidental buildings lined the street.

There were strangely few people. The street was quiet and empty all the way to the Palace moat. The dazzlingly bright streetcars too were quiet.

Looking down from the crowded train, he felt that the avenue alone floated in this strange time of evening, that it had been dropped here from some foreign country.

He had the illusion that the Inamura girl was walking in the shade of the trees, the pink kerchief and its thousand white cranes under her arm. He could see the cranes and the kerchief vividly.

He sensed something fresh and clean.

His chest rose – the girl might even now be arriving at his door.

But what had Chikako had in mind, telling him to bring friends, and, when he refused, suggesting that she call the Inamura girl? Had she meant from the start to call the girl? Kikuji did not know.

Chikako came hurrying to the door. 'You're alone?'

Kikuji nodded.

'It's better that way. She's here.' Chikako took his hat and briefcase. 'You made a stop on your way home, I see.' Kikuji wondered if his breath smelled of liquor. 'Where was it? I called the office again and was told you had left, and I knew how much time it would take you to get home.'

'I wouldn't be surprised at anything you do, I suppose.'

She made no apology for having come uninvited and taken over the house.

She evidently meant to go with him to his room and help him to change to the kimono the maid had laid out.

'Don't bother. I can manage by myself.' In shirt sleeves, Kikuji withdrew to his room.

But Chikako was still waiting when he came out.

'Aren't bachelors remarkable.'

'Very.'

'But it's not a good way to live. Let's make a change.'

'I learned my lesson from watching my father.'

She glanced up at him.

She had borrowed an apron from the maid, and her sleeves were pushed up. The apron had belonged to Kikuji's mother.

The flesh of her arms was disproportionately white and full, and the muscle at the inside of the elbow was like cord. Very strange, thought Kikuji. The flesh seemed hard and heavy.

'I suppose the cottage would be best.' Her manner became more businesslike. 'I have her in the main house now.'

'Is there a light out there? I don't remember having seen one.'

144

'We might eat by candlelight. That would be even more interesting.'

'Not for me.'

Chikako seemed to remember something. 'When I spoke to Miss Inamura over the telephone, she asked if I meant that her mother was to come too. I said it would be still better if we could have the two of them. But there were reasons why the mother couldn't come, and we made it just the girl.'

'"We made it," you say, but you did it all by yourself. Don't you suppose she thought it just a little rude, being summoned out with no warning?'

'No doubt. But here she is. She's here, and doesn't that cancel out my rudeness?'

'Why should it?'

'Oh, it does. She's here, and that means that as far as she's concerned matters are going beautifully. I can be forgiven if I seem a little odd along the way. When everything is settled, the two of you can have a good laugh over what an odd person Kurimoto is. Talks that are going to be settled are going to be settled, whatever you do in the process. That's been my experience.'

Thus Chikako made light of her behaviour. It was as if she had read Kikuji's mind.

'You've talked it over with her then?'

'That I have.' And don't you be dodging the issue, her manner seemed to say.

Kikuji walked down the veranda toward the parlour. A large pomegranate tree grew half under the eaves. He struggled to control himself – he must not show displeasure when he received the Inamura girl.

As he looked into the deep shadow of the pomegranate, he thought again of Chikako's birthmark. He shook his head. The last of the evening sunlight shone on the garden stones below the parlour.

The doors were open, and the girl was near the veranda.

Her brightness seemed to light the far corners of the large, dusky room.

There were Japanese irises in the alcove.

There were Siberian irises on the girl's obi. Perhaps it was coincidence. But irises were most ordinary flowers for the season, and perhaps she had planned the combination.

The Japanese irises sent their blossoms and leaves high into the air. One knew that Chikako had arranged them a short time before.

The next day, Sunday, was rainy.

In the afternoon, Kikuji went alone to the tea cottage, to put away the utensils they had used.

And he went too in search of the fragrance of the Inamura girl.

He had the maid bring an umbrella, and as he stepped down into the garden he noticed that there was a leak in the rain gutter on the eaves. A stream of water fell just in front of the pomegranate tree.

'We'll have to have that repaired,' he said to the maid.

'Yes, sir.'

Kikuji remembered that for some time the sound of falling water had bothered him on rainy nights.

'But once we start making repairs, there'll be no end to them. I ought to sell the place before it falls apart.'

'People with big houses all seem to be saying that. The young lady yesterday was very surprised at the size of this house. She spoke as if she might live here some day.'

The maid was telling him not to sell it.

'Miss Kurimoto mentioned the possibility?'

'Yes, sir. And when the young lady came, Miss Kurimoto seems to have shown her through the house.'

'What will she do next!'

The girl had said nothing to Kikuji of having seen the house.

He thought she had gone only from the sitting-room to the tea cottage, and now he wanted to go from the sitting-room to the cottage himself.

He had not slept the night before.

He had felt that the scent of the girl would still be in the cottage, and he had wanted to go out in the middle of the night.

'She will always be far away,' he had thought, trying to make himself sleep.

146

He had not suspected that Chikako had marched her through the house.

Ordering the maid to bring the charcoal embers, he went out over the stepping stones.

Chikako, who lived in Kamakura, had left with the Inamura girl. The maid had cleaned the cottage.

Kikuji's only duty was to put away the utensils piled in one corner. But he was not sure where they all belonged.

'Kurimoto would know,' he muttered to himself, looking at the picture in the alcove. It was a small Sōtatsu* wash in light ink, delicately coloured.

'Who is the poet?' the Inamura girl had asked the evening before, and Kikuji had not been able to answer.

'I wouldn't know, I'm afraid, without a poem. In this sort of portrait, every poet looks exactly like every other poet,' he said.

'It will be Muneyuki,'† said Chikako. '"Forever green, the pines are yet greener in the spring." The painting is already a little out of season, but your father was very fond of it. He used to take it out in the spring.'

'But from the picture it could be Tsurayuki‡ just as well as Muneyuki,' Kikuji objected.

Even today, he could find nothing distinctive about the vague figure.

But there was power, a suggestion of mass and weight, in the few quick lines. Looking at it for a time, he seemed to catch a faint perfume, something clean and clear.

The painting and the irises in the sitting-room brought back the Inamura girl.

'I'm sorry to have taken so long. I thought it would be best to let the water boil a little while.' The maid came with charcoal and a tea kettle.

Because the cottage was damp, Kikuji had meant to warm it. He had not thought of making tea.

The maid, however, had used her imagination.

*An early Edo Period painter the dates of whose birth and death are uncertain.

†Minamoto Muneyuki, died 939.

‡Kino Tsurayuki, died 945.

Kikuji absent-mindedly arranged the charcoal and put on the kettle.

Keeping his father company, he had often been through the tea ceremony. He had never been tempted to take up the hobby himself, however, and his father had never pressed him.

Even with the water boiling, he only pushed the lid open a little and sat staring at it.

There was a smell of mildew. The mats too seemed to be damp.

The deep, subdued colour of the walls had brought the figure of the Inamura girl out to even better effect than usual; but today they were only dark.

There had been a certain incongruity, as when someone living in a European house wears a kimono. Kikuji had said to the girl: 'It must have upset you, being called out by Kurimoto. And it was Kurimoto's idea to bring us out here.'

'Miss Kurimoto says that this is the day of your father's tea ceremony.'

'So it would seem. I had forgotten about it myself.'

'Do you suppose she's being funny, inviting someone like me on a day like this? I haven't been practising, I'm afraid.'

'But I gather that Kurimoto herself only remembered this morning, and came to clean the cottage. Smell the mildew?' He half swallowed the next words: 'If we are to be friends, I can't help thinking we would have done better to have someone besides Kurimoto introduce us. I should apologize to you.'

She looked at him suspiciously. 'Why? If it hadn't been for Miss Kurimoto, who could have introduced us?'

It was a simple protest, and yet very much to the point.

If it had not been for Chikako, the two would not have met in this world.

Kikuji felt as if a glittering whip had lashed at him.

The girl's way of speaking suggested that his proposal was accepted. So it seemed to Kikuji.

The strangely suspicious look in her eyes therefore came blazing at him.

How did she take it when he dismissed Chikako as 'Kurimoto'? Did she know that Chikako had been his father's woman, though for but a short time?

148

'I have bad memories of Kurimoto.' Kikuji's voice was near trembling. 'I don't want that woman's destinies to touch mine at any point. It's hard to believe that she introduced us.'

Having served the others, Chikako came with a tray for herself. The conversation broke off.

'I hope you won't mind if I join you.' Chikako sat down. Bending slightly forward, as though to recover her breath from having been up and at work, she looked into the girl's face. 'It's a little lonely, being an only guest. But I'm sure Kikuji's father is happy too.'

Unaffectedly, the girl looked at the floor. 'I'm hardly qualified to be in Mr Mitani's cottage.'

Chikako ignored the remark and talked on, as memories came to her, of Kikuji's father and the cottage.

Apparently she thought the marriage already arranged.

'Suppose you visit Miss Inamura's house sometime, Kikuji,' she said as the two left. 'We'll see about making an appointment.' The girl only looked at the floor. She evidently wanted to say something, but the words would not come. A sort of primeval shyness came over her.

The shyness was a surprise to Kikuji. It flowed to him like the warmth of her body.

And yet he felt that he was wrapped in a dark, dirty, suffocating curtain.

Even today he could not throw it off.

The dirtiness was not only in Chikako, who had introduced them. It was in Kikuji too.

He could see his father biting at her birthmark with dirty teeth. The figure of his father became the figure of Kikuji himself.

The girl did not share his distrust of Chikako. This was not the only reason for his own irresolution, but it seemed to be one reason.

While Kikuji was indicating his dislike for Chikako, he was making it seem that she was forcing the marriage through. She was a woman who could so be used.

Wondering whether the girl had sensed all this, Kikuji again felt the lash of that whip. He saw himself, the figure at which it struck, and he was repelled.

When they had finished dinner, Chikako went to prepare the tea utensils. 'So it's our fate, is it, to have Kurimoto managing us,' said Kikuji. 'You and I do not seem to have the same view of that fate.' The remark, however, sounded like an attempt to vindicate himself.

After his father's death, Kikuji had not liked to see his mother go into the cottage alone. His father and his mother and Kikuji himself, he saw now, had had each his own separate thoughts in the cottage.

Rain spattered against the leaves.

With the rain on the leaves came the sound of rain on an umbrella. The maid called through the closed door. He gathered that someone named Ota had come.

'The young lady?'

'No, sir, the mother. She's terribly thin. I wonder if she's been ill.'

Kikuji quickly got up. He only stood there, however.

'Where shall I take her?'

'The cottage here will do.'

'Yes sir.'

Mrs Ota did not have an umbrella. Perhaps she had left it in the main house.

He thought that rain had struck her face; but it was tears.

He knew that it was tears from the steady flow over the cheeks.

And he had thought they were raindrops – that was the measure of his heedlessness. 'What's the matter?' he almost shouted as he came up to her.

Mrs Ota knelt on the veranda with both hands on the floor before her.

She sank down softly, facing Kikuji.

Drop by drop the veranda near the lintel was wet.

The tears fell steadily, and Kikuji again wondered if they might be raindrops.

Mrs Ota did not turn her eyes from him. The gaze seemed to keep her from falling. Kikuji too felt that she would be in danger if her eyes were to leave him.

There were hollows and small wrinkles around the eyes, and dark spots below. The fold of the eyelids was emphasized in a strangely morbid way, and the pleading eyes glowed with tears. He felt an indescribable softness in them.

'I'm sorry. I wanted to see you, and I couldn't stay away,' she said quietly.

There was softness in the figure too.

She was so thin that he could hardly have borne to look at her if it had not been for the softness.

Her suffering pierced him through. Although he was the cause of the suffering, he had the illusion that in the softness his own suffering was lightened.

'You'll get wet. Come inside.' Kikuji suddenly took her in a deep, almost cruel embrace from back to breast, and pulled her to her feet.

She tried to stand by herself. 'Let me go, let me go. See how light I am.'

'Very light.'

'I'm so light. I've lost weight.'

Kikuji was a little surprised at himself, abruptly taking the woman in his arms.

'Won't your daughter be worried?'

'Fumiko?'

'Is she with you?' She had called out as though the girl were near by.

'I didn't tell her I was coming.' The words were little sobs. 'She won't take her eyes off me. At night she is awake if I make the slightest move. She's been strange herself lately, thanks to me.' Mrs Ota was now kneeling upright. 'She asked me why I had only one child. She said I should have had a child by Mr Mitani. She says such dreadful things.'

Kikuji sensed from Mrs Ota's words how deep the girl's sadness must be.

He could not feel it as the mother's sadness. It was Fumiko's.

The fact that Fumiko had spoken of his father's child pierced him like a spear.

Mrs Ota was still gazing at him. 'Maybe she'll even come after me today. I slipped out while she was away. It's raining, and she thought I wouldn't leave.'

'Because of the rain?'

'She seems to think I'm too weak now to go out in the rain.'

Kikuji only nodded.

'Fumiko came to see you the other day?'

'I did see her. She said I must forgive you, and I couldn't think of an answer.'

'I know how she feels. Why have I come, then? The things I do!'

'But I've felt grateful to you.'

'It's good to hear you say that. It's quite enough, just that. But I've been very unhappy. You must forgive me.'

'What is there to make you feel guilty? Nothing at all, I should think. Or maybe my father's ghost.'

The woman's expression did not change. Kikuji felt as if he had clutched at air.

'Let's forget everything,' said Mrs Ota. 'I'm ashamed of myself. Why should I have been so upset at a call from Miss Kurimoto?'

'Kurimoto telephoned you?'

'Yes. This morning. She said that everything was settled between you and Mrs Inamura's Yukiko. I wonder why she had to tell me.'

Her eyes were moist, but she suddenly smiled. It was not the smile of one weeping. It was a simple, artless smile.

'Nothing at all is settled,' he answered. 'Do you suppose Kurimoto has guessed about us? Have you seen her since?'

'No. But she's a person you have to be careful with, and she may know. I must have sounded strange when she telephoned this morning. I'm no good at pretending. I almost fainted, and I suppose I screamed at her. She could tell, I know she could, even over the telephone. She ordered me not to interfere.'

Kikuji frowned. He had nothing to say.

'Not to interfere – why, I've only thought of the harm I've done Yukiko. But since this morning I've been frightened at Miss Kurimoto. I couldn't stay in the house.' Her shoulders quivered as if she were possessed. Her mouth was twisted to one side, and some outside force seemed to pull it upward. All the unsightliness of her years came to the surface.

Kikuji stood up and laid a hand on her shoulder.

She clutched at the hand.

'I'm frightened, frightened.' She looked around the room and shrank away, and suddenly her strength left her.

'In this cottage?'

Confused, Kikuji wondered what she might mean. 'Yes,' he answered vaguely.

'It's a very nice cottage.'

Did she remember that her dead husband had occasionally had tea here? Or was she remembering Kikuji's father?

'This is the first time you've been in the cottage?' he asked.

'Yes.'

'What are you looking at?'

'Nothing. Not at anything.'

'The painting there is a Sōtatsu.'

She nodded, and her head remained bowed in the act.

'And you've never been in the main house?'

'Never.'

'Can that be true, I wonder.'

'I was there once. Your father's funeral.' Her voice trailed off.

'The water is boiling. Suppose we have tea. You'll feel better afterwards, and as a matter of fact I'd like a bowl myself.'

'Is it all right?' She started to get up, and reeled slightly.

Kikuji took tea bowls and other utensils from the boxes in the corner. He remembered that the Inamura girl had used them the evening before, but he took them out all the same.

Mrs Ota's hand was trembling. The lid clicked against the kettle.

She bent over to take up the bamboo tea-measure, and a tear wet the shoulder of the kettle.

'Your father was good enough to buy this kettle from me.'

'Really? I hadn't known.'

Kikuji found nothing displeasing in the fact that the kettle had belonged to the woman's husband. And he did not think her words strange, so simply had she said them.

'I can't bring it to you.' She had finished making tea. 'Come for it.'

Kikuji went to the hearth, and drank the tea there.

The woman fell across his lap as if in a faint.

He put his arm around her shoulder. The shoulder quivered, and her breathing grew fainter. In his arms, she was soft as a small child.

He shook her roughly.

As if to strangle her, he grasped her with both hands between throat and collarbone. The collarbone stood out sharply.

'Can't you see the difference between my father and me?'

'You mustn't say that.'

Her eyes were closed, and her voice was soft.

She was not yet ready to return from the other world.

Kikuji had spoken less to her than to his own disquieted heart.

He had been led easily into the other world. He could only think of it as another world, in which there was no distinction between his father and himself. So strong was the sense of the other world that afterwards this disquietude came over him.

He could ask himself if she was human. If she was pre-human, or again if she was the last woman in the human race.

He could imagine her in this other world, making no distinction between her dead husband and Kikuji's father and Kikuji.

'You think of my father, don't you, and my father and I become one person?'

'Forgive me. The things I've done. The things I've been guilty of.' A tear spilled over from the corner of her eye. 'I want to die. It would be so pleasant to die now. You were about to strangle me. Why didn't you?'

'You aren't to joke about it. But I do feel a little like strangling someone.'

'Oh? Thank you.' She arched her long throat. 'It's thin. You should have no trouble.'

'Could you die and leave your daughter behind?'

'It makes no difference. I'll wear out and die soon in any case. Take care of Fumiko.'

'If she is like you.'

Suddenly she opened her eyes,

154

Kikuji was astonished at his own words. They had been quite involuntary.

How had they sounded to the woman?

'See? See how my heart is beating? It won't be long now.' She took Kikuji's hand and held it to her breast.

Perhaps her heart had started in surprise at Kikuji's words.

'How old are you?'

Kikuji did not answer.

'Still in your twenties? It's wrong. I'm very unhappy. I don't understand myself.'

Pressing one hand to the floor, she half pushed herself up. Her legs were curled beneath her.

Kikuji sat up.

'I didn't come here to spoil things for you and Yukiko. But it's done.'

'I haven't decided to marry her. But the truth is that you've washed my whole past for me – or so it seemed when you said that.'

'Really?'

'Kurimoto was my father's woman too, and she's the go-between. All the poison from the old days is concentrated in that woman. My father was lucky to have you for the last.'

'You must hurry and marry Yukiko.'

'That's a question for me to decide.'

She stared vacantly at him. The blood left her cheeks, and she pressed a hand to her forehead.

'The room is spinning around.'

She had to go home, she said. Kikuji called a cab and got in with her.

She leaned back in one corner, her eyes closed, a thoroughly helpless figure. The last embers seemed in danger of going out.

Kikuji did not see her into the house. As she left the cab, her cold fingers simply left his.

At two the next morning, there was a telephone call from Fumiko.

'Hello. Mr Mitani? My mother has just ...' The voice broke for an instant, then continued firmly. 'Has just died.'

'What! What happened?'

'Mother is dead. She had a heart attack. She has been taking a great deal of sleeping medicine lately.'

Kikuji did not answer.

'I'm afraid I – must ask a favour, Mr Mitani.'

'Yes?'

'If there is a doctor you know well, and if it seems possible, could you bring him here?'

'A doctor? You need a doctor? I'll have to hurry.'

Kikuji was astonished that no doctor had yet been called. Then, suddenly, he knew.

Mrs Ota had killed herself. The girl was asking him to help hide the fact.

'I understand.'

'Please.'

She had thought carefully before calling him, he knew, and she had therefore been able to state the essentials of her business with something like formal precision.

Kikuji sat by the telephone with his eyes closed.

He saw the evening sun as he had seen it after the night with Mrs Ota: the evening sun through the train windows, behind the grove of the Hommonji Temple.*

The red sun seemed about to flow down over the branches.

The grove stood dark against it.

The sun flowing over the branches sank into his tired eyes, and he closed them.

The white cranes from the Inamura girl's kerchief flew across the evening sun, which was still in his eyes.

*In the southern outskirts of Tokyo.

Figured Shino*

On the day after the seventh-day memorial services, Kikuji made his visit.

It would be evening if, following his usual schedule, he stopped by on his way home from the office. He had therefore meant to leave work a little early, but the day was over before he was able to collect himself for the task.

Fumiko came to the door.

'Oh!'

She knelt in the raised entranceway and looked up at him. Her hands were pressed to the floor, as though to steady her shoulders.

'Thank you for the flowers yesterday.'

'Not at all.'

'I thought I wouldn't see you.'

'Oh? But people do sometimes send flowers ahead, and go themselves later.'

'Even so, I didn't expect you.'

'I sent them from a florist's very near here.'

Fumiko nodded simply. 'There was no name, but I knew immediately.'

Kikuji remembered how he had stood among the flowers and thought of Mrs Ota.

He remembered that the smell of the flowers had softened the guilt.

And now, softly, Fumiko was receiving him.

She had on a plain cotton dress. Except for a touch of lipstick on her dry lips, she wore no cosmetics.

'I thought it would be best to stay away yesterday,' he said.

Fumiko turned slightly to one side, inviting him in.

Perhaps because she was determined not to weep, she

*A ware from the Oribe kilns (see page 130).

157

limited herself to the most ordinary greetings; but it seemed that she would weep anyway unless she moved or remained silent.

'I can't tell you how happy I was to have the flowers. But you should have come.' She stood up and followed him in.

'I didn't want to upset your relatives,' he answered – lightly, he hoped.

'That sort of thing doesn't worry me any more.' The words were firm and clear.

In the sitting-room, there was a photograph before the urn.

There were only the flowers Kikuji had sent the day before.

He thought this strange. Had Fumiko left only his and taken away all the others? Or had it been a lonely memorial service? He suspected that it had.

'A water jar, I see.'

He was looking at the vase in which she had arranged his flowers. It was a water jar for the tea ceremony.

'Yes. I thought it would be right.'

'A fine Shino piece.' For a ceremonial jar, it was rather small.

He had sent white roses and pale carnations, and they went well with the cylindrical jar.

'Mother sometimes used it for flowers. That's why it wasn't sold.'

Kikuji knelt to light incense before the urn. He folded his hands and closed his eyes.

He was apologizing. But love flowed into the apology, to coddle and mollify the guilt.

Had Mrs Ota died unable to escape the pursuing guilt? Or, pursued by love, had she found herself unable to control it? Was it love or guilt that had killed her? For a week Kikuji had debated the problem.

Now, as he knelt with closed eyes before the ashes, her image failed to come to him; but the warmth of her touch enfolded him, making him drunk with its smell. A strange fact, but, because of the woman, a fact that seemed in no way unnatural. And although her touch was upon him, the sensation was less tactile than auditory, musical.

Unable to sleep since her death, Kikuji had been taking

sedatives with *saké*. He had been quick to awaken, however, and he had had many dreams.

They had not been nightmares. On awakening, he would be drowsy and sweetly drunk.

That a dead woman could make her embrace felt in one's dreams seemed eerie to Kikuji. He was young, and unprepared for such an experience.

'The things I've done!' She had said it both when she spent the night with him in Kamakura and when she came into the tea cottage. The words had brought on the delicious trembling and the little sobs, and now, as he knelt before her ashes and asked what had made her die, he thought he might grant for the moment that it had been guilt. The admission only brought back her voice, speaking of her guilt.

Kikuji opened his eyes.

Behind him he heard a sob. Fumiko seemed to be fighting back tears – one sob had escaped, but only one.

Kikuji did not move. 'When was the picture taken?' he asked.

'Five or six years ago. I had a snapshot enlarged.'

'Oh? It was taken at a tea ceremony?'

'How did you know?'

The photograph had been cut at the throat, showing only a little of the kimono and nothing of the shoulders.

'How did you know it was a tea ceremony?'

'It has that feeling. The eyes are lowered, and she seems to be busy at something. You can't see the shoulders, of course, but you can feel a sort of concentration in her manner.'

'I wondered if it would do. It was taken a little from the side. But it's a picture Mother was fond of.'

'It's a very quiet picture. A very good picture.'

'I can see now that it was a mistake, though. She doesn't look at you when you offer incense.'

'Oh? That's true, I suppose.'

'She's looking away, and down.'

Kikuji thought of the woman making tea the day before she died.

As she measured out the tea, a tear fell on the shoulder of the kettle. He went for the tea bowl – she did not bring it to

him. The tear on the kettle had dried by the time he had drunk
the tea. She fell across his lap the moment he laid down the
bowl.

'Mother weighed more when the picture was taken.' She
hurried over the next words: 'And it would have embarrassed
me to have the picture too much like myself.'

Kikuji looked around at her.

Her eyes, now on the floor, had been fixed on his back.

He had to leave the urn and photograph, and face her.

How could he apologize?

He saw his escape in the Shino water jar. He knelt before it
and looked at it appraisingly, as one looks at tea vessels.

A faint red floated up from the white glaze. Kikuji reached
to touch the voluptuous and warmly cool surface.

'Soft, like a dream. Even when you know as little as I do
you can appreciate good Shino.'

'Like a dream of a woman,' he had thought, but he had sup-
pressed the last words.

'Do you like it? Let me give it to you in memory of Mother.'

'Oh, no. Please.' Kikuji looked up in consternation.

'Do you like it? Mother will be happy too, I know she will.
It's not a bad piece, I should imagine.'

'It's a splendid piece.'

'So Mother said. That's why I put your flowers in it.'

Kikuji felt hot tears coming to his eyes. 'I'll take it, then, if
I may.'

'Mother will be happy.'

'But it doesn't seem likely that I'll be using it for tea. I'll
have to turn it into a flower vase.'

'Please do. Mother used it for flowers too.'

'I'm afraid I don't mean tea flowers. It seems sad for a tea
vessel to be leaving the tea ceremony.'

'I'm thinking of giving up tea myself.'

Kikuji turned to face her, and stood up as he did so.

There were cushions near the doors to the breakfast room.
He pushed one out towards the veranda and sat down.

She had been kneeling deferentially on the bare straw matting.

Only Kikuji moved. Fumiko was left in the middle of the room.

Her hands, gently folded at her knees, seemed about to tremble. She clutched them tightly together.

'Mr Mitani, you must forgive Mother.' Her head sank to her breast.

Kikuji started up, afraid that in the motion she would fall over. 'What are you saying? It is I who must ask to be forgiven. I've been trying to think of the right words. But there's no way to apologize, and I'm ashamed to be here with you.'

'We are the ones who should be ashamed.' The shame came over her face. 'I wish I could just disappear.'

The flush spread from the unpowdered cheeks over the white throat; and all the wear and anguish came to the surface.

The faint blood colour only made the pallor more striking.

A dull pain ran through his chest. 'I thought how you must hate me.'

'Hate you? Do you think Mother hated you?'

'No. But wasn't it I who made her die?'

'She died because of herself. That is what I think. I worried over it for a whole week.

'You've been here alone all the time?'

'Yes. But that is the way we were, Mother and I.'

'I made her die.'

'She died because of herself. If you say it was you who made her die, then it was I even more. If I have to blame anyone, it should be myself. But it only makes her death seem dirty, when we start feeling responsible and having regrets. Regrets and second thoughts only make the burden heavier for the one who has died.'

'That may be true. But if I hadn't met her . . .' Kikuji could say no more.

'I think it's enough if the dead person can be forgiven. Maybe Mother died asking to be forgiven. Can you forgive her?' Fumiko stood up.

At Fumiko's words, a curtain in Kikuji's mind seemed to disappear.

Was there also a lightening of the burden for the dead? he wondered.

Worrying oneself over the dead – was it in most cases a mistake, not unlike berating them? The dead did not press moral considerations upon the living.

Kikuji looked again at Mrs Ota's photograph.

Fumiko brought in two bowls on a tray.

They were cylindrical, a red Raku and a black Raku.

She set the black before Kikuji. In it was ordinary coarse tea.

Kikuji lifted the bowl and looked at the potter's mark. 'Who is it?' he asked bluntly.

'Ryōnyū,* I believe.'

'And the red?'

'Ryōnyū too.'

'They seem to be a pair.' Kikuji looked at the red bowl, which lay untouched at her knee.

Though they were ceremonial bowls, they did not seem out of place as ordinary teacups; but a displeasing picture flashed into Kikuji's mind.

Fumiko's father had died and Kikuji's father had lived on; and might not this pair of Raku bowls have served as teacups when Kikuji's father came to see Fumiko's mother? Had they not been used as 'man-wife' teacups, the black for Kikuji's father, the red for Fumiko's mother?

If they were by Ryōnyu, one could be a little careless with them. Might they not also have been taken along on trips?

Fumiko, who knew, was perhaps playing a cruel joke on him.

But he saw no malice, indeed no calculation, in her bringing out the two bowls.

He saw only a girlish sentimentality, which also came to him.

He and Fumiko, haunted by the death of her mother, were unable to hold back the grotesque sentimentality. The pair of Raku bowls deepened the sorrow they had in common.

Fumiko too knew everything: Kikuji's father and her mother, her mother and Kikuji, her mother's death.

*Raku, a Kyoto ware, was first produced in the sixteenth century. Ryōnyū (1756–1834) was the ninth master of the Raku kiln.

And they had shared the crime of hiding the suicide.

Fumiko had evidently wept as she made tea. Her eyes were a little red.

'I'm glad I came today,' said Kikuji. 'I could take what you said a few minutes ago to mean that between the living and the dead there can be no forgiving and not forgiving; but I may think instead that I've been forgiven by your mother?'

Fumiko nodded. 'Otherwise Mother can't be forgiven. Not that she could forgive herself.'

'But in a way it's rather terrible that I'm here with you.'

'Why?' She looked up at him. 'You mean it was wrong of her to die? I was very bitter myself – I thought that no matter how she had been misunderstood, death could not be her answer. Death only cuts off understanding. No one can possibly forgive that.'

Kikuji was silent. He wondered if Fumiko too had pushed her way to a final confrontation with the secret of death.

It was strange to be told that death cut off understanding.

The Mrs Ota whom Kikuji knew now was rather different from the mother Fumiko knew.

Fumiko had no way of knowing her mother as a woman.

To forgive or to be forgiven was for Kikuji a matter of being rocked in that wave, the dreaminess of the woman's body.

It seemed that the dreaminess was here too in the pair of Raku bowls.

Fumiko did not know her mother thus.

It was strange and subtle, the fact that the child should not know the body from which she had come; and, subtly, the body itself had been passed on to the daughter.

From the moment she had greeted him in the doorway, Kikuji had felt something soft and gentle. In Fumiko's round, soft face he saw her mother.

If Mrs Ota had made her mistake when she saw Kikuji's father in Kikuji, then there was something frightening, a bond like a curse, in the fact that, to Kikuji, Fumiko resembled her mother; but Kikuji, unprotesting, gave himself to the drift.

Looking at the uncared-for little mouth, the lower lip thrust

163

forward as if in a pout, he felt that there was no fighting the girl.

What could one do to make her resist?

That question would have to be asked about Kikuji himself. 'Your mother was too gentle to live,' he said. 'I was cruel to her, and I suspect that I was hitting at her with my own moral weakness. I'm a coward.'

'Mother was wrong. Mother was so wrong. Your father, then you – but I have to think that Mother's real nature was different.' She spoke hesitantly, and flushed. The blood colour was warmer than before.

Avoiding Kikuji's eyes, she bowed and turned slightly away.

'But from the day after Mother died, she began to seem more beautiful. Is it just in my mind, or is she really more beautiful?'

'The two are the same, I suppose, with the dead.'

'Maybe Mother died from not being able to stand her own ugliness.'

'That doesn't seem likely.'

'It was too much – she couldn't bear it.' Tears came to Fumiko's eyes. Perhaps she wanted to speak of her mother's love for Kikuji.

'The dead are our property, in a way. We must take care of them,' said Kikuji. 'But they all died in such a hurry.'

She seemed to understand: he meant her parents and his own.

'You're an orphan now, and so am I.' His own words made him aware that if Mrs Ota had not had this daughter, Fumiko, he would have had darker, more perverse thoughts about her.

'You were very good to my father. Your mother told me so.' He had said it, and he hoped it had seemed unaffected.

He saw nothing wrong in talking of the days when his father had come to this house as the lover of Fumiko's mother.

Suddenly, Fumiko made a deep bow.

'Forgive her. Mother was really too sad. After that, I hardly knew from one minute to the next when she might die.' Her head was still bowed. Motionless, she began to weep, and the strength left her shoulders.

Because she had not expected visitors, she was barefoot.

164

Her feet were curled beneath her, half hidden by her skirt, and she presented a thoroughly shrunken, helpless figure.

The red Raku bowl was almost against her hair, so long that it fell to the floor matting.

She left the room with both hands pressed to her face.

Moments passed, and she did not come back. 'I believe I'll be leaving, then,' said Kikuji.

She came to the door with a bundle.

'I'm afraid it will be heavy, but try not to mind too much.'

'Oh?'

'The Shino.'

He was astonished at her quickness: she had emptied the jar, dried it, found a box for it, and wrapped it in a kerchief.

'I'm to take it already? But it had flowers in it.'

'Please do take it.'

'If I may, then,' said Kikuji. The quickness, he sensed, had come from an excess of grief.

'But I won't come to see how you use it.'

'Why not?'

Fumiko did not answer.

'Well, take care of yourself.' He started out.

'Thank you. It was good of you to come. And – don't worry about Mother. Hurry and get married.'

'I beg your pardon?'

He turned back towards her, but she did not look up.

Kikuji tried putting white roses and pale carnations in the Shino jar.

He was haunted by the thought that he was falling in love with Mrs Ota, now that she was dead.

And he felt that the love was made known through the daughter, Fumiko.

On Sunday, he telephoned her.

'You're at home by yourself?'

'Yes. It's a little lonely, of course.'

'You shouldn't be alone.'

'I suppose not.'

'I can almost hear the quiet.'

Fumiko laughed softly.

'Suppose we have a friend look in on you.'

'But I keep thinking that whoever comes will find out about Mother.'

Kikuji could think of no answer. 'It must be inconvenient. You have no one to watch the house when you want to go out.'

'Oh, I can always lock it.'

'Suppose you come and see me, then.'

'Thank you. One of these days.'

'Have you been well?'

'I've lost weight.'

'And are you able to sleep?'

'Hardly at all.'

'That will never do.'

'I'm thinking of closing the house and taking a room in a friend's house.'

'Soon – when will that be?'

'As soon as I can sell the house.'

'The house?'

'Yes.'

'You mean to sell it?'

'Don't you think I should?'

'I wonder. As a matter of fact, I'm thinking of selling my own.'

Fumiko did not answer.

'Hello? There's no use talking about these things over the telephone. It's Sunday and I'm at home. Can you come over?'

'Yes.'

'I have flowers in the Shino, but if you come I can try putting it to the use it was meant for.'

'A tea ceremony?'

'Not a real ceremony. But it's a great waste not to use Shino for tea. You can't bring out the real beauty of a tea piece unless you set it off against its own kind.'

'But I look even worse than when you were here. I can't see you.'

'There will be no other guests.'

'Even so.'

'You won't reconsider?'

'Good-bye.'

'Take care of yourself. Excuse me – there seems to be some-one at the door. I'll call again.'

It was Kurimoto Chikako.

A grim look came over Kikuji's face. Had she heard?

'It's been so gloomy. Rain, rain. The first good day in such a long time, and I'm taking advantage of it.' She was already looking at the Shino. 'From now into the summer, I'll have more time from lessons, and I thought I'd like to come and sit in your cottage for a while.'

She brought out her offerings, sweets and a folding fan. 'I suppose the cottage will be all mildewed again.'

'I suppose so.'

'Mrs Ota's Shino? May I look at it?' She spoke casually, and turned to examine the Shino.

As she bent towards it, the heavy-boned shoulders fell back. She seemed to exude venom.

'Did you buy it?'

'It was a present.'

'Quite a present. A keepsake?' She raised her head and turned back to him. 'Really, shouldn't you have paid for a piece like this? I'm a bit shocked that you took it from the girl.'

'I'll give the question some thought.'

'Do. You have all sorts of tea pieces that belonged to Mr Ota, but your father paid for every one of them. Even after he was taking care of Mrs Ota.'

'That's not a matter I want to discuss with you.'

'I see, I see,' said Chikako airily, and stood up. He heard her talking to the maid, and she emerged in an apron.

'So Mrs Ota committed suicide.' The show of unconcern was no doubt designed to catch him off guard.

'She did not.'

'Oh? But I knew immediately. There was always something weird about that woman.' She looked at him. 'Your father used to say that he would never understand her. To another woman, of course, the problem was a little different, but there was something childish about her, no matter how old she got. Well, she wasn't my sort. Sticky and clinging, somehow.'

'May we ask you to stop slandering the dead?'

'Oh, please do. But isn't this particular dead person still trying to ruin your marriage? Your father suffered a great deal at the hands of that woman.'

It was Chikako who had suffered, thought Kikuji.

Chikako was his father's plaything for a very short time. She had no cause to indict Mrs Ota. Still, one could imagine how she had hated the woman who was with his father to the end.

'You're too young to understand such people. For your sake, it was good of her to die. That's the truth.'

Kikuji turned aside.

'Were we to stand for it, having her interfere with your marriage plans? She died because she couldn't keep down the devil in her even when she knew she was doing wrong. That's the truth too. And then being the woman she was, she thought she would die and go to meet your father.'

Kikuji felt cold.

Chikako stepped down into the garden. 'I'm going out to the cottage and quieten my nerves.'

He sat for a time looking at the flowers.

The white and the pale pink seemed to melt into a mist with the Shino.

The figure of Fumiko, weeping alone in her house, came to him.

Her Mother's Lipstick

Back in his bedroom after brushing his teeth, Kikuji saw that the maid had hung a gourd in the alcove. It contained a single morning glory.

'I'll be getting up today,' he said, though he got into bed again. Throwing his head back, he looked up at the flowers.

'There was a morning glory in bloom,' said the maid from the next room. 'You'll be at home again today, then, sir?'

'One more day. But I'll be getting up.' Kikuji had been away from work for several days with a headache and cold. 'Where was the morning glory?'

'It had climbed the ginger at the far side of the garden.'

It was a plain indigo morning glory, probably wild, and most ordinary. The vine was thin, and the leaves and blossom were small.

But the green and the deep blue were cool, falling over a red-lacquered gourd dark with age.

The maid, who had been with the family from his father's time, was imaginative in her way.

On the gourd was a fading lacquer seal-signature, and on its ancient-looking box the mark of the first owner, Sōtan,* which, if authentic, would make it three hundred years old.

Kikuji knew nothing about tea flowers, nor was the maid likely to be well informed. For morning tea, however, it seemed to him that the morning glory was most appropriate.

He gazed at it for a time. In a gourd that had been handed down for three centuries, a flower that would fade in a morning.

Was it more fitting than all those Occidental flowers in the three-hundred-year-old Shino?

*Sen Sōtan (1578–1658), a tea master, was the grandson of Sen Rikyū (page 130).

But there was something unsettling in the idea of a cut morning glory.

'You expect it to wither right in front of your eyes,' he said to the maid at breakfast.

He remembered that he had meant to put peonies in the Shino.

It had already been past the peony season when Fumiko gave him the jar, but he could have found them if he had hunted.

'I'd even forgotten that we had the gourd. You were clever to think of it.'

The maid only nodded.

'You saw my father put morning glories in it?'

'No. But morning glories and gourds are both vines, and I thought . . .'

'Both vines!' Kikuji snorted. The poetry had quite vanished.

His head grew heavy as he read the newspaper, and he lay down in the breakfast room.

'Don't bother to make the bed.'

The maid, who had been doing the laundry, came in drying her hands. She would clean his room, she said.

When he went back to bed, there was no morning glory in the alcove.

Nor was there a gourd hanging from the pillar.

'Well.' Perhaps she had not wanted him to see the fading flower.

He had snorted at the association of the two vines, and yet his father's way of living seemed to survive in the maid.

The Shino jar stood naked in the middle of the alcove. Fumiko, if she were to see it, would no doubt think this treatment unkind.

Upon receiving it, he had put white roses and pale carnations in it, because she had done the same before her mother's ashes. The roses and carnations were flowers that Kikuji had sent for the seventh-day memorial services.

He had stopped and bought flowers at the shop from which, the day before, he had sent flowers to Fumiko.

His heart would rise even at the touch of the jar, and he had put no more flowers in it.

Sometimes he would be drawn to a middle-aged woman in the street. Catching himself, he would frown and mutter: 'I'm behaving like a criminal.'

He would look again and see that the woman did not resemble Mrs Ota after all.

There was only that swelling at the hips.

The longing at such moments would almost make him tremble; and yet intoxication and fear would meet, as at the moment of awakening from a crime.

'And what has turned me into a criminal?' The question should have shaken him loose from whatever it was; but instead of an answer there came only intenser longing.

He felt that he could not be saved unless he fled those moments when the touch of the dead woman's skin came to him warm and naked.

Sometimes too he wondered if moral doubts had not sharpened his senses to the point of morbidness.

He put the Shino in its box and went to bed.

As he looked out over the garden, he heard thunder.

It was distant but strong, and at each clap it was nearer.

Lightning came through the trees in the garden.

But when the rain began, the thunder seemed to withdraw.

It was a violent rain. White spray rose from the earth of the garden.

Kikuji got up and telephoned Fumiko.

'Miss Ota has moved.'

'I beg your pardon?' He was startled. 'Excuse me, but might I . . .' She must have sold the house. 'I wonder if you could tell me where she is living.'

'Just a moment, please.' It seemed to be a maid.

She came back immediately and gave him the address, which she was evidently reading from a notebook. 'In care of Mr Tozaki.' There was a telephone.

Fumiko's voice was bright. 'Hello. I'm sorry to have kept you waiting.'

'Fumiko? This is Mitani. I called your house.'

'I'm sorry.' Her voice fell, and it was like her mother's.

'When did you move?'

'I . . .'

'And you didn't tell me.'

'I've been staying with a friend for several days now. I sold the house.'

'Oh?'

'I didn't know whether I should tell you or not. At first I thought I shouldn't, but lately I've begun to feel guilty.'

'You ought to.'

'Really? You're kind enough to think so?'

As they talked on, Kikuji felt fresh and new, washed clean. There could be this feeling from a telephone conversation, then?

'The Shino you gave me. When I look at it I want to see you.'

'Oh? I have another, a little cylindrical tea bowl. I thought of letting you have that too, but Mother used it as an everyday teacup. It has her lipstick on it.'

'Oh?'

'Or so Mother used to say.'

'The lipstick was just left there?'

'Not "just left there." The Shino was reddish to begin with, but Mother used to say that she couldn't rub lipstick from the rim, no matter how hard she tried. I sometimes look at it now that she is dead, and there does seem to be a sort of flush in one place.'

Was this only idle talk?

Kikuji could hardly bear to listen. 'We're having a real storm. How is it there?'

'Terrible. I was terrified at the thunder.'

'But it should be pleasant afterward. I've been away from work for several days, and I'm at home now. If you have nothing else to do, why not come over?'

'Thank you. I'd been meaning to stop by, but only after I found work. I'm thinking of going to work.' Before he could answer, she continued. 'I'm so glad you called. I *will* see you. I shouldn't see you again, of course.'

Kikuji got out of bed when the shower was over.

He was surprised at the outcome of the telephone conversation.

And it was strange that his guilt in the Ota affair seemed to disappear when he heard the daughter's voice. Did it make him feel that the mother was still living?

He shook his shaving brush among the leaves at the veranda, wetting it with rain water.

The doorbell rang shortly after lunch. It would be Fumiko – but it was Kurimoto Chikako.

'Oh, you.'

'Hasn't it got warm. I've been neglecting you, and I thought I should look in.'

'Your colour isn't good.' She scowled at him.

It had been foolish, he thought, to associate the sound of wooden clogs with Fumiko. Fumiko would be wearing European dress.

'Have you had new teeth made?' he asked. 'You look younger.'

'I had spare time during the rainy season. They were a little too white at first, but they turn yellow in a hurry. They'll be all right.'

He led her into the sitting-room, which also served as his bedroom. She looked at the alcove.

'I've always found empty alcoves pleasant,' said Kikuji. 'No hangings to weigh you down.'

'Very pleasant, with all this rain. But maybe a few flowers at least.' She turned back to him.

'What did you do with Mrs Ota's Shino?'

Kikuji did not answer.

'Shouldn't you send it back?'

'That I think is up to me.'

'I'm afraid not.'

'It's hardly your place to be giving orders.'

'That's not quite true either.' She laughed and showed her white teeth. 'I came today to tell you what I think.' In a quick gesture, she thrust both hands before her, then spread them as if to brush something away. 'If you don't get rid of that witch.'

'You sound very threatening.'

'But I'm the go-between, and I'm to have my say.'

'If you're talking about the Inamura girl, I'm sorry to have to refuse your proposal.'

'Now, now. That's very small of you, refusing a girl you

173

like just because you don't like the go-between. The go-between is a bridge. Go ahead, step on the bridge. Your father was quite happy to.'

Kikuji did not hide his displeasure.

When Chikako put herself into an argument, she threw her shoulders back. 'I'm telling you the truth. I'm different from Mrs Ota. As things went with your father, I was a very light case. I see no reason to hide the truth – I was unfortunately not his favourite game. Just when it started, it was over.' She looked down. 'But I have no regrets. He was good enough to use me afterwards, when it was convenient for him. Like most men, he found it easier to use a woman he had had an affair with. And so, thanks to him, I developed a good, healthy strain of common sense.'

'I see.'

'You should make use of my healthy common sense.'

Kikuji was almost tempted to feel safe with her. There was something in what she said.

She took a fan from her obi.

'When a person is too much of a man or too much of a woman, the common sense generally isn't there.'

'Oh? Common sense goes with neuters, then?'

'Don't be sarcastic. But neuters, as you call them, have no trouble understanding men and women too. Have you thought how remarkable it is that Mrs Ota was able to die and leave an only daughter? It seems just possible that she had something to fall back on. If she died, mightn't Kikuji look after the daughter?'

'What are you talking about?'

'I thought and thought, and all of a sudden I came up against a suspicion: she died to interfere with your marriage. She didn't just die. There was more to it.'

'Your inventions can be monstrous sometimes.' But even as he spoke, he had to gasp at the force of the invention.

It came like a flash of lightning.

'You told Mrs Ota about the Inamura girl, didn't you?'

Kikuji remembered, but feigned ignorance. 'It was you, wasn't it, who told her that everything was arranged?'

'I did. I told her not to interfere. It was the night she died.'

Kikuji was silent.

'How did you know I telephoned? Did she come weeping to you?'

'Of course she did. I can guess from the way she screamed at me over the telephone.'

'Then it's very much as if you killed her, isn't it?'

'I suppose that conclusion makes things easier for you. Well, I'm used to being the villain. When your father needed a villain, he found me quite ideal. It's not exactly that I'm returning an old favour, but I'm here to play the villain today.'

Kikuji knew that she was giving vent to the old, deep jealousy.

'But we won't worry about what goes on back-stage.' She looked down her nose. 'I don't care in the least if you sit there glowering at the nasty old woman who comes meddling. Before long I'll have got rid of the witch and made a good marriage for you.'

'I must ask you to stop talking about this good marriage you're making for me.'

'Certainly. I don't want to talk about Mrs Ota any more than you do.' Her voice softened. 'I don't mean that she was bad. She was only hoping that when she died the daughter would naturally go to you.'

'The nonsense begins again.'

'But isn't it the truth? Do you really think that while she was alive she didn't once think of marrying the daughter off to you? That's very absent-minded of you. Waking and sleeping, brooding over your father, almost bewitched, I used to think – if you want to call her emotions pure I suppose they were. She was half out of her mind, and she managed to involve the daughter too, and finally she gave her life. Pure she may have been, but to the rest of us it all sounds like some terrible curse, some witch's net she was laying for us.'

Kikuji's eyes met hers.

Her small eyes rolled up at him.

Unable to shake them off, Kikuji looked away.

He withdrew into himself and let her talk on. His position had been weak from the start, and that strange remark had shaken him.

Had the dead woman really thought of marrying her daughter to him? Kikuji did not want to linger over the possibility. It was unreal, a product of that venomous jealousy. Of ugly suspicions, clinging to her breast like the ugly birthmark.

He was deeply uneasy.

Had he not hoped for the same thing?

One's heart could indeed move from mother to daughter; but, if, still drunk in the embrace of the mother, he had not sensed that he was being passed on to the daughter, had he not in fact been the captive of witchcraft?

And had his whole nature not changed after he met Mrs Ota?

He felt numb.

The maid came in. 'Miss Ota said she would stop by again if you were busy.'

'She left, then?' Kikuji stood up.

'It was good of you to telephone this morning.' Fumiko looked up at him, showing the full curve of her long, white throat.

There was a yellowish shadow in the hollow from throat to breast.

Whether it was a play of light or a sign of weariness, it somehow gave him rest.

'Kurimoto is here.'

He was able to speak calmly. He had come out feeling tense and constrained, but at the sight of Fumiko the tension strangely left him.

She nodded. 'I saw Miss Kurimoto's umbrella.'

'Oh. That one?'

There was a long-handled grey umbrella by the door.

'Suppose you wait in the cottage. Old Kurimoto will be leaving soon.'

He wondered why, knowing that Fumiko was coming, he had not sent Chikako away.

'It doesn't make any difference as far as I'm concerned.'

'Come on in, then.'

Shown into the drawing-room, Fumiko greeted Chikako as

if she did not suspect the hostility. She thanked Chikako for her condolences.

Chikako hunched her left shoulder and threw her head back, as when she watched a pupil at tea.

'Your mother was such a gentle person. I always feel when I see someone like her that I'm watching the last flowers fall. This is no world for gentle people.'

'Mother wasn't as gentle as all that.'

'It must have troubled her to die and leave an only daughter behind.'

Fumiko looked at the floor.

The mouth with its pouting lower lip was drawn tight.

'You must be lonely. Suppose you take up tea again.'

'But . . .'

'It will give you something to think about.'

'But I'm afraid I can't afford such luxuries.'

'Come, now.' Chikako dismissed the remark with a sweep of her hands, which had been folded on her knees. 'As a matter of fact, I'm here to air the cottage. The rains seem to be over.' She glanced at Kikuji. 'Fumiko is here too. Shall we?'

'I beg your pardon?'

'I thought I might be allowed to use the Shino piece you have in memory of Fumiko's mother.'

Fumiko looked up.

'And we can all exchange memories.'

'But I'll only weep if I go into the cottage.'

'Let's weep. We'll all have a good cry. I won't have my way with the cottage once Kikuji is married. It's full of memories, of course, but then . . .' Chikako laughed shortly, and was sober again. 'Once we've arranged everything with Mrs Inamura's Yukiko, you know.'

Fumiko nodded. Her face was expressionless.

There were signs of fatigue, however, on the round face that so resembled her mother's.

'You'll only embarrass the Inamuras, talking of plans that aren't definite,' said Kikuji.

'I'm speaking of a possible engagement. But you're right. It's the good things that attract the villains. You must pretend you've heard nothing, Fumiko.'

'Of course.' Fumiko nodded again.

Chikako summoned the maid and went out to clean the cottage.

'Be careful,' she called back from the garden. 'The leaves are still wet here in the shade.'

'It was raining so hard here that you must have heard it over the telephone.'

'Can you hear rain over the telephone? But I wasn't listening. Could you hear the rain in my garden?'

Fumiko looked out towards the shrubbery, from beyond which they could hear Chikako's broom.

Kikuji too looked out. 'I didn't think so at the time, but afterwards I began to wonder. It was a real cloudburst.'

'I was terrified at the thunder.'

'So you said over the telephone.'

'I'm like my mother in all sorts of trivial ways. When I was little, Mother used to cover my head with her kimono sleeves whenever it thundered. And when she went out in the summertime, she would look up at the sky and ask if anyone thought it would thunder. Even now, sometimes, I want to cover my head.' Shyness seemed to creep in from her shoulders toward her breast. 'I brought the Shino bowl.' She stood up.

She laid the bowl, still wrapped in a kerchief, at Kikuji's knee.

Kikuji hesitated, however, and Fumiko herself untied it.

'I suppose your mother used the Raku for an everyday cup? It was Ryōnyū?'

'Yes. But Mother didn't think ordinary tea looked right in either red or black Raku. She used this bowl instead.'

'You can't see the colour against black Raku.'

Kikuji made no motion towards taking up the Shino before him.

'I doubt if it's a very good piece.'

'I'm sure it's very good indeed.' But he still did not reach for it.

It was as Fumiko had described it. The white glaze carried a faint suggestion of red. As one looked at it, the red seemed to

178

float up from deep within the white.

The rim was faintly brown. In one place the brown was deeper.

It was there that one drank?

The rim might have been stained by tea, and it might have been stained by lips.

Kikuji looked at the faint brown, and felt that there was a touch of red in it.

Where her mother's lipstick had sunk in?

There was a red-black in the crackle too.

The colour of faded lipstick, the colour of a wilted red rose, the colour of old, dry blood – Kikuji began to feel queasy.

A nauseating sense of uncleanness and an overpowering fascination came simultaneously.

In black enamel touched with green and an occasional spot of russet, thick leaves of grass encircled the waist of the bowl. Clean and healthy, the leaves were enough to dispel his morbid fancies.

The proportions of the bowl were strong and dignified.

'It's a fine piece.' Kikuji at length took it in his hand.

'I don't really know, but Mother liked it.'

'There's something very appealing about tea bowls for women.'

The woman in Fumiko's mother came to him again, warm and naked.

Why had Fumiko brought this bowl, stained with her mother's lipstick?

Was she naïve, was she tactless and unfeeling? Kikuji could not decide.

But something unresisting about her seemed to come over to him.

He turned the cup round and round on his knee. He avoided touching the rim, however.

'Put it away. There will be trouble if old Kurimoto sees it.'

'Yes.' She put it back in the box and wrapped it up.

She had evidently meant to give it to him, but she had lost her chance to say so. Perhaps she had concluded that he did not like it.

She took the package out to the hall again.

Shoulders thrust forward, Chikako came from the garden. 'Would you mind taking out Mrs Ota's water jar?'

'Couldn't you use one of ours, with Fumiko here and all?'

'I don't understand. Can't you see that I want to use it because she is here? We'll have this keepsake with us while we exchange memories of her mother.'

'But you hated Mrs Ota so.'

'Not at all. We just weren't meant for each other. And how can you hate a dead person? We weren't meant for each other, and I couldn't understand her. And then in some ways I understood her too well.'

'You've always been fond of understanding people too well.'

'They should arrange not to be understood quite so easily.'

Fumiko appeared at the veranda, and sat down just inside the room.

Hunching her left shoulder, Chikako turned to face the girl.

'Fumiko, suppose we use your mother's Shino.'

'Please do.'

Kikuji took the Shino jar from a drawer.

Chikako slipped her fan into her obi, tucked the box under her arm, and went back to the cottage.

'It was something of a shock to hear that you'd moved.' Kikuji too went toward the veranda. 'You sold the house all by yourself?'

'Yes. But it was very simple. I knew the people who bought it. They were living in Oiso while they looked for something permanent, and they offered to trade houses. Theirs was very small, just right for me, they said. But I could never live by myself, no matter how small the house, and if I'm to work it will be easier to live in a rented room. I decided to have a friend take me in.'

'Have you found work?'

'No. When I'm being honest with myself, I have to admit that there's nothing I'm qualified to do.' Fumiko smiled. 'I'd been meaning to come by, once I found work. I hated the thought of talking to you while I was still drifting, no house, no work, nothing.'

At such times you should talk to me, Kikuji wanted to say. He thought of Fumiko by herself. It was not a lonely figure he saw.

'I'm thinking of selling this house too, but I put it off and put it off. But wanting to sell, I've left the leaves untended, and you can see how long it's been since I had the mats refaced.'

'You'll be married here, I suppose,' she said unaffectedly. 'You can have them done then.'

Kikuji looked at her. 'Kurimoto's story? Do you think I could marry now?'

'Because of Mother? Mother has made you suffer enough. You should think of her as something finished long ago.'

Cleaning the cottage took the practised Chikako very little time.

'How do you like the company I've put the Shino in?' she asked. Kikuji did not know.

Fumiko too was silent. They both looked at the Shino.

Before Mrs Ota's ashes it had been a flower vase, and now it was back at its old work, a water jar in a tea ceremony.

A jar that had been Mrs Ota's was now being used by Chikako. After Mrs Ota's death, it had passed to her daughter, and from Fumiko it had come to Kikuji.

It had had a strange career. But perhaps the strangeness was natural to tea vessels.

In the three or four hundred years before it became the property of Mrs Ota, it had passed through the hands of people with what strange careers?

'Beside the iron kettle, the Shino looks even more like a beautiful woman,' Kikuji said to Fumiko. 'But it's strong enough to hold its own against the iron.'

The lustre glowed quietly from the white depths.

Kikuji had said over the telephone that when he looked at this Shino he wanted to see Fumiko. In the white skin of her mother, had he sensed the depths of woman?

It was a warm day. Kikuji slid open the doors of the cottage.

The maples were green in the window behind Fumiko. The shadow of the maple leaves, layer upon layer, fell on Fumiko's hair.

Her head and her long throat were in the light of the window, and her arms, below the short sleeves of a dress she was apparently wearing for the first time, were white with a touch of green. Although she was not plump, there was a round fullness in the shoulders, and a roundness too in the arms.

Chikako was gazing at the jar. 'You can't bring a water jar to life unless you use it for tea. It's a great waste, cramming foreign flowers in it.'

'Mother used it for flowers too,' said Fumiko.

'It's like a dream, sitting here with this souvenir of your mother. I'm sure she is as happy to see it here as we are.' Was she being sarcastic?

Fumiko, however, seemed not to notice. 'I gather that Mr Mitani means to use it as a flower vase, and I've given up tea myself.'

'Oh, you mustn't say that.' Chikako looked around the cottage. 'I do feel most at peace when I'm allowed to sit here. I go to all sorts of tea cottages, of course.' She looked at Kikuji. 'Next year will be the fifth anniversary of your father's death. We must have a tea ceremony.'

'I suppose so. It would be fun to invite all sorts of connoisseurs and use imitation pieces from beginning to end.'

'Oh, come. There isn't an imitation piece in your father's whole collection.'

'Oh? But don't you think that would be fun?' he asked Fumiko. 'This cottage always smells of some mouldy poison, and a really false ceremony might drive the poison away. Have it in memory of Father, and make it my farewell to tea. Of course I severed relations with tea long ago.'

'What you're saying is that a meddlesome old woman comes to air the place?' Chikako was stirring tea with a bamboo whisk.

'Perhaps I am.'

'You mustn't. But then I suppose it's all right to sever old relations when you've struck up new.' She brought him tea like a waitress filling an order.

'Listen to his jokes, Fumiko. You must wonder whether this souvenir of your mother hasn't come to the wrong place. I almost feel that I can see your mother's face in it.'

Kikuji drank and put the bowl down, and glanced at the Shino.

Perhaps Fumiko could see Chikako's figure reflected in the black lacquer lid.

But Fumiko only sat there absently.

Kikuji did not know whether she was resisting Chikako or ignoring her.

It seemed odd that she could be here in the cottage with Chikako and show no resentment.

She had remained impassive when Chikako spoke of Kikuji's marriage.

From long hostility toward Fumiko and her mother, Chikako made every remark an insult.

Was Fumiko's sorrow so deep that the insults flowed over the surface?

Had her mother's death driven her beyond them?

Or had she inherited her mother's nature, was there in her, too, a strange childishness that left her unable to resist, whether the challenge came from herself or another?

Kikuji did not seem disposed to guard her from Chikako's venom.

He noted the fact, and thought himself odd.

And Chikako, now serving herself, struck him as an odd figure too.

She took a watch from her obi. 'These little watches are no good when you're far-sighted. Suppose you give me your father's pocket watch.'

'He had no pocket watch.'

'Oh, but he did. He often had one with him. When he went to Fumiko's house too, I'm sure.' Chikako goggled at her own watch.

Fumiko looked down.

'Ten past two, is it? The hands are running together in one

183

big blur.' Her manner became brisk and businesslike. 'Miss Inamura has been kind enough to organize a tea group, and they practise at three. I thought I'd just stop by for your answer before I went.'

'Tell her very clearly that I'll have to refuse.'

'I see. I'm to tell her very clearly.' Chikako met the crisis with a laugh. 'I must have the group practise in this cottage sometime.'

'Maybe we could have Miss Inamura buy the house. I'll be selling it anyway.'

Chikako ignored him, and turned instead to Fumiko. 'Fumiko, suppose we go at least part of the way together.'

'Yes.'

'I'll be just a minute putting things away.'

'Let me help you.'

'You'll help me, will you?' But Chikako hurried into the pantry without waiting for her.

There was a sound of water.

'You still have time,' said Kikuji in a low voice. 'Don't go off with her.'

Fumiko shook her head. 'I'm afraid.'

'There's nothing to be afraid of.'

'I'm afraid.'

'Suppose you go out, then, and come back when you've got rid of her.'

But Fumiko again shook her head. She smoothed the back of her summer dress, wrinkled from kneeling.

Kikuji, still kneeling, was about to put out his hand.

He thought she was going to fall. She flushed crimson.

She had reddened slightly at the mention of the pocket watch, and now all the shame seemed to blaze forth.

She took the Shino water jar into the pantry.

'So you brought your mother's Shino, did you?' came Chikako's husky voice.

Double Star

Kurimoto Chikako came by to tell Kikuji that Fumiko and the Inamura girl were both married.

With daylight-saving time, the sky was still bright at eight-thirty. Kikuji lay on the veranda after dinner, watching the caged fireflies the maid had bought. Their white light took on a yellow tinge as evening became night. He did not get up to turn on the light, however.

He had been vacationing for some days at a friend's villa on Lake Nojiri, and he had come back that afternoon.

The friend was married and had a baby. Not used to babies, Kikuji did not know whether it was large for its age, or indeed how old it was.

'A well-developed baby,' he finally said.

'Not really,' the wife answered. 'It was tiny when it was born. Now, of course, it's beginning to catch up.'

Kikuji passed a hand before the baby's face. 'It doesn't blink.'

'It can see, but blinking comes a little later.'

He had thought it would be perhaps six months old, but in fact it was barely a hundred days old. He understood why the hair of the young wife seemed thin, why her colour was bad – she was still recovering from childbirth.

The life of the couple centred upon the baby. They seemed to have time only for the baby, and Kikuji felt a little left out. But on the train back, the thin figure of the wife, worn and somehow drained of life, absently holding the baby in her arms – a quiet, docile young woman, one knew immediately – the figure was with him and would not leave. The friend lived with his family, and perhaps the wife, thus alone with her husband at a lakeside villa after the birth of this first child, felt a security that gave her a dreamy respite from thought.

At home now, lying on the veranda, Kikuji remembered the wife with a poignant, almost reverent affection.

Chikako came upon him there.

She marched into the room. 'Well. In pitch dark.'

She knelt on the veranda, at Kikuji's feet. 'It's hard being a bachelor. You have to lie in the dark, and no one will turn on the light for you.'

Kikuji curled his legs. He lay thus for a time, and sat up in distaste.

'No, please. Stay as you are.' She held out her right hand as if to motion him down, then made her formal bow. She had been to Kyoto and she had stopped at Hakone on the way back. In Kyoto, at the house of her tea master, she had met one Oizumi, a dealer in tea wares. 'We talked and talked about your father. Really, it was the first good talk in such a long time. Oizumi said he'd show me the inn your father used for secret meetings, and off we went to a little inn on Kiyamachi. I suppose your father stayed there with Mrs Ota. And what did Oizumi do but suggest that I stay there myself? Very insensitive of him. With your father and Mrs Ota both dead, even someone like me would feel a little strange there in the middle of the night.'

Kikuji said nothing. Chikako was hardly demonstrating her own sensitiveness, he thought.

'You've been to Lake Nojiri?' She already knew the answer. It was her style to examine the maid the moment she arrived, and to come in unannounced.

'I got back just a few minutes ago,' Kikuji answered sullenly.

'I've been back several days.' Chikako's answer too was curt. Abruptly, she hunched her left shoulder. 'And I found when I got back that something very unfortunate had happened. I was shocked. A terrible thing – I don't know how to face you.'

She told him that the Inamura girl was married.

In the darkness, Kikuji did not have to hide his surprise.

He was able to answer coolly. 'Oh? When?'

'Says he, just as if it didn't concern him.'

'But I gave you my refusal more than once.'

'At least on the surface you did. So you wanted it to seem.

You weren't interested, you wanted it to seem, and a meddle-some old woman came bustling in, and pushed and pushed. Very annoying. But the girl herself was all right.'

'What are you talking about?' Kikuji laughed sardonically.

'I imagine you liked the young lady well enough.'

'A very nice young lady.'

'I saw it all.'

'The fact that I think she's a nice girl doesn't mean that I want to marry her.'

Yet he had felt a stabbing at the heart, and, as if with a violent thirst, he struggled to draw the girl's face in his mind.

He had met her only twice.

To put her on display, Chikako had had her make tea in the Engakuji Temple. Her performance had been simple and elegant, and the impression was still vivid of the shoulders and the long kimono sleeves, and the hair too, radiant in light through paper doors. The shadows of leaves on the paper, the bright red tea napkin, the pink crêpe handkerchief under her arm as she walked through the temple grounds to the tea cottage, the thousand white cranes – all of these floated fresh-ly into his mind.

The second time she had come here, and Chikako had made tea. Kikuji had felt the next day that the girl's perfume lin-gered on, and even now he could see her obi with its Siberian irises; but her face eluded him.

He could not call up the faces of his own mother and father, who had died three or four years before. He would look at a picture, and there they would be. Perhaps people were pro-gressively harder to paint in the mind as they were near one, loved by one. Perhaps clear memories came easily in propor-tion as they were ugly.

Yukiko's eyes and cheeks were abstract memories, like im-pressions of light; and the memory of that birthmark on Chik-ako's breast was concrete as a toad.

Although the veranda was now dark, Kikuji could see that Chikako was wearing a white crêpe singlet under her kimono. Even if it had been daylight he could not have seen through to the birthmark; but it was there before him, all the more dis-tinct for the darkness.

'Well, most men wouldn't let a girl get away while they were thinking what a nice girl she was. After all, there's only one Yukiko in this world. You won't find her again if you spend your whole life looking. It's the simple things you don't understand.' Her manner was openly scolding. 'You're inexperienced and you pamper yourself. Well, this has changed her life and it's changed yours. She was very interested. We can't really say, can we, that you're not responsible if her marriage isn't happy?'

Kikuji did not answer.

'You took a good look at her, I suppose. It doesn't bother you to think that years and years from now a girl like her will remember you and think how much better it would have been if she could have married you?'

There was poison in her voice.

But if the girl was already married, why was all this necessary?

'Fireflies? At this time of the year?' She thrust her head forward. 'It's almost autumn. There are still fireflies, are there? Like ghosts.'

'The maid bought them.'

'That's the sort of thing maids do. If you were studying tea, now, you wouldn't put up with it. You may not know, but in Japan we are very conscious of the seasons.'

There was indeed something ghostly about the fireflies. Kikuji remembered that autumn insects had been humming on the shores of Lake Nojiri. Very strange fireflies, alive even now.

'If you had a wife, she wouldn't depress you with end-of-the-season things.' Suddenly her tone was soft and intimate. 'I thought of arranging your marriage as a service to your father.'

'A service?'

'Yes. And what else happens while you lie in the dark staring at fireflies? The Ota girl gets married too.'

'When?' Kikuji was even more startled.

His show of composure struck him as remarkable, but something in his voice must have given him away.

'I was just as shocked as you are, coming back from Kyoto and hearing about it. Both of them running off and getting married, as if they'd talked it over beforehand – young people don't give much notice, do they? There I was, feeling pleased that Fumiko had kindly removed herself, and wasn't the Inamura girl married too? And the way she did it. She might as well have slapped me in the face. Well, it's all because of your indecisiveness.'

Kikuji had trouble believing that Fumiko was married.

'Did Mrs Ota succeed in ruining your marriage after all, even if she had to die to do it? But maybe the witch will leave us, now that Fumiko is married.' Chikako looked out toward the garden. 'Suppose you settle down, and give the trees a good pruning. Even in the dark I can see how you've let them grow. The gloomiest garden I've ever been in.'

Kikuji had not called a gardener in the four years since his father's death. He had indeed let the garden grow. There was a dank smell from it that brought back the full heat of the day.

'And I suppose the maid does nothing about sprinkling. You might mention that, at least.'

'I'm not sure it's your business.'

But though he scowled fiercely at each remark, he let her talk on. So it was whenever he saw her.

Even while she was annoying him, she was seeking to ingratiate herself, and probing. He was used to the trick. He showed his displeasure openly, and he was on guard. Chikako knew all this and for the most part feigned ignorance. Occasionally she let him see how much she did know.

Even while she was annoying him, she rarely said things that startled by their incongruity. Everything went with the self-loathing that had become a part of Kikuji's nature.

Tonight she was probing to see how he had reacted to her news. He was on guard – what could be her reason? She had sought to marry him to Yukiko and to drive Fumiko away; and, although it was hardly her place to wonder how he might feel now, she went on digging into the shadows.

He thought of turning on the lights in the room and at the veranda. It was strange to be here in the dark with Chikako. They were hardly that intimate. She gave him advice about the garden, and he dismissed it as the sort of thing she did. Yet it seemed a nuisance to get up and turn on the lights.

And Chikako, though she had spoken of the darkness the moment she came in, made no motion towards getting up. It was her habit, and indeed her art, to be of service; but Kikuji could see that her ardour in serving him had dimmed. Perhaps she was getting old. Perhaps, again, she had her dignity as a mistress of tea.

'I'm just passing on a message from Oizumi in Kyoto,' she said nonchalantly, 'but if you ever decide to sell your father's collection he'd like to manage the sale. If you mean to pull yourself together and start a new life now that Yukiko has run away, I don't suppose you'll be in a mood for tea. It makes me a little sad to give up work I had when your father was alive, but I suppose the tea cottage gets only the airings I give it.'

Well, well – Kikuji saw everything.

Her aims were only too clear. Having failed to arrange the marriage with Yukiko, she would see no more of Kikuji, and, as her farewell, she would form a partnership with Oizumi to take over the collection. She had discussed the terms in Kyoto.

Kikuji felt less angry than relieved.

'I'm thinking of selling the house too. I may well call on you one of these days.'

'We can feel safe with someone who's been in and out of the house since your father's time.'

Kikuji suspected that she knew better than he what was in the collection. Possibly she had already calculated the profits.

He looked out towards the cottage. In front of it there was a large oleander, heavy with blossoms, a vague white blur. For the rest, the night was so dark that he had trouble following the line between trees and sky.

About to leave his office one evening, Kikuji was called back to the telephone.

'This is Fumiko.' He heard a very small voice.

'Hello.'

'This is Fumiko.'

'Oh yes, I recognized you.'

'I ought to see you in person, but there's something I must apologize for. If I don't telephone it will be too late.'

'I beg your pardon?'

'I mailed a letter yesterday, and I seem to have forgotten the stamp.'

'Oh? It hasn't come yet.'

'I bought ten stamps when I mailed it, and I still had ten when I got home. I must have been thinking of something else. I wanted to apologize before you got the letter.'

'Is that all? Really, you shouldn't worry.' Kikuji wondered if the letter was to tell of her marriage. 'It calls for congratulations?'

'I beg your pardon? We've always talked over the telephone and this is the first time I've written. I must have forgotten the stamp while I was wondering whether to mail it.'

'Where are you calling from?'

'A public telephone. Tokyo Central Station. Someone is waiting for the booth.'

'A public telephone?' Kikuji was not quite satisfied. 'Congratulations.'

'What? Thank you. I did finally – but how did you know?'

'Kurimoto told me.'

'Miss Kurimoto? How could she know? What a frightening person.'

'I don't suppose you see Kurimoto any more. The last time – remember? – I heard rain over the telephone.'

'So you said. I had just moved, and I was wondering whether to tell you. This time it's the same.'

'You should have told me. Ever since I had it from Kurimoto I've been wondering whether I should congratulate you.'

'And I just disappeared? It's a little sad, isn't it? One of the missing.' Her voice, trailing off, was like her mother's.

Kikuji fell silent.

'But I have to be one of the missing.' There was a pause. 'It's a dirty little room. I found it when I found work.'

'I beg your pardon?'

'It wasn't easy, beginning work in the hottest part of the year.'

'I'd imagine not. And newly married too.'

'Married? Did you say married?'

'Congratulations.'

'Me? Married?'

'You *are* married, aren't you?'

'Me?'

'Didn't you get married?'

'No, no! Could I possibly? With mother just dead?'

'I see.'

'Miss Kurimoto said I was married?'

'She did.'

'Why? Why did she say it? And did you believe it?' The question seemed to be directed half at Fumiko herself.

'It's no good over the telephone.' Kikuji spoke with decision. 'Can't I see you?'

'Yes.'

'I'll go to Tokyo Central. Wait for me there.'

'But . . .'

'Is there somewhere you'd rather meet?'

'I don't like meeting people in strange places. I'll go to your house.'

'Shall we go together?'

'That would mean meeting somewhere.'

'Can't you come here?'

'No. I'll go to your house by myself.'

'Oh? Well, I'm leaving now. If you get there first go on inside.'

Taking a train from Tokyo Central, she would be there ahead of him. He wondered, however, if they might not be on the same train. He looked for her in the crowd.

She had indeed reached his house ahead of him.

She was in the garden, said the maid. Kikuji went around the house and saw her sitting on a rock in the shade of the white oleander.

Since Chikako's visit some days before, the maid had been careful to sprinkle the shrubbery before Kikuji came home. She used an old faucet in the garden. The rock seemed damp at Fumiko's sleeve.

When a red oleander floods into bloom, the red against the thick green leaves is like the blaze of the summer sky; but when the blossoms are white, the effect is richly cool. The white clusters swayed gently, and enveloped Fumiko. She was wearing a white cotton dress trimmed at the pockets and the turned-down collar with narrow bands of deep blue.

The light of the western sun fell on Kikuji from over the oleander.

'It's good to see you.' There was nostalgia in his voice as he came up to her.

She had been about to speak. 'Over the telephone, a few minutes ago ...' She seemed to shrink away from him as she stood up. Perhaps she had felt that unless she stopped him he would take her hand. 'You said that, and I've come to deny it.'

'That you're married? I was very surprised.'

'Surprised that I was or that I wasn't?' She looked at the ground.

'Well, both. When I heard that you were married, and again when I heard that you weren't.'

'Both times?'

'Shouldn't I have been?' Kikuji walked on over the stepping stones. 'Suppose we go in from here. You could just as well have waited inside, you know.' He sat on the veranda. 'I'd come back from a trip and I was lying here, and in marched Kurimoto. It was at night.'

The maid called Kikuji into the house, probably to confirm the dinner instructions he had telephoned from the office. While he was inside he changed to a white linen kimono.

Fumiko seemed to have repowdered her face. She waited for him to sit down again.

'What exactly did Miss Kurimoto say?'

'Just that you were married.'

'Did you believe it?'

'Well, it was the sort of lie I could hardly believe anyone would tell.'

'You didn't even doubt it?' The near-black eyes were moist. 'Could I get married now, possibly? Do you think I could? Mother and I suffered together, and with the suffering still here ...' It was as if the mother were still alive. 'Mother and I both presume a great deal on people, but we expect them to understand us. Is that impossible? Are we seeing our reflections in our own hearts?' Her voice wavered on the edge of tears.

Kikuji was silent for a time. 'Not long ago I said the same

thing. I asked if you thought I could possibly marry. The day of the storm, was it?'

'The day of the thunder?'

'And now you say it to me.'

'But it's different.'

'You said several times that I would be getting married.'

'But your case is so different.' She gazed at him with tear-filled eyes. 'You're different from me.'

'How?'

'Your position, your place.'

'My position?'

'Your position is different. Shouldn't I say position? I'll say the degree of darkness, then.'

'In a word, the guilt? But mine is deeper.'

'No.' She shook her head violently, and a tear spilled over, drawing a strange line from the corner of her left eye to her ear. 'The guilt was Mother's and she died – if we have to talk about guilt. But I don't think it was guilt. Only sorrow.'

Kikuji sat with bowed head.

'If it was guilt,' she continued, 'it may never go away. But sorrow will.'

'When you talk about darkness, aren't you making your mother's death darker than you need to?'

'I should have said the degree of sorrow.'

'The degree of sorrow.'

'The degree of love,' he wanted to add; but he stopped himself.

'And there is the question of you and Yukiko. That makes you different from me.' She spoke as if she meant to bring the conversation back to reality. 'Miss Kurimoto thought Mother was trying to interfere, and she thought I stood in the way too. And so she said I was married. I can't think of any other explanation.'

'But she said that the Inamura girl was married too.'

For a moment her face seemed to collapse. Again she shook her head violently. 'A lie, a lie. That's a lie too. When?'

'When did she get married? Very recently, I suppose.'

'It's sure to be a lie.'

'When I heard that the two of you were married, I thought

it might be true about you,' he said in a low voice. 'But the other may really be true.'

'It's a lie. No one gets married in this heat. In a summer kimono, sweat pouring off – can you imagine it?'

'There's no such thing as a summer wedding?'

'Only now and then. People put weddings off to autumn, or ...' For some reason, tears came to her eyes again, and fell to her knee. She gazed at the wet spot. 'But why should Miss Kurimoto tell such lies?'

'She cleverly took me in, did she?' Kikuji deliberated for a time.

But what had brought the tears?

It was certain that at least the report about Fumiko was a lie.

Had Chikako said that Fumiko was married to drive her off, the Inamura girl in fact being married? He weighed the possibility.

There was something in it he could not accept, however. He, too, began to feel that she had lied.

'Well, as long as we don't know whether it's a lie or the truth, we don't know the extent of Kurimoto's prankishness.'

'Prankishness?'

'Suppose we call it that.'

'But if I hadn't telephoned today I'd have been left married. A fine prank.'

The maid called Kikuji again.

He came back with a letter in his hand.

'Your letter, and no stamp.' He lightly turned it over.

'No, no. You're not to look at it.' She brought herself toward him, still kneeling, and tried to take it from his hand. 'Give it back to me.'

Kikuji whipped his hands behind him.

Her left hand fell on his knee, and her right hand reached for the letter. With left hand and right hand thus making contradictory motions, she lost her balance. The left hand was behind her to keep her from falling against Kikuji, the right was clutching at the letter, now behind Kikuji's back. Twisting to the right, she was about to fall. The side of her face would be against his chest – but she turned supplely away. The touch of her left hand on his knee was unbelievably light. He could not see how she had supported the upper part of her body, twisted as it was and about to fall.

He had stiffened abruptly as she threw herself upon him; and now he wanted to cry out at the astonishing suppleness. He was intensely conscious of the woman. He was conscious of Fumiko's mother, Mrs Ota.

At what instant had she recovered and pulled away? Where had the force spent itself? It was a suppleness that could not be. It was like the deepest instinct of woman. Just as he was expecting her to come down heavily upon him, she was near him, a warm odour. That was all.

The odour was strong. It came richly, the odour of a woman who had been at work through the summer day. He felt the odour of Fumiko, and of her mother. The smell of Mrs Ota's embrace.

'Give it back to me.' Kikuji did not resist. 'I'm going to tear it up.'

She turned away and tore her letter to small bits. The neck and the bare arms were damp with perspiration.

She had suddenly paled as she fell toward him and recovered herself. Then, kneeling again, she had flushed; and in that time, it seemed, the perspiration had come out.

Dinner, from a near-by caterer, was uninteresting, exactly what one would have expected.

Kikuji's teacup was the cylindrical Shino bowl. The maid brought it to him as usual.

He noticed, and Fumiko's eyes too were on it. 'You have been using that bowl?'

'I have.'

'You shouldn't.' He sensed that she was not as uncomfortable as he. 'I was sorry afterwards that I'd given it to you. I mentioned it in my letter.'

'What did you say?'

'What ... Well, I apologized for having given you a bad piece of Shino.'

'It's not a bad piece at all.'

'It can't be good Shino. Mother used it as an ordinary tea-cup.'

196

'I don't really know, but I'd imagine that it's very good Shino.' He took the bowl in his hand and gazed at it.

'There is much better Shino. The bowl reminds you of another, and the other is better.'

'There don't seem to be any small Shino pieces in my father's collection.'

'Even if you don't have them here, you see them. Other bowls come into your mind when you're drinking from this, and you think how much better they are. It makes me very sad, and Mother too.'

Kikuji breathed deeply. 'But I'm moving farther and farther from tea. I have no occasion to see tea bowls.'

'You don't know when you might see one. You must have seen much finer pieces.'

'You're saying that a person can give only the very finest?'

'Yes.' Fumiko looked straight at him, affirmation in her eyes. 'That is what I think. I asked you in my letter to break it and throw away the pieces.'

'To break it? To break this?' Kikuji sought to divert the attack that bore down upon him. 'It's from the old Shino kiln, and it must be three or four hundred years old. At first it was probably an ordinary table piece, but a long time has gone by since it became a tea bowl. People watched over it and passed it on – some of them may even have taken it on long trips with them. I can't break it just because you tell me to.'

On the rim of the bowl, she had said, there was a stain from her mother's lipstick. Her mother had apparently told her that once the lipstick was there it would not go away, however hard she rubbed, and indeed since Kikuji had had the bowl he had washed without success at that especially dark spot on the rim. It was a light brown, far from the colour of lipstick; and yet there was a faint touch of red in it, not impossible to take for old, faded lipstick. It may have been the red of the Shino itself; or, since the forward side of the bowl had become fixed with use, a stain may have been left from the lips of owners before Mrs Ota. Mrs Ota, however, had probably used it most. It had been her everyday teacup.

Had Mrs Ota herself first thought of so using it? Or had Kikuji's father? Kikuji wondered.

There had also been his suspicion that Mrs Ota, with his father, had used the two cylindrical Raku bowls, the red and the black, as everyday 'man-wife' teacups.

His father had had her make the Shino water jar a flower vase, then – he had had her put roses and carnations in it? And he had had her use the little Shino bowl as a teacup? Had he at such times thought her beautiful?

Now that the two of them were dead, the water jar and the bowl had come to Kikuji. And Fumiko had come too.

'I'm not just being childish. I really do wish you would break it. You liked the water jar I gave you, and I remembered the other Shino and thought it would go with the jar. But afterwards I was ashamed.'

'I shouldn't be using it as a teacup. It's much too good.'

'But there are so many better pieces. You'll drink from this and think of them. I'll be very unhappy.'

'But do you really believe that you can't give away anything except the finest pieces?'

'It depends on the person and the circumstances.'

The words had rich overtones.

Was Fumiko kind enough to think that for a souvenir of her mother, a souvenir of Fumiko herself – perhaps something more intimate than a souvenir – only the finest would do?

The desire, the plea, that only the finest be left to recall her mother came across to Kikuji. It came as the finest of emotions, and the water jar was its witness.

The very face of the Shino, glowing warmly cool, made him think of Mrs Ota. Possibly because the piece was so fine, the memory was without the darkness and ugliness of guilt.

As he looked at the masterpiece it was, he felt all the more strongly the masterpiece Mrs Ota had been. In a masterpiece there is nothing unclean.

He looked at the jar and he wanted to see Fumiko, he had said over the telephone that stormy day. He had been able to say it only because the telephone stood between. Fumiko had answered that she had another Shino piece, and brought him the bowl.

It was probably true that the bowl was weaker than the jar.

'I seem to remember that my father had a portable tea chest.

He used to take it with him when he went travelling,' mused Kikuji. 'The bowl he kept in it must be much worse than this.'

'What sort of bowl is it?'

'I've never seen it myself.'

'Show it to me. It's sure to be better. And if it is, may I break the Shino?'

'A dangerous gamble.'

After dinner, as she dexterously picked seeds from the watermelon, Fumiko again pressed him to show her the bowl.

He sent the maid to open the tea cottage, and went out through the garden. He meant to bring the tea chest back with him, but Fumiko went along.

'I have no idea where it might be,' he called back. 'Kurimoto knows far better than I.'

Fumiko was in the shadow of the blossom-heavy oleander. He could see, below the lowest of the white branches, stockinged feet in garden clogs.

The tea chest was in a cupboard at the side of the pantry.

Kikuji brought it into the main room and laid it before her. She knelt deferentially, as though waiting for him to untie the wrapping; but after a time she reached for it.

'If I may see it, then.'

'It's a bit dusty.' He took the chest by the wrapping and dusted it over the garden. 'The pantry is alive with bugs, and there was a dead cicada in the cupboard.'

'But this room is clean.'

'Kurimoto cleaned it when she came to tell me that you and the Inamura girl were married. It was night, and she must have shut a cicada in the cupboard.'

Taking out what appeared to be a tea bowl, Fumiko bent low to undo the sack. Her fingers trembled slightly.

The round shoulders were thrown forward, and to Kikuji, looking at her in profile, the long throat seemed even longer.

There was something engaging about the pouting lower lip, which pushed forward in proportion as the mouth was drawn earnestly shut, and about the plain swell of the ear lobes.

She looked up at him. 'It's Karatsu.'*

Kikuji came nearer.

*A Kyūshū ware of Korean origin.

'It's a very good bowl.' She laid it on the floor matting.

It was a small, cylindrical Karatsu bowl, which, like the Shino, could be used for everyday.

'It's strong. Dignified – much better than the Shino.'

'But can you compare Shino and Karatsu?'

'You can tell if you see them together.'

Held by the power of the Karatsu, Kikuji took it on his knee and gazed at it.

'Shall I bring the Shino, then?'

'I'll get it.' Fumiko stood up.

They put the Shino and the Karatsu side by side. Their eyes met, and fell to the bowls.

'A man's and a woman's.' Kikuji spoke in some confusion. 'When you see them side by side.'

Fumiko nodded, as if unable to speak.

To Kikuji too the words had an odd ring.

The Karatsu was undecorated, greenish with a touch of saffron and a touch too of carmine. It swelled powerfully towards the base.

'A favourite your father took with him on trips. It's very much like your father.'

Fumiko seemed not to sense the danger in the remark.

Kikuji could not bring himself to say that the Shino bowl was like her mother. But the two bowls before them were like the souls of his father and her mother.

The tea bowls, three or four hundred years old, were sound and healthy, and they called up no morbid thoughts. Life seemed to stretch taut over them, however, in a way that was almost sensual.

Seeing his father and Fumiko's mother in the bowls, Kikuji felt that they had raised two beautiful ghosts and placed them side by side.

The tea bowls were here, present, and the present reality of Kikuji and Fumiko, facing across the bowls seemed immaculate too.

Kikuji had said to her, on the day after the seventh-day services for her mother, that there was something terrible in his being with her, facing her. Had the guilt and the fear been wiped away by the touch of the bowls?

'Beautiful,' said Kikuji, as if to himself. 'It wasn't Father's nature to play with tea bowls, and yet he did, and maybe they deadened his sense of guilt.'

'I beg your pardon?'

'But when you see the bowl, you forget the defects of the old owner. Father's life was only a very small part of the life of a tea bowl.'

'Death, waiting at your feet. I'm frightened. I've tried so many things. I've tried thinking that with death itself at my feet I can't be forever held by Mother's death.'

'When you're held by the dead, you begin to feel that you aren't in this world yourself.'

The maid came with a kettle and other tea utensils.

She had evidently concluded that, so long in the cottage, they needed water for tea.

Kikuji suggested to Fumiko that they use the Shino and the Karatsu here as if they themselves were on a trip.

Fumiko nodded simply. 'May I use the Shino one last time before I break it?' She took the tea whisk from the box, and went to wash it.

The long summer day was still bright.

'As if on a trip,' said Fumiko, twirling the small whisk in the small bowl.

'Off on a trip – and are we at an inn?'

'It doesn't have to be an inn. A river bank, or a mountain top. Maybe cold water would have been better, to make us think of the mountains.' As she lifted the tea whisk, her near-black eyes rose and for an instant were on Kikuji. Then she looked down at the Karatsu, which she turned in the palm of one hand.

The eyes moved forward with the bowl, to a spot before Kikuji's knee.

He felt that she might come flowing over to him.

When she started to make tea in her mother's Shino, the whisk rustled against the bowl. She stopped.

'It's very hard.'

'It must be hard in such a small bowl,' said Kikuji. But the trouble was that Fumiko's hands were trembling.

Once she had stopped, there was no making the whisk move again.

Fumiko sat with bowed head, her eyes on her taut wrist.

'Mother won't let me.'

'What!' Kikuji started up and took her by the shoulders, as if to pull her from the meshes of a curse.

There was no resistance.

Unable to sleep, Kikuji waited for light through the cracks in the shutters, and went out to the cottage.

The broken Shino lay on the stepping stone before the stone basin.

He put together four large pieces to form a bowl. A piece large enough to admit his forefinger was missing from the rim.

Wondering if it might be somewhere on the ground, he started looking among the stones. Immediately he stopped.

He raised his eyes. A large star was shining through the trees to the east.

It was some years since he had last seen the morning star. He stood looking at it, and the sky began to cloud over.

The star was even larger, shining through the haze. The light was as if blurred by water.

It seemed dreary in contrast to the fresh glimmer of the star, to be hunting a broken bowl and trying to put it together.

He threw the pieces down again.

The evening before, Fumiko had flung the Shino against the basin before he could stop her.

He had cried out.

But he had not looked for the pieces in the shadows among the stones. He had rather put his arm round Fumiko, supporting her. As she fell forward in the act of throwing the Shino, she seemed herself about to collapse against the basin.

'There is much better Shino,' she murmured.

Was she still sad at the thought of having Kikuji compare it with better Shino?

He lay sleepless, and an echo of her words came to him, more poignantly clean in remembrance.

Waiting for daylight, he went out to look for the pieces.

Then, seeing the star, he threw them down again.

And looking up, he cried out.

There was no star. In the brief moment when his eyes were

on the discarded pieces, the morning star had disappeared in the clouds.

He gazed at the eastern sky for a time, as if to retrieve something stolen.

The clouds would not be heavy; but he could not tell where the star was. The clouds broke near the horizon. The faint red deepened where they touched the roofs of houses.

'I can't just leave it,' he said aloud. He picked up the pieces again, and put them in the sleeve of his night kimono.

It would be sad to leave them there. And besides, Kurimoto Chikako might come calling.

He thought of burying the bowl beside the stone basin, because Fumiko had broken it there in such obvious desperation. Instead, he wrapped the pieces in paper, put them in a drawer, and went back to bed.

What had she so dreaded having him compare the Shino with?

And why had the possibility so worried her? Kikuji could think of no reason.

Now, even more than the evening befo e, he could think of no one with whom to compare her.

She had become absolute, beyond comparison. She had become decision and fate.

Always before, she had been Mrs Ota's daughter. Now, he had forgotten – the idea had quite left him that the mother's body was in a subtle way transferred to the daughter, to lure him into strange fantasies.

He had at length made his way outside the dark, ugly curtain.

Had the breach in her cleanness rescued him?

There had been no resistance from Fumiko, only from the cleanness itself.

That fact, one might think, told how deep he had sunk into the meshes of the curse, how complete the paralysis was; but Kikuji felt the reverse, that he had escaped the curse and the paralysis. It was as if an addict had been freed of his addiction by taking the ultimate dose of a drug.

Kikuji called Fumiko from his office. She worked for a wool wholesaler in Kanda.

She was not at work. Kikuji had left home sleepless. Had Fumiko fallen into a deep sleep at perhaps dawn? Or, in her shame, had she shut herself up for the day?

In the afternoon she still was not at work, and he asked where she lived.

Her new address would have been on the letter yesterday; but Fumiko had torn it up envelope and all and put the pieces in her pocket. At dinner they had talked of her work, and he remembered the name of the firm. He had not asked where she lived. It had been as if her dwelling were Kikuji himself.

On his way home, he looked for the rooming house. It was behind Ueno Park.

Fumiko was not there.

A girl twelve or thirteen, just back from school to judge from her student uniform, came to the door and went inside again.

'Miss Ota is out. She said she was going away with a friend.'

'Away? She went on a trip? What time was it? And where did she say she was going?'

The girl went inside again, and this time she did not come to the door. 'I really don't know. Mother is out.' She seemed afraid of Kikuji. She had thin eyebrows.

Kikuji looked back as he went out the gate, but he could not tell which was Fumiko's room. It was a fairly decent two-storey house with a little garden.

She had said that death was at her feet. Kikuji's own feet were suddenly cold.

He wiped his face with his handkerchief. The blood seemed to leave as he wiped, and he wiped more violently. The handkerchief was wet and dark. He felt a cold sweat at his back.

'She has no reason to die,' he muttered.

There was no reason for Fumiko to die, Fumiko who had brought him to life.

But had the simple directness of the evening before been the directness of death?

Was she, like her mother, guilt-ridden, afraid of the directness?

'And only Kurimoto is left.' As if spitting out all the accumulated venom on the woman he took for his enemy, Kikuji hurried into the shade of the park.